THE SHAKER MURDERS

A Selection of Titles by Eleanor Kuhns

The Will Rees Series

A SIMILE MURDER
DEATH OF A DYER
CRADLE TO GRAVE
DEATH IN SALEM
THE DEVIL'S COLD DISH
THE SHAKER MURDERS *

* available from Severn House

THE SHAKER MURDERS

MURDERS

Eleanor Kuhns

Severn House Large Print
London & New York

This first large print edition published 2019
in Great Britain and the USA by
SEVERN HOUSE PUBLISHERS LTD of
Eardley House, 4 Uxbridge Street, London W8 7SY.
First world regular print edition published 2018 by
Severn House Publishers Ltd.

British Library Cataloguing in Publication Data
A CIP catalogue record for this title is available from the British Library.

ISBN-13: 9780727829948

Severn House Publishers support the Forest Stewardship Council™
[FSC™], the leading international forest certification organisation. All
our titles that are printed on FSC certified paper carry the FSC logo.

MIX
Paper from
responsible sources
FSC
www.fsc.org   FSC® C013056

Typeset by Palimpsest Book Production Ltd.,
Falkirk, Stirlingshire, Scotland.
Printed and bound in Great Britain by
T J International, Padstow, Cornwall.

One

'What is that?' asked Jabez, the Shaker Brother with whom Rees would be sharing his room. Rees turned to the man in surprise. He had previously tried to initiate a conversation by introducing himself, but Jabez had silenced Rees with a sharp reprimand. 'No unnecessary speech!'

'Well?' Jabez said now. Rees glanced down at the canvas-wrapped bundle. 'My loom,' he said.

Or rather, the pieces of one. During the persecution directed at Rees and his family in Dugard, Rees's loom had been purposely broken. He still wasn't entirely sure how serious the damage was.

'You're a weaver?' Jabez asked. Rees nodded. 'Well, I hope you do not intend to weave in here, in our bedchamber. That is work that should be accomplished in the Weaving House.'

'This is my livelihood,' Rees said, feeling irritation burn at the back of his mind. He had spent the last two days driving from Dugard to Zion as fast as he could, and that had been after some very difficult weeks battling constant harassment. He had been blamed for a murder he did not commit, and his wife accused of witchcraft. After she'd been threatened with hanging, Rees had brought her and the children to Zion. And now he was too tired to treat foolishness with courtesy.

'And you're dirty,' Jabez continued, his lip

curling as he inspected Rees. 'You'd better wash before supper. As Mother Ann said, cleanliness is a necessary accomplishment for a civilized person.'

'I've been traveling hard,' Rees said curtly, suppressing the urge to strike the other man. Rees had certainly not expected to arrive at this refuge only to jump into another argument. After safeguarding his family's safety, he had spent more than a week running for his life before finally identifying the malicious intelligence behind his persecution. He inhaled a deep breath and added, 'And the loom is broken.'

Jabez, catching the edge to Rees's voice, turned. 'Watch your temper, Rees. We do not approve of anger here.' Rees took an involuntary step forward, his heart beginning to thud in his chest.

With a slight smile, Jabez clapped his straw hat over his reddish-brown curls and left the room. Going to supper, no doubt.

Rees stood there for a few seconds, waiting for his heartbeat to return to normal. He was annoyed with himself for reacting to Jabez's baiting. He knew better. But there was something about this Shaker that got under his skin.

Blowing out a long breath, Rees moved the loom pieces into the corner where he hoped Jabez would not notice them. Defiant now, Rees was determined not to move his loom to the Weaving Shed. He put his satchel on his bed to claim it. Then he went to the ewer and basin on the table assigned to him and began to wash. As he dried his face and hands, a sharp knock

2

sounded on the door and it opened to reveal another of the Brethren. Rees recognized Brother Jonathan, one of the Elders. He was still wearing the navy-blue vest he and all of his fellows wore to Sunday meeting.

'Better,' Jonathan said, eyeing Rees's face and hands approvingly. 'I'll accompany you to supper. Then you'll bathe in the laundry tub before bed.'

Rees nodded, feeling the faint heat of shame in his cheeks. He had not meant to arrive dirty. But since it was Sunday the inn in Durham had been closed, so he had been unable to stop and bathe before continuing on to Zion.

As soon as Rees followed Jonathan into the Dining Hall his gaze went unerringly to the Sisters' side. He found his wife, Lydia, easily as she was the only woman not wearing the square Shaker's cap. And she was still with child. Rees breathed a sigh of relief. He had not missed the birth.

Then he looked to the children's tables, and found Simon and Jerusha in their respective seats. The three youngest were harder to discover in the midst of the bigger children, Joseph most difficult of all. His head barely reached above the table.

With his family found, Rees claimed the nearest empty seat and sat down for supper. Sisters began bringing out platters of beef, johnnycake, and beans from the garden. As a young girl deposited the plates upon the table, she met Rees's eyes. He recognized her; she was the Sister who upon his arrival in Zion had taken him to Brother Jonathan. She made a quick motion as though washing her face. Rees shared a smile with her as he remembered the woman they had seen on their way to the Meetinghouse.

The road that ran north to south through the center of the village had been so crowded with vehicles of all descriptions that Rees and his Shaker chaperone had had to pick their way around them. All these people from the World had come to see the Shaker service, as though it were some kind of show.

Rees almost collided with one of the visitors, a well-dressed woman making her way toward her own carriage. Garbed in one of the unstructured pastel gowns from Paris and a large feathered hat, she had buried her face in a handkerchief. Her shoulders shook uncontrollably and at first Rees, who had jumped quickly aside, thought she was weeping. But as a new gust of hilarity shook her, he realized she was laughing. When she looked up, Rees had seen tears of mirth running down her face, streaking her rouged cheeks. The woman was made up after the French fashion, à la Josephine, that upstart Napoleon's wife. While her maquillage might be the latest word in Europe, it was an unfamiliar sight in Maine and Rees grinned as he remembered the woman's strange appearance.

But his amusement faded as he recalled his subsequent behavior.

'Oh dear me!' the woman had said, barely able to force the words through her giggles, 'I did not see you there.' She attempted to wipe away the tears from her cheeks, and red paint stained the white linen in her hand. Although Rees knew it was only carmine, he couldn't help thinking of blood and shuddered. 'Forgive me, please.' Another gust of merriment shook her. 'I found the scene in the Meetinghouse so risible.' Although gowned and made up like a fashionable Parisian woman, she spoke English without an accent.

'I'm certain,' Rees had said in such a sharp tone she took a step backwards, 'that you would not care to have your services the subject of ill-informed amusement.' Although he found some of the Shaker beliefs and practices odd, he was irritated that she should laugh at people he saw as human beings. 'I know them as good neighbors and honest men. Your response displays your ignorance.' Offended, the woman had brushed past him and climbed into an elegant coach with a medallion on the door.

Rees shook his head at himself, embarrassed by his anger. Such a powerful response for something so minor. Why had he been so rude? Although he had spoken only what he felt was the truth, he was not usually so disrespectful.

The Sister, once the platters were delivered to the table, gave him a final twinkling smile before departing for the kitchen. Rees's comment that the painted visitor should wash her face had elicited a chuckle from the Sister and she was still enjoying it.

The hearty meal, instead of energizing Rees, had the opposite effect and he felt almost too tired to eat the bowl of blueberries and cream that was put before him. He ate more and more slowly. When he glanced to the other side of the room, he saw that the children and Lydia were watching him. The cut on her forehead had healed and left a white scar that was visible even from this distance. Rees smiled at them, and applied himself to his dessert. He had come for them and wanted to spend a little time with them before Jonathan drew him away.

Elder Solomon rose to dismiss his Family from the meal. He was gray-haired and, although the Shakers did not use ranks, Rees suspected Solomon was senior to Jonathan. Solomon also wore a long gray beard. Rees was surprised to see it. Although the Shakers, like the people in the World, followed their own internal fashions, and sometimes beards were approved, most of the other Brothers here in Zion were clean-shaven. Had Solomon won special permission from the Maine Ministry? The gray beard marked Solomon as different, and that was unusual.

As the community scattered to their evening chores, Rees quickly finished his berries. Lydia was trying to keep the children on the other side of the Dining Hall, but they were not obedient. Although Lydia had a grip on Judah's arm, Nancy and Joseph had already begun running toward Rees. He scraped his spoon over the bottom of the bowl for the last morsels and stood up. As he started for his children, he was conscious of raised voices behind him. Angry voices. They were a shocking sound in the silence of the Shaker Dining Room. Rees turned. Jonathan and

Jabez were leaning in toward one another. Jonathan's cheeks were scarlet. Jabez, smiling in a condescending manner, said something in a low voice. It caused Jonathan to interrupt, his words carrying clearly to Rees's ears.

'How dare you say that? I will . . .' And then Solomon reached them, his back concealing Jonathan's face, and the younger Shaker's voice ceased. Losing interest, Rees turned around and started toward his children.

Nancy hurled herself into Rees's arms and Joseph clutched him around his knees. Jerusha and Simon were not far behind. With an exasperated sigh, Lydia released Judah so he could join his siblings.

'I'm in school,' Jerusha said. 'I'm learning to read.'

'Me too,' Nancy said in an excited voice. 'Me too.'

'When can we go home?' Simon asked at the same moment. 'I miss David.' Rees almost did not hear Simon's admission in the cacophony of other voices. Looking down at the boy, Rees put his hand on Simon's head. He worshipped David and, like Rees's older son, loved farming, something Rees would never understand.

'Children,' Lydia said, 'be quiet, please. We must speak one at a time. Jerusha, Simon.' She eyed them sternly. When the chatter had subsided a little, she leaned forward. 'Is the crisis in Dugard over then?' she asked with a frown.

Rees hesitated a few seconds, not sure what he could tell her. 'Mostly,' he said finally, reaching across the space to run his thumb lightly over the white scar on her forehead. Worry flooded her eyes.

'I know your family missed you and are grateful for your safe return.' Jonathan's voice came from behind him. Rees turned, Nancy clutched in his arms. Red still tinted Jonathan's cheeks and the tip of his nose, but he seemed calmer. 'There will be time to visit with them tomorrow.'

Rees tried to set Nancy down but she clung to him, her hands clutching at his shirt and her legs tightening around his waist. Lydia came forward. To Rees's eyes, she appeared far more pregnant than she had just a few weeks ago. She smiled at him, but Rees saw the shadow in her eyes.

'Come, Nancy. Come, children. Your father will still be here tomorrow.' She detached Nancy and put her on the floor. Rees reached out to touch her wrist. Jonathan clucked disapprovingly.

'The water is hot now,' he said. 'It is time to go.'

'I'll see you all tomorrow,' Rees promised his family as he reluctantly turned to follow Jonathan.

Rees paused at the men's door and looked back over his shoulder. All of his family watched him as he left. Lydia had caught her lower lip in her teeth and Joseph was wailing loudly, his face screwed up and his mouth wide open. Rees realized how hard the separation had been on them. They couldn't know what had been happening to him – and he was glad of that – or when he would return. And now he was leaving again, and every face betrayed the fear he would not come back. Rees lifted a hand in reassurance and followed Jonathan from the Dining Hall.

The two men walked down the main street in silence. Although Jonathan did not speak, Rees felt as though he was the target of the Brother's serious disapproval. Once they crossed the bridge over the creek and went into the thicket of trees, the shadows made it almost too dark to see. 'You have about an hour of light left,' Jonathan said. Rees nodded. He hoped he would not be expected to do anything else today; he was so tired he thought he might go to bed immediately after his bath.

Inside the laundry shed the Brother gestured to the large tub, which in Rees's opinion resembled a stone coffin with the lid missing. Rees examined it doubtfully. 'What is this usually used for?' he asked. The last time he'd visited the laundry shed, several years ago now, the space had been filled with large copper cauldrons.

'Laundry,' Jonathan said, sounding surprised. Rees examined the tub with more attention. Constructed at the proper height for washing clothes, the tub's edges had been smoothed and rounded so the Sisters could bend over it comfortably. Steam rose into the air from the hot water. 'With a community this size,' Jonathan continued, 'a lot of laundry is produced. A washtub this size enables the Sisters to wash many pieces at the same time. Cleanliness is one of the instructions from our Mother, Ann Lee.' His gaze lighted briefly, but pointedly, upon Rees. 'You know the way to the Dwelling House,' he added as he left.

Rees knew he'd been judged and found wanting. For a moment he considered calling after Jonathan but elected not to. Not tonight, when he couldn't trust himself to remain calm. Stripping off his clothing, he dipped his hand in to test the hot water. It felt wonderful. He climbed inside the enormous tub and leaned back with a sigh. He was accustomed to bathing with his knees up to his chin, unless it was summer and he could swim in the pond. But in this long hollowed-out obelisk he could stretch out full length. He dunked his head below the surface of the water and used the hard yellow soap to scrub his hair and body. Then he lay back with his head resting on the tub's edge. As he reclined in the warm water, he allowed his worries about David, still in Dugard and alone, to recede. For the first time in several weeks, Rees felt safe. No one would threaten him or his family here. They had found a refuge. He relaxed and before he knew it, he was asleep.

Two

Rees awoke with the sound of screams ringing in his ears. David, he thought in terror. He was half out of the bed before he remembered he was safe in Zion, and David was far away in Dugard. Despite Rees's fatigue and the relaxing bath, his fear for his son had taken over his sleeping mind and his dreams had been filled with running and hiding from angry pursuers. As his memory of arriving at the Shaker community returned, Rees turned to look for his roommate. Brother Jabez was already gone and his bed was empty.

Another scream sounded outside and now Rees could hear the sobbing that followed. He swung his legs over the bed's side. He was still in his borrowed Shaker's shirt. As another scream ripped through the still early morning air, he quickly pulled on his borrowed breeches. In too much of a hurry to bother with socks, he thrust his feet into his shoes. Then he ran out of his room, running toward the source of those wild cries.

It was just daybreak and the Brothers who were emerging from the stable and the barns, as well as the Sisters from the kitchen, had already begun their daily work. A sobbing Esther stood in the road, at the center of a cluster of Sisters. Despite the disapproving looks directed Rees's way, he joined the circle of women.

'What happened?' he asked Esther. He had never seen her so distraught. An escaped slave, she carried herself with the air of one who has seen everything and survived and so was not prone to displays of emotion.

'Something happened in the laundry room,' said Lydia, cutting through the crowd to join her husband. She put a hand on the sobbing woman's arm and shook it gently. 'Esther, Esther. Tell us what happened.' Esther sniffled and tried to pull herself together.

'A body,' she quavered. 'In the l-laundry tub.' The Shaker Brethren drew closer.

'Bathing?' Rees said, although he knew that could not explain Esther's distress. She shook her head.

'There was blood on the stone.' She tried to still her shivering by wrapping her arms around herself.

'Sister Esther,' Jonathan said sternly, 'calm yourself. I'm certain there is some simple explanation. Do you know who is in the tub?'

She shook her head. Jonathan's tartness had some effect, though, and when she spoke again her voice was steadier. 'He's face down in the water.' Now her gaze went to Rees. 'I know he's dead. He couldn't be turned over like that and still live.' She gulped and clutched at Lydia's hand.

Rees directed a look at Jonathan. He was frowning at Sister Esther and appeared more irritated by her emotion than anything. Elder Solomon, standing behind Jonathan, brushed a hand over his eyes. The silvery beard softened the lines of his chin, but Rees could see the older man's lips trembling. 'This is monstrous,' he said, turning away from the cluster of people. 'Such upset.' Rees glanced at him but spoke to the others.

'I'm going to the laundry shed,' he said. 'This may be a prank but I want to see for myself.'

'It is not a prank,' Esther said in a sharp voice. She sounded almost like her usual self.

Rees started down the street with Jonathan. Daniel, young but already a Deacon, and far too young for that post in Rees's opinion, fell into step with them. Rees glanced at the youth,

12

wondering why this boy had chosen to join them. His face was contorted with both revulsion and fascination.

After a momentary hesitation Solomon hurried to follow, and together the four men walked down to the laundry room.

The laundry shed had been built a good distance away from the main part of the village. As the men filed through the thick screen of trees, Rees realized it would be an easy job to attack someone here with no one the wiser.

The door to the stone shed stood open. Rees exchanged a glance with Jonathan and then, taking the lead, stepped through the opening. Just beyond the foot of the tub lay Rees's discarded dirty clothing, exactly where he'd left them. He jumped back, suppressing a gasp. Although he was very much aware that he had bathed in this tub the night before, seeing his clothing made the death feel personal. The tub felt as if it was part of his own space. Maybe this was even the same water he had used. He gagged.

'Are you all right?' Jonathan asked. Rees nodded, not trusting himself to speak.

A bundle of sticks lay scattered across the dirt floor where Esther had dropped them. Rees looked around and understood what had happened. Esther had come to the shed early to start the fires under the coppers so that the water would be good and hot when the Sisters came to start the laundry after breakfast. Monday was always laundry day. Then she had crossed the floor to the tub – Rees suited action to his thoughts – and looked down into the full tub with the body floating in the water. Esther's candle had dropped into a large puddle on the floor and gone out. There was enough light seeping though the door for Rees to see the blood streaked across the stone tub. The water in the tub had a distinct reddish tint.

Rees took a series of deep, calming breaths. He could taste the metallic, coppery flavor of blood in the air.

'Maybe he just fell in,' Solomon said. His shoes were already soaked with water.

'He did not just fall in,' Rees said tersely. 'There's blood.'

'An accident then?' Jonathan suggested.

Rees stared at the body in the water. He could imagine, just barely, a possibility in which the victim slid on the wet floor and somehow toppled into the tub. But Rees knew the man would have climbed out again if he were conscious. Rees leaned forward a little. It was hard to tell, but he thought there might be a wound on the back of the dead man's head.

All right, he thought, suppose the victim slid on the wet floor and cracked the back of his head on the tub. Wouldn't he have fallen on the floor? On his back?

Rees did not see any way this could have been an accident.

'We need to get him out of the water,' he said.

'We should identify him,' said Daniel without making any effort to approach the tub.

'He's a Shaker,' Rees said, sternly quelling his

14

unruly stomach as he peered at the body. 'You can see that by the clothing.'

'Not necessarily,' Solomon said, glancing at Rees. 'You are wearing our clothing.'

'Have you heard of anyone missing, Daniel?' Jonathan asked, turning to look at the Deacon. His mouth a tight line, Daniel shook his head.

'Somebody, help me,' Rees said, grasping the back of the body's sodden shirt. The man had been well-nourished and now his clothing was heavy with water. Even as strong as Rees was, he could not lift the victim by himself. After a second's hesitation, Daniel hurried over and then Jonathan. Grunting with effort, they lifted the corpse from the water and half laid him, half dropped him on the floor. He hit the dirt with a wet thud, and red-tinted water began running across the packed earth. Rees took several deep breaths. There had been too many deaths these past few weeks, but he would not crumble here, in front of the Brothers, and disgrace himself. Daniel ran for the door and veered into the bushes. Rees could hear him retching. Jonathan and Solomon also stepped outside. Rees followed them, but stopped at the door.

When Daniel returned, wiping his mouth, Rees said, 'Did anyone recognize the . . .' He jerked his head at the body by the tub. The corpse had landed on its belly and Rees did not recognize the sliver of face.

Daniel shook his head. 'I didn't look,' he confessed. Rees turned to Jonathan and Solomon.

'He is one of yours,' he said. They both shook

15

their heads. 'You should go back inside and take a closer look.'

'He could be visiting from another community,' Daniel said. Hopefully, Rees thought.

'Or one of our new converts.' Jonathan's sour tone drew an inquiring glance from Rees. 'A Winter Shaker,' Jonathan clarified. Rees nodded in understanding, familiar with the regular influx of new people in the fall. They joined knowing they would be offered three meals each day and a warm shelter with a bed each night. Usually they spent only the winter in the community and disappeared with the coming of spring. But the Shakers tolerated them, and sometimes one of the Winter Shakers became a valued member of the Family.

'Somebody must know who he is.' Rees returned to what he felt was most important now. 'We must go back inside and examine him.'

'I can't do it,' Brother Solomon said. His voice was trembling so much the words were almost impossible to understand. Rees turned to look at the older man. His skin had taken on an alarming grayish pallor and he was swaying.

'Sit down,' Jonathan said, gently pressing him down on to a large rock. Solomon put his head between his knees.

'I'll do it,' Daniel said, straightening up. 'If someone is with me.' He looked at Rees. Since neither of the older men moved, Rees nodded. Daniel took several deep breaths, and Rees could see he was preparing himself for what was to come.

They crossed the floor together to the body

lying by the washtub. Now Rees could clearly see the bloody wound upon the victim's crown. 'He'd been hit,' he said as his gaze traveled slowly around the laundry room. And hit hard, too. But with what? A shovel? Rees saw nothing appropriate. The weapon must have been carried away, and that spoke to intent and cover-up. As Rees had begun to suspect, the dead man had been murdered.

'Help me . . .' Daniel stopped. He was very pale. Rees bent and together they pulled the body on to its back.

Daniel shot a quick glance at the corpse. Then, with a quick intake of breath, he bent over and stared into the pallid face. 'Brother Jabez,' he muttered in surprise.

'Who?' Rees asked. 'You mean my roommate from last night?'

Daniel nodded. 'Indeed.' He nodded his head slowly 'It is no surprise Solomon and Jonathan did not recognize him. When I was a boy, several years ago, Jabez was a member of Zion. Then he transferred to one of the New York settlements. Maybe Niskayuna? I don't know. Anyway, he was gone for many years. We did hear that when Mother Lucy Wright called for volunteers to serve as missionaries into the World, Jabez was one of the first to answer.'

'Mother Lucy Wright,' Rees repeated. He remembered Lydia telling him Brother Joseph Meachum, the successor to Mother Ann Lee, had passed away and a new spiritual head would be chosen. Although Rees knew the Shakers believed in the equality of men and women – they

17

worshipped God as both masculine and feminine – he was still surprised that a woman had been selected. That would set the Shakers even further apart from the World. 'That must have caused comment,' he said.

Daniel nodded. 'Not everyone is happy about the elevation of a woman to such an exalted position,' he said, confirming Rees's own thoughts. 'And many of the Shakers resent her efforts to reach out and actively look for converts as well.'

'What do you think?' Rees asked.

Daniel opened his mouth several times, but was clearly having difficulty formulating his thoughts. Finally he said, 'I don't know. We need converts to grow, since we do not marry or produce children of our own. But some of the new members do not have the passion for our beliefs and find our rules hard to follow. I wonder if this effort of Mother Lucy's is not already doomed to failure.'

Perhaps, thought Rees, one of the Shakers in the Zion community felt more strongly than Daniel and had taken out his frustration and anger on Brother Jabez. That was one avenue he would investigate.

'Jabez was always known for his piety,' Daniel added.

Rees stared into the pale face. Maybe if the hair, darkened and slicked down by water, had been dry, the reddish-brown curls Rees remembered would have identified the victim sooner. 'I don't remember him,' he said. 'From before, I mean, when I was first here.'

'No, he wasn't here then. He did not return to Zion until just this past Friday. He seemed quite surprised by Brother Solomon's elevation to Elder, and he and Jonathan . . .'

Daniel stopped short, the color rising into his cheeks. Rees nodded, now recalling the heated quarrel he himself had witnessed the previous night at supper. Maybe one of the Shakers knew exactly how Jabez had come to be in the tub. But it was too early to voice that suspicion, so instead he said, 'Let's find something to cover him up. And then we'd better tell the others that Brother Jabez was murdered.'

'No,' said Brother Jonathan. 'We will not involve Simon Rouge, even if he is the constable in Durham. He does not know our ways.'

Rees did not speak until he'd mastered his frustration. He'd met this attitude before. 'It is clear,' he said very slowly, 'that Brother Jabez, a member of your community, has been murdered. The constable should be informed and given permission to search for the guilty party.'

Jonathan and Solomon stared at one another in horror.

'I don't like your tone,' Jonathan said at the same time Solomon spoke.

'You should know, Mr Rees, Rouge can't come into Zion and question our members,' Solomon said in a trembling voice. 'This was simply an accident. Regrettable, of course, but nothing that need involve an outsider.'

Jonathan nodded emphatically in agreement. 'Zion is not the World,' he said. 'Here we are

19

spared the temptations and sins of the non-believers. We do not even have a jail, nor do we need one.'

'Doesn't Brother Jabez deserve justice?' Rees asked, trying another tack. 'He was a community member. One of you. From what I can discern, someone hit him on the head and rendered him unconscious. Then put Jabez in the tub, where he died. That is murder . . .'

'It was a simple accident,' Jonathan said.

'But—' Rees began to argue.

'Mr Rees,' Brother Solomon said in his soft, gentle voice, 'please remember you are a guest here. You and your family. Please respect our wishes.'

Rees swallowed, the words he had not said a choking ball of disappointment. When he did not protest further, Solomon nodded.

'Good. We will arrange to remove the body to the icehouse. And now, it must be past time for breakfast.'

Solomon and Jonathan, with an embarrassed-looking Daniel following behind them, left the laundry shed. Rees waited a few seconds, until the footsteps of the other men had faded away, before following in his turn.

He knew Jabez's death had been murder but felt he had no choice but to accept the Elders' terms, at least outwardly. They had been taking care of his family and tolerated him only because they hoped he would gift the Ellis farm, Lydia's inheritance from her first husband, to them. How he hated to be dependent on this community, but he had nowhere else to take his family. Not now, anyway, when he'd given David his Dugard farm.

But most of all Rees grieved for the death of his hopes. He'd expected to find refuge in Zion, a safe harbor where he could lick his wounds after the past summer of betrayal and revenge. Instead, after just a few short hours, the ills of the outside world had come calling.

Three

When the four men entered the Dining Hall, every person except for a few of the younger children, turned to stare. Some youngster started to ask a question, and was quickly shushed since the prohibition on unnecessary speech was rigidly enforced. But Rees saw questions on every countenance. And the rustling of so many people turning in their chairs sounded like rain hitting pebbles.

Brother Solomon did not speak. He crossed the floor to an available chair and sat down. Daniel glanced at Jonathan, then they struck out across the room to find vacant seats. Rees chose a table close to the women's side so he could see Lydia, and deposited himself in the empty chair. A full dish was put before him. He stared at the eggs and bacon and the buckwheat pancakes, his stomach flipping over. He was too upset to be hungry and didn't think he could eat anything at all. He picked up his fork, but instead of eating he pushed the food around on his plate.

21

Finally breakfast ended. Rees found himself tensing in expectation of Solomon's speech. The Elder put aside his napkin and rose to his feet. A hush fell upon the Shakers. It was as if everyone had forgotten to breathe. 'I am very sorry to report,' said Solomon in his quiet voice, 'that Brother Jabez was found drowned in the washtub this morning.' Involuntary gasps hissed through the room.

'Drowned?' Rees thought, rising in protest from his seat. If Jabez had drowned, it was after someone had smashed him in the head. Solomon directed a stern glare at him and Rees subsided reluctantly into his chair.

'Drowned,' Solomon said firmly.

'His feet were wet.' A childish treble sounded clearly through the room, cracking on the final word. Rees looked around, trying to identify the speaker, but he couldn't see the children's table very well. An adult whispered 'Hush!'

When the room was quiet once again, Solomon glanced around and asked, 'Does anyone know why Brother Jabez was in the laundry room?'

'His feet were wet,' said the youthful speaker once again.

'You cannot speak,' said a woman softly. 'Do not say that.'

'Her feet were wet,' the child suggested, sounding almost certain. 'I saw them.' Solomon threw an annoyed glance at the children's table. Rees could not see what happened, but silence resumed. Brother Solomon continued.

'Brother Jabez will be greatly missed,' he said. 'But we can take comfort in knowing he will be going home to Mother.' He looked down and touched his napkin. 'Our Brother will be interred later today.' For several seconds no one moved, and then the sound of chairs scraping across the floor broke the silence. Rees did not see any signs of grief on the men's faces.

Rees looked over at Lydia and found her staring at him, her eyebrows raised to her hairline. He pointed to the door, trying to convey the message that he would meet her outside at the meal's conclusion.

As soon as the Shakers began rising from their chairs, Rees jumped up and hurried toward the door. He did not make it before Jonathan intercepted him. 'I hope you recall our ways,' he said, his tone severe.

'We will restrain ourselves,' Rees said, not very politely. He knew the rules but right now, after so many weeks without seeing his wife and children, he found those Shaker strictures lying heavily upon him. He brushed past Jonathan, and went through the door and to the street outside.

Lydia had gathered the children around her, and as Rees approached she pointed to him. All of the children raced straight to him, except for Jerusha. She followed more decorously, as a young lady should. Rees went down on his knees and tried to hug them all at once, kissing Nancy's fine silky hair and Judah's cheek and finally swinging Joseph high into the air. Jerusha wept with excitement and joy, wiping her eyes upon her sleeve until Lydia handed her a handkerchief.

'Oh, how I've missed you all!' Rees said.

'Are we going home today?' Simon asked, jumping up and down.

'I don't think we will be leaving today,' Rees said, glancing up at Lydia. 'I'd like a day or two to rest.' He sounded false to his own ears. He knew he would have to answer Simon's question eventually. But Rees didn't know how he could tell Lydia all that had happened, culminating in the loss of the farm. 'Besides,' and here he cast a glance down at his wife's pregnant belly, 'I want to talk to the midwife. It may be unwise to leave right now.'

'Oh, I fancy I have two weeks or so until the baby comes,' Lydia said, examining her husband's expression with concern. 'But perhaps it will be safer to wait.' She paused and then mouthed at him, 'What's wrong?' Rees was very glad that the throng of children around him prevented him from replying.

'Simon.' Jonathan paused a few feet away. 'Where's Deacon Daniel? You should be with the other boys. Back to the barns now.'

'But I've only just seen my father,' Simon protested.

'Listen to the wise counsel of your superiors and yield strict obedience,' Jonathan said. Rees could hear the quotes.

'Brother Jonathan,' Rees began. 'Can't he stay for a few more minutes?' He put his hand on the boy's dark hair. Jonathan frowned.

'You may visit your son later this evening. Now, Simon has chores. We do not want to encourage idleness, lest the young become like the children of the World. Come on now, Simon.'

Ducking his head, the boy unwillingly obeyed, dragging his feet through the dirt as he went to Jonathan. Rees watched in consternation as the boy disappeared down the path. Simon loved farm work, cows especially. What had happened to elicit that sullen reluctance?

'What's the matter with the boy?' Rees asked Lydia.

'I'm not sure,' she admitted. 'I've been told he's disobedient.'

Rees tried to imagine it, but couldn't. Simon was such a hard worker, a responsible boy who knew more about farming than Rees ever would. 'He's like a different child,' he muttered. A child with no joy.

'I love it here,' Jerusha said, clutching at Rees's sleeve. 'I'm in school . . .'

'And doing very well,' Lydia added.

'Will we remain here until October?' Jerusha asked, her face screwing up into an anxious frown. 'I'm learning to read and I'd like to continue as long as I may.' She turned pleading eyes upon Rees.

'But of course you'll attend school in Dugard,' Lydia said. 'All of you will.' She fixed her gaze on Rees. He did not speak. How could he tell her they could not return to Dugard anymore? 'Something's wrong,' Lydia said, and this time it was a statement.

'Everyone will learn to read,' Rees said, forcing a heartiness he did not feel into his voice.

'Will, what's the matter?' Lydia asked. Rees

shook his head at her. He did not want to discuss his bad news in front of the children.

'And here's Annie,' he said instead, gesturing at the young girl coming toward them. 'You look well. Happy.' Three months ago he and Lydia had rescued her from almost certain prostitution in Salem and brought her here to reside among the Shakers. She had gained weight and her cheeks were round and rosy. Like the other children, she was scrubbed clean; and her clothing, although faded with much washing, was sturdy. She was not the hungry, dirty maid he'd first met. 'I'm glad to see you are safe in Zion. Still waiting for Billy?' Annie nodded, her face beginning to shine.

'I had a letter from him a few weeks ago,' she said, taking a battered and grimy sheet of paper from her sleeve. 'Sent from the Ile de France.'

'And is he enjoying his new profession?' Rees asked. Annie frowned and then she bit her lip.

'I'm not sure,' she admitted at last. 'Maybe not so much as he expected. But,' and her face lit up with joy, 'he is still planning to fetch me when he returns.' She looked at the children around her, 'I'll miss them when they go home.'

Lydia turned an anxious glance upon her husband and tucked her hand into Rees's elbow, despite the knowledge she would bring the community's opprobrium down upon them. It was forbidden for men and women to touch one another. 'What's wrong, Will?' she asked in a soft voice. 'Is David all right?'

'Yes. He's fine. He and Abigail are planning to wed in November.'

26

'Oh, they're so young!' Lydia said as Jerusha clapped her hands.

'A wedding! I must have a new dress,' she said.

'Perhaps.' Lydia returned her attention to Rees. 'We aren't surprised, are we? But that's a happy occasion.' The happy light faded from her eyes. 'Is something wrong with the bees?' After the vandalism last month and the fiery destruction of several skeps, she had cause for apprehension.

'They're fine,' Rees said. 'The remaining hives seem to be thriving. No further harm was done to them. Or anything else.' He sighed involuntarily and Lydia stared at her husband, her expression sharpening.

'You're frightening me, Will!' she whispered.

'Nothing to be frightened of,' he said. 'In a week or so I may return to Dugard to check on David. But first . . .' He stopped. Lydia turned to examine Rees's face.

'Is there more to Brother Jabez's death than a simple drowning? There is, isn't there?' Rees, relieved by her curious question, nodded.

'Yes. The Elders want to believe Jabez's death was an accident, but it wasn't. He was struck on the head.' He hesitated, not wanting to share all of the details within earshot of the children. None of them, however, seemed to be listening. Annie was tickling Joseph until he squealed with laughter, and Judah and Nancy were running up and down the street shouting as they stooped to pick up stones. Rees looked around. He was even more wary of the Shakers overhearing him. But there were only a few Brothers and Sisters on the main street and they were all hurrying to their various chores. Every single one was carefully avoiding directing even the slightest glance toward Rees and his family. Nevertheless, Rees lowered his voice even further. 'I think he was struck by a shovel or something.'

'Maybe he slipped and hit his head on the edge of the tub?' Lydia suggested.

'If Jabez slipped and hit his head, how did he climb into the tub and drown?' Rees asked rhetorically. 'He would have been unconscious. And he didn't slip *in* the tub. It has round edges. Lydia, I saw the wound. The injury to Jabez's head was defined, sharp.' Rees paused and thought. 'But not as deep or narrow as it would have been if he'd been struck by a shovel. It had to be something else. Which was carried away. I didn't see it in the laundry room.'

'When Brother Solomon claimed this was an accident and I saw your expression, I wondered.' She tapped her fingers on Rees's arm and added, 'You know, Will, you can't blame the Elders for wanting to believe Brother Jabez's death was an accident. They're people of peace. And a murder would bring all ugliness of the outside world into Zion.'

Rees dipped his head in agreement but said, 'It's more than that. If Jabez's death is murder, as I believe, the murderer must be someone here. In Zion. One of the Shakers. There's no one else.'

Lydia shook her head. 'That's not quite true. Some of our guests wandered all through the village.' Rees looked at her, understanding the tone in her voice. Like the Shakers, she had not liked seeing all of those who came to mock.

'They were all dressed in their finest clothes. Blood or water stains would have been visible upon them,' Rees said. 'Besides, I know Jabez was alive at nine o'clock. We shared a room, remember? So Jabez was murdered sometime between bedtime and dawn. Is it possible a visitor returned then and made his way through the village, found his way in the dark to the laundry shed, which is not only distant from the main street but is also hidden behind a screen of trees?' Raising his brows, Rees fixed a look upon his wife.

'Yes, I see. So no visitor is guilty then. Oh,' she said passionately, 'I am so eager to go home.'

Rees could not look at her.

As Rees and his family reached the end of the buildings and turned around to start back the other way, Brother Solomon exited the Dwelling House. He looked up and down the street. When he spotted Rees and his family he trotted down the steps and hurried toward them. He frowned at the sight of Lydia's arm slipped through Rees's, and she hastily withdrew it and stepped away from him. Solomon looked at the children, one after the other, carefully inspecting each face as though committing them to memory. Finally he said, 'Don't you children have chores? Or school?'

'Yes Brother Solomon,' the children said in unison. Rees watched in amazement as the kids scurried obediently away. Solomon watched them a moment before turning to face Rees. He glanced at Lydia. Although he did not speak, she ducked her head.

'I am expected at the kitchen,' she said in a low voice to her husband.

'We will speak later,' he said and watched her turn and walk away. Then he turned to face Solomon. But the Elder smiled at him.

'You have a fine family,' Solomon said. 'We have so enjoyed having them all here.' Rees, who'd expected the kind of disapproval he'd received from Jonathan, was too surprised to speak. 'What are you planning to do this morning?'

'I thought I'd look at the body,' Rees lied. He had planned to search around the laundry and see if he could find the tool that had hit Jabez. The murderer might have thrown it away. Solomon's mouth and the corners of his eyes turned down.

'For what purpose?' Solomon asked. 'Idle curiosity?' Rees stared at the dusty road, unwilling to continue the argument over whether or not Jabez had been murdered. 'He was a fine man,' Solomon continued. 'A honorable and faithful Believer. He does not deserve prurient inquisitiveness or ignorant mockery—'

'Do you completely entirely believe Jabez's death was an accident?' Rees interrupted, stung. He looked up, catching the Elder's surprise and a flicker of uncertainty. 'I do not. And if the death was not an accident, I want to be sure Jabez finds justice. We owe him that at least.'

'Are you certain this is not about you and some quest for vengeance?' Solomon asked.

'I did not even know him,' Rees said, his voice rising. He inhaled, forcing himself to calm down. 'Jabez will attain his just reward in Heaven,' Solomon said. 'His death was an accident.' He turned and continued up the road toward the workshops at the other end. Rees watched until Solomon was almost out of sight and too far away to see what he was doing. Then Rees broke into a trot and headed south, to the laundry room.

Four

Once he'd crossed the stream, Rees decided to stop at the icehouse and take a look at the body. He wanted to refresh his memory of the wound. And anyway, doing so would make him less of a liar.

The icehouse had been placed over a particularly fast-moving part of the stream to cool the interior. Ice chunks, wrapped in sawdust and transported from Northern Maine, were scattered upon the shelves. As soon as Rees stepped inside, he felt chilled. A variety of foodstuffs, milk and cream primarily, waited here until the Sisters could devote some attention to them. The body of Brother Jabez reclined upon the central counter. Rees took in a breath and blew it out. It seemed only yesterday that he'd come inside this very shack to examine the body of Sister Chastity. And yet so much had happened in those intervening few years. Most notably his marriage, and now Lydia was expecting their first child . . .

He pulled his thoughts back to the present and approached the bier. He hadn't liked Jabez, and from the reactions of the Zion community deduced that no one else had either. But still, the man had been murdered and deserved justice. Surely, somewhere there was someone who missed him.

Jabez had been put on his back, and his bloodless face was calm and at repose. But Rees couldn't see the wound. The stiffening corpse proved more difficult to turn than Rees expected. Grunting, he pushed the upper body over. The left arm dropped to the side of the wooden shelf with a thud. Rees shivered and stepped back. He gulped several times to swallow his bile. God, how he hated handling dead bodies.

But once he'd leaned over to peer at the wound he lost his squeamishness. Blood matted Jabez's red-brown hair, and when Rees ran the tips of his fingers over the wound he felt a long, narrow indentation. As he'd thought, this blow would have left Jabez dizzy or unconscious. Rees wiped his hand on his borrowed breeches and retreated. Now all he had to do was find the weapon.

Although early September was not unusually warm, the air felt hot and steamy after the chill in the icehouse. Rees walked the few steps to the main path and headed to the laundry.

Even before he reached the clearing, he could smell the pungent odor of vinegar. The Sisters were scrubbing washtub, coppers, floor, and everything else before beginning the laundry. 'Mind the fire,' a woman's voice said from inside. 'I need more kindling . . .'

Rees moved around to the rear of the laundry shed. The Shakers had built it perched on the edge of the hill so the dirty water would go through the pipe and cascade down the slope to the stream below. Rees reckoned that if he had struck someone he would not leave the weapon lying in plain sight. Therefore his best chance of finding it was to search the tree-covered rocky hillside behind the shed.

Rees started descending the slope, leaping from rock to rock. Exposed tree roots snarled the expanses between the boulders, ready to trip the unwary. But Rees hoped he would find the murder weapon caught somewhere in this rough terrain. After all, the murderer would have been hurried and probably jittery. Killing another man – even if by accident, and Rees was not sure that was the case here – was not easy.

He crisscrossed the slope, estimating the distance you could throw something from the top. And finally, halfway down, he found a poker, one end stained dark. Although Rees picked it up, he didn't touch the stained end. When he peered at it more closely he saw strands of hair: curly and red-brown just like Brother Jabez's.

He began the climb back to the top. When he crested the slope, he found Esther waiting for him, arms akimbo and hands on her hips. 'What are you doing?' she demanded.

'Uh, nothing,' Rees said, putting the poker behind his back.

'What you got there?' She stared at him with her brows raised. Rees hesitated. 'You better show me. I know you were looking for something. And knowing you, it was something relating to the death of Brother Jabez.' With a sigh Rees took the poker out from behind his back. She looked at it and then raised her eyes to his face. 'I knew, as soon as I saw you sneaking through the trees, that you thought Jabez's death was murder. I just knew.'

'Yes,' Rees said.

She sucked in her breath. 'So, Solomon was lying when he said Jabez drowned.'

'Not necessarily,' Rees said, considering the soft-spoken Brother. 'Jabez probably did drown. But someone hit him on the head before putting him in the tub.'

'What are you going to do now?'

'I thought I would show this poker to Solomon and Jonathan.' Rees offered Esther a humorless grin. 'And press them to allow me to investigate. Jabez was murdered. That means there's a killer here.'

Esther nodded. 'The Elders will have to discuss this. But you have my support.'

'I want to start now,' Rees said. 'Jabez's murderer was here, in Zion. Has anyone left suddenly? Or is one of the Brethren behaving strangely?'

'I really do not want to believe anyone I know is guilty,' Esther said as she covered her face with her hands. Sighing, she rubbed her eyes. 'But we do have a few hired men. And some new converts.' She looked up at the sky. 'Jonathan is probably making brooms now. Solomon would be next door, in the leather shop, making whips. For sale, you know?' Rees nodded. The Shakers went on regular journeys into the World to sell their wares.

'I'll take this to them now then,' he said.

Rees crossed the stream and walked north on the main street until he reached the workshops. They were lined up in a row behind the Meetinghouse. The woodworking shop was first, and through the open door Rees could see Jonathan turning wooden broom handles on the lathe. The sweet smell of fresh wood perfumed the air inside and out. Rees went up the few steps and into the interior. The younger Brother working beside Jonathan looked up and smiled at Rees, but Jonathan displayed no sign at all that he knew Rees was there.

'I found the murder weapon,' Rees said. Jonathan continued working. 'I said,' Rees raised his voice, 'I found the poker that struck Jabez. He was murdered.'

Now Jonathan looked up. And Brother Solomon, who had been working in the next room on attaching whips to their wooden handles, dropped the leather strap and ran through the connecting door.

'You did what?'

Rees held out the poker. 'I found this near the laundry, on the hill in back where it had been thrown. Look at it.' Jonathan darted a quick glance at the poker, but Solomon turned his head aside. 'Can you see the hair? It is exactly the color of Brother Jabez's. Someone struck Jabez in the head and then put his body into the tub. It is time to alert the constable.'

'No, no,' Solomon said. 'The upset to this peaceful community, it does not bear imagining.'

'You've done investigating before,' Jonathan said to Rees, sounding as though the words were choking him. 'Would you look into the death?'

'Yes,' agreed Solomon, jumping on the suggestion with eagerness. 'That is a much better solution. I am persuaded that one of our visitors, maybe someone who knew Jabez previously, killed him. Not one of us.'

'Maybe so,' Rees said politely. 'Although the visitors had been gone many hours when Jabez made his ill-fated trip to the laundry. I spoke with Esther. She suggested that the hired men be questioned. And also any of the new members here.'

Solomon's white brows rose and he smiled. 'Of course. The hired men. I should have considered such a possibility. Maybe Jonathan,' he looked at him, 'might prepare a list of the newest members.'

Jonathan frowned. Rees suspected that the Brother would have argued, despite the rule of obedience, but for Rees standing right there. 'I'll make the list immediately and bring it to you,' Jonathan muttered, his tanned face scowling at the floor.

'Thank you,' Rees said, disposed to be gracious now that he'd gotten his way. 'I'll talk to the hired men straightaway. Where might I find them?'

36

'In the orchards,' said Solomon. 'You'll find them in the orchards.'

The orchards filled all the land between the blacksmith and the Surry Road. As Rees approached, he saw most of the Brothers carrying baskets from tree to tree and filling them with apples. They had been at this for some time. Most of the lower branches were bare; the remaining apples were high at the top. The Sisters would use some for baked goods, but most would be turned into the Shakers' excellent cider. The air was sweet with the winey scent of rotting fruit.

To one side, separated by several rows, were three men. Although in this case they were doing the same work as the Brothers, the division between them could not have been more obvious.

Rees crossed the orchard. As he neared the men, the youngest one climbed down from the tree, and the boys – for boys they were, the oldest could not have been more than early twenties – lined up shoulder to shoulder to face him. Rees looked at them thoughtfully. All were stocky and dark-haired, and their faces bore a strong resemblance. Clearly brothers, and already accustomed to facing a hostile world as one. 'What do you want?' asked the eldest. He was shorter than his younger brothers, but responsibility had put lines in his forehead.

'Just to ask a few questions,' Rees said with an easy smile. 'You're not in any trouble.'

'Huh,' replied the young man in a scornful voice. 'If a pie go missing, we get the blame.'

'What's your name?' Rees asked.

'Palmer.'

'All right, Misters Palmer. Well, this morning, one of the Brothers was found dead in the laundry tub.'

'See?' cried the eldest Palmer. 'What did I say? Next they'll be accusing us.'

'Nobody's accusing you,' Rees said. Yet. 'Did any of you see anything?'

'No.'

'What time do you begin your chores?' Rees could see that breaking through the crust of suspicion was going to be difficult.

'We gets up before dawn. The bell rings.' The eldest Palmer paused. Rees nodded to encourage him. Everyone on a farm arose early to begin chores; milking usually began by four. 'Then we go to breakfast at five.'

'Five? The Shakers are called to eat at six,' Rees said. The young man nodded.

'We eat before this lot.' He scowled. 'I suppose they think we'll contaminate them if we eat together. We're "too much of the World".' Rees clearly heard the quote and pity washed over him. These poor boys. Besides the work and the food, they needed some kind of family.

'I'm sorry,' Rees said, knowing that was inadequate.

'At least the food be good and there be plenty of it,' said the second oldest. He was probably twenty or so. Rees looked at the third brother who never raised his eyes from the ground. How old was he? Eighteen?

'So, you continue your chores after breakfast? Six?' Rees asked. The three young men nodded.

'Little before. One of the Brothers tells us what to do that day.'

Rees pondered. Zion began coming alive before dawn; by four or so the Brothers and Sisters were awake and beginning their daily work. Rees knew Jabez had gone to bed the previous night. Well, Rees had seen the other man lie down as though ready for slumber. Jabez could have arisen again as soon as Rees fell asleep. 'What time do you go to bed?' he asked.

For the first time the elder boy looked at his siblings before speaking. 'We goes to bed before dark,' said the second brother. 'But our Ned likes to do a bit of reading before he sleeps.'

Rees looked at the youngest boy with more interest. If asked, Rees would have guessed the boys were illiterate. Ned looked up, met Rees's gaze for a fleeting second, and looked down again. 'I read the paper for a few minutes,' he muttered. 'Not long. Have to save the candle. But I didn't see anything. I wouldn't, would I? We sleep clear on the other side of the village, next to the Infirmary.'

'And none of us wake until the bell rings,' said the older brother. 'These two,' he gestured at the younger boys, 'sleep like the dead.' Rees thought they probably did. The work was hard and went from before sun up to sun down.

He wondered now if Jabez could have gotten up very early to meet his killer in the laundry room. 'Where do you wash?' he asked suddenly. The oldest boy looked surprised.

'In the bowl in our room.' He paused and then added, 'I don't know what you're getting at, but

39

we always be together. We sleep in the same room. We eat together. And we work together.'
Rees turned to look at the other two boys. The second eldest was nodding. The youngest continued staring at the dirt. He certainly seemed used to having his elder brothers speak for him.

'Did you ever meet anyone called Brother Jabez?'

As one, all three of the boys shook their heads. Rees guessed they wouldn't recognize him if they had seen him. All the Shakers were identically garbed and Jabez had been here only a few days.

'Do you recognize this poker?' Rees asked. The three boys glanced at it and then back to Rees.

'It looks like every other poker,' said the oldest brother.

'And you didn't see anything unusual? On your way to the Dining Hall maybe?'

'What would that be?' The elder boy's mouth turned down at the corners. 'They all be strange to us. Didn't see anyone but them, though.'

Rees nodded. He saw no reason why these boys would lie and they had only corroborated what he thought himself: no stranger had come into Zion property and murdered Brother Jabez. 'Well, thank you,' he said and turned back toward the village.

Five

Rees crossed the wooden bridge over the stream and headed up toward the center of town. It was mid-morning, approaching ten or ten thirty, and the sun was already hot on his shoulders. Rees planned to hitch Hannibal to the wagon and drive into town. Although the Elders had agreed Rees should look into the death, he knew they still wished to exclude the constable. But, their command or no, he felt Rouge should know about Jabez's death.

He didn't reach the stables before Jonathan intercepted him. 'Wait, Mr Rees. Brother Solomon tasked me with drawing up a list of all the new members or future members of our Family.' Jonathan handed a square of paper to Rees. It had been folded over, the creases sharp and the edges lined up. When he unfolded it, he realized this was a full sheet, not just a scrap torn from a larger piece, and that the handwriting flowed elegantly across the page. Jonathan's desire for perfection extended even to this informal document.

Rees looked at the four names inscribed upon the paper, two women and two men. 'Tell me something about these people, please,' he said.

'I know little about Sister Deborah. She is just a young girl.'

Rees nodded. Lydia might know her. And if she didn't, probably Annie would.

41

'Sister Elizabeth and Brother Robert are older, a married couple, who say they wish to spend their final days in the service of God.' As Jonathan spoke, Deacon Daniel crossed the road to join them.

'How old?' Rees asked.

Jonathan looked at Daniel. The younger man shrugged and said, 'Elderly. Fifties perhaps. Their children are almost grown, I believe. And of course Sister Elizabeth is ill.'

Rees thought he knew this story: two white-haired old people in poor health searching for a safe and comfortable berth for their declining years. He mentally moved them to the bottom of his list. It would have taken some strength to push Jabez, although he was not a tall or husky man, into the washtub.

'Then there is Brother Calvin.' Jonathan's voice flattened out and Rees raised his brows inquiringly. 'I prefer you interview him yourself and make your own determination,' he said. Rees could see there was something, some problem maybe, with Calvin.

'Don't forget Brother Aaron,' Daniel said.

'He's not a new member,' Jonathan said, his black eyebrows snapping together. 'Aaron's been one of us for ten years or more.'

'But he just returned from a selling trip,' Daniel persisted. 'He's been gone several months, almost all summer. You know what he's like, perhaps he offended one of the World's People.'

'Daniel,' Jonathan said. His quiet voice was sharp with reproof. Daniel ducked his head, his lips pressed tight into a stubborn line.

'Where are these men now?' Rees asked.

'Brother Robert is in the smithy,' Jonathan said, gesturing to the stables behind Rees, directly across from the Dwelling House. Rees nodded. He knew where the smithy was. It was at the bottom of the path that led to the cottage where Lydia had once resided. 'He was a blacksmith by trade, so it seemed fitting to ask him to work at a craft he knows. As for Aaron?' Jonathan looked at Daniel once again.

'Brother Aaron is mucking out the barn,' Daniel said. Rees wondered if Aaron had done something to deserve a punishment, but he knew Daniel would not say, especially not now, in Jonathan's presence. 'Calvin is supposed to be helping him.'

'I don't know where the girl Deborah is, but Sister Elizabeth is in the infirmary,' Daniel continued. Rees whistled silently. Elizabeth had to be critically ill if she was in the Infirmary. Believers, if they were not too sick, preferred to remain in their rooms.

'How old is Deborah?' Jonathan asked. 'Isn't she in school?' Daniel shrugged. He didn't know.

Rees hoped that were so. He could visit the school under the pretext of seeing his daughters and Annie, and at the same time speak to this Deborah. He expected a few sentences to be sufficient – a young girl would never have the strength to lift a grown man. But Rees would interview her anyway, as he would Sister Elizabeth in the infirmary, just in case one of them had seen or heard something important.

Rees glanced up at the sky just as Jonathan

43

said, 'It's going on eleven. Prayers will begin soon.' With brief nods in Rees's direction, the two Brothers began walking toward the Meetinghouse. They would be early. Few others had left their work yet, although in a short while the street would be thronged with people on their way there.

Rees turned around and walked to the smithy. Pausing at the door, he waited for a moment to allow his eyes to adjust. Despite the morning sun streaming through the door in a bright square patch, the rest of the interior of the smithy was dim and shadowy. Supplies of bar iron and wood framed the door through which Rees had entered. On the back wall, opposite the entrance, was a loft with a ladder rising to the upper level. Rees couldn't see what the Brothers had stored there.

To Rees's right was located a pipe kiln as well as a barrel of broken white pieces. These were discards, the manufacture of pipes being a major source of revenue. But the three Brothers who labored here were gathered around the anvil that dominated the center of the smithy.

They were all muscular specimens and all hatless, but only one of them had white hair. 'Brother Robert?' Rees asked, raising his voice to be heard over the banging of the hammer upon a horseshoe. The clang – clang – clang ceased and all three Brothers turned.

'What?' said the man with the white hair.

'I'm Will Rees.' The Shaker tilted his head, the better to hear, and Rees repeated himself, raising his voice as he added, 'Brother Jonathan gave me your name. I was hoping you could help me.'

'Oh yes? Why do you want to talk to me?'

Rees gestured to the street outside. No conversation could be held in a smithy. Brother Robert dropped the wood he was holding near the fire and followed Rees into the yard outside. He appeared much younger in the bright light. Although his hair was white and his face creased, the arms revealed by his rolled-up shirtsleeves were solid. His broad shoulders stretched the vest to the limit. With a hat covering his hair, he would appear much younger than described by Solomon. In fact Rees suspected Robert was no older than forty-five, if that.

'Not what you were expecting?' Robert asked in a dry voice. Rees could think of no response. The task of questioning a feeble old man had now become something quite different. 'My father lived well into his eighties.'

'A great age,' Rees said. 'Why did you join the Shakers?' He was too curious to be tactful. Robert inclined his head and gestured to his ears. Rees repeated the question, more loudly this time. Robert smiled.

'A common question. I met my wife Elizabeth in 1782, during Mother Lee's journey through New York to Boston. We were both widowed and my children were already older. They're adults now, of course. Anyway, Mother Ann's devotion to God and the oratory of her brother William converted us. It was there we met Solomon, Solomon and his brother Abraham Vors.'

45

'Elder Solomon?' Rees asked. Robert nodded.
'He was a passionate follower of Mother Ann. Still is. His brother didn't stay within the fold for very long, though. Too much obedience, I always thought.'

'You left as well, didn't you?' Rees interrupted with a question. 'What happened?'

Robert shrugged. 'You should know. Didn't you marry a Shaker Sister?' He grinned at Rees as though they were comrades. 'We fell in love. Those were heady days, Brother Rees.'

'Just Rees.'

'Very well, *just* Rees. You must understand there were few of us then, in Mother's party. We were hounded on all sides by non-believers, physically attacked by those who branded us heretics and in frequent danger of our lives.' He stopped short and shook his head. 'But you don't want to hear all this. In summary, by the time Mother Ann returned to New York, Elizabeth and I knew we wished to be man and wife. So we left and married. But we never forgot Mother Ann or the faith she established. When Elizabeth fell ill . . .'

He stopped talking again, and this time Rees saw the moisture in Robert's eyes.

'Do you have children of your own?' Rees asked.

'Elizabeth and I have only the two sons, and the eldest is already almost thirteen. How time slips from us. We left them in the care of my brother, with the farm as their inheritance. And we came here, to recommit our lives to God.'

Rees had several other questions. His own son

David had been treated badly by his uncle. Was Robert really sure his sons would be well cared for? And why had Robert and his wife come to Zion, the Shaker community in Maine, when there were several communities in New York? But these questions seemed far too personal; and anyway, he knew they were irrelevant for his purposes. Instead he asked, 'Did you know Brother Jabez?'

'No. I met him for the first time when he arrived last week. And then we spoke little. He was very devout. No unnecessary speech, you know.' He smiled again, this time ruefully. 'I fear I have become much more talkative after living in the World these last fifteen years. Jabez was a passionate Believer, quick to note the faults of others. And he was prone to . . . making judgments when faced with our human flaws.' Rees, who had felt Jabez's censure himself, inclined his head in agreement. 'So,' Robert continued, leaning forward and dropping his voice to a whisper, 'what is the truth of Jabez's death? I know Brother Solomon described it as a drowning, but surely you would not be asking questions if that were the case.'

Rees eyed Robert with close attention, wondering how well the smith would fare in this community. Robert thought for himself, he was curious, and would probably find the rules governing obedience difficult to follow. Rees hesitated but decided, since the truth would get out soon enough, that he might as well answer. 'Jabez probably did drown,' he said. 'But before he went into that tub someone hit him. He had a wound

47

on the back of his head.' He held up the poker as though Robert might want to examine it. Robert took a step back.

'He couldn't have slipped and fallen?' he asked.

'He could. But why then was he face down in the water?'

'Yes,' Robert said, drawing out the word. 'He criticized many people. In a closed community such as this, such comments might fester. People take umbrage. Slights are not easily forgiven.'

Rees found it interesting that Robert immediately assumed the murderer was one of the community members. 'Brother Solomon suggested one of the visitors might have slipped into Zion,' Rees said. 'I've already spoken to the hired men.'

'A visitor? Hmmm.' Robert did not sound convinced. 'I don't see how a visitor . . . Well, never mind.'

'Was there anyone here in Zion who took a particular dislike to Jabez?' Rees asked.

Robert shrugged. 'I saw him in heated discussions with several Brothers. Raised voices – and one never hears that in this village. It's not permitted.'

'Who?' Rees demanded. 'Who were the Brothers? Names, please.'

'Brothers Jonathan and Aaron,' Robert said. Rees nodded. He'd witnessed Jabez's quarrel with Jonathan himself. And now, with a second mention of Brother Aaron, especially after Daniel's attitude of wariness and dislike, Rees was beginning to wonder about him. 'You should talk to my wife,' Robert continued. 'She's more sensitive to the undercurrents than I am. Especially the emotional ones. Women generally are, aren't they?'

'Yes,' Rees agreed. 'They are. I'll talk to your wife.' He often found the female perspective valuable, and Lydia's insights had frequently shown the way to a murderer. He suddenly missed her with a sharp pang and wished he could cross the road and haul her out of the kitchen. His separation from her seemed almost more terrible now when he knew she was physically close by.

'It may not be permitted,' Robert warned him. 'I'm allowed to visit my wife. Brother Solomon has been very kind, and at least they tolerate that. But you, a strange man? Visiting a Sister?' He shook his head, his face furrowed with doubt under that shock of white hair.

Rees wondered whether Robert's wife Elizabeth was expected to recover, but refrained from asking. It seemed insensitive, especially since a trip to the Infirmary frequently meant the patient was on his deathbed. 'Well, thank you,' he said. 'I may have more questions.'

'Anything I can do to help,' Robert said, turning as his fellow smiths, both exhibiting signs of recent washing, joined him. 'Although I can't imagine what I could offer.' The three men joined the silent throng walking to the Meetinghouse.

Rees remained standing in the street for a minute or two, replaying the conversation in his head. He wondered what undercurrents Robert's wife had sensed.

As the Brothers and Sisters disappeared into the Meetinghouse, the streets emptied. Within just a few minutes, Rees found himself standing on a deserted road. Zion looked like a ghost town. But he knew one area where the activity would be at its height: the kitchen. And that was where Lydia was working.

Rees went into the Dwelling House to put the poker in his bedchamber. He had hoped someone would betray himself with a guilty look when he displayed the weapon that had struck down Jabez. But no one had.

The Sisters had already finished cleaning, and Rees's bed was neatly made. The second bed and all of Jabez's possessions had been removed. A space designed for two was now fitted out for only one, and it felt too large and uncomfortably empty. Rees shivered – told himself a goose had just walked over his grave – and shook off the inexplicable chill that had swept over him. If it had not been for the loom in the corner, the loom that made the room familiar and anchored Rees to the person he was, he would have quit this chamber and demanded a different one. Rees pulled off the canvas covering and looked at the tool that supported his livelihood.

Now that the shroud was off he saw the damage anew, not just the marks and scars left by the boots that had kicked the pieces apart, but also the broken reed. Bent by one of the mob that had thudded through his house searching for Lydia, the reed could now not be fitted into the frame. Until it was repaired, Rees's loom was unusable. Just thinking about it made him so frightened and angry he began to shake. Closing his eyes, he took in several deep breaths and told himself his time in Dugard was over. He and all his family were safe here with the Shakers. Finally his heart rate began to slow. He would ask one of the Brothers to help him mend the reed; after all, that was the reason he'd brought the loom with him in the first place.

Finally, Rees opened his eyes. Pushing his personal concerns from him, he looked around the room. He had to hide the poker. This was, so far, his only proof that Jabez had been murdered. He saw no hiding places at all. Finally, after some thought, he slid it between the fine feather mattress and the rope springs below. He did not feel secure leaving it there, but at least it was out of sight and perhaps that would be enough for a few hours.

Then he went outside and turned down the path to the kitchen. The strong sweet smell of boiling cider permeated the area, enveloping Rees and submerging even the meaty aroma of roasting beef. The boiled cider would be used to sweeten pies and cakes and doughnuts; in fact Rees wouldn't be surprised if something flavored with the cider turned up at dinner.

As soon as he started up the steps into the kitchen, Lydia came to the open door and looked out. It was almost as though she'd been waiting for him. With a smile, she stepped out on to the small porch. 'I can't talk long,' she said. 'We're busy now.' Perspiration dotted her flushed cheeks, and ropes of sweaty hair were glued to her cheeks and neck.

51

Rees looked over her head. Besides Lydia, most of the kitchen staff was made up of the hired girls and the younger Sisters. Only one or two older women, sweating in this stifling room, had sacrificed noon prayers so that their Family would have a hot dinner to eat.

Lydia came down the steps and dropped to the boulder with a sigh of relief. 'I don't like having you work in such heat,' Rees said, eyeing her scarlet face in worried dismay. 'Isn't there some other way you can help here that will not be so strenuous?'

'I have been offered the chance to assist with cheesemaking,' Lydia said. 'And I may accept. I tire so quickly now.'

'Of course you do,' Rees said, taking her hand in his. 'You've got to take care, both for the baby and yourself.'

'You didn't come just to visit me,' Lydia said, fixing him with her steady gaze.

'I did want to visit you,' Rees said. Lydia laughed.

'Uh-huh. I think you have a question for me?'

'I wondered if the hired men are in the Dining Hall eating dinner.'

'No,' Lydia said, looking at him in surprise. 'One of the Sisters took them a basket. As usual. They always eat near the fields.'

'I wish . . .' Rees turned to look at her. 'They shouldn't be ostracized.'

'It is thought they are too much of the World.'

'But they are only boys.'

Lydia regarded him in silence for several seconds. 'I never thought of that. Your compassion does you credit.' She hesitated and then went on. 'I suppose by your comment that you don't believe they are guilty of Brother Jabez's death?'

Rees began to shake his head, but stopped and thought about it. What did he think? 'No,' he said at last, 'I doubt they had anything to do with the murder. I would like to question the youngest boy further, but without his brothers. He stays up later and just might have seen something.'

Lydia nodded her head, her eyes fixed upon the kitchen garden. Although most of the plants were still producing, browning leaves and dying stalks said it wouldn't be long before the garden had to be taken down for the winter. But Rees didn't think Lydia was thinking about the garden. Even so, her next remark took him by surprise.

'I know something is bothering you,' she said. 'I can see it. What's wrong? What happened after the children and I left Dugard? Did you not discover the villain behind the murders?'

'I did,' Rees said. 'And Constable Farley now knows I am not guilty of the murders. But . . .'

He stopped abruptly, not sure how to continue. The new constable in Dugard was a superstitious fool.

'There is so much I have to tell you,' he said at last. She clutched at his arm and Rees saw that her imaginings were beginning to frighten her, probably more than the reality would.

'Yes, I have been found innocent of murder,' he said, 'but Lydia, you are still suspected of witchcraft. Farley is still looking for you. He has a writ in your name.' Lydia sucked in her breath.

'But surely most people know how foolish that is,' she said, shaking her head in disbelief. 'That I would be a witch.'

'Farley remains in the position of constable and he is a believer in all things supernatural. I don't know what will ever persuade him of your innocence.'

'And Magistrate Hanson? He must know the accusation came out of malice.' Except for two scarlet spots on her cheeks, Lydia's face was white.

'Yes. But he has not suspended the charge against you.' Rees stared helplessly at his wife.

Lydia shook her head several times. 'What does that mean for going home?' she asked at last.

'I don't know. I mean I'm not sure.' He tried to think of something reassuring to say. 'Maybe after enough time away, Farley – and others – will reconsider. But still . . .'

How could he tell her he'd given the farm to David and that, despite his son's promises to put them up, Rees and his family had no home of their own anymore?

'Besides, with the baby due within a week or two . . .' Rees's voice petered out. He was hesitant to tell her all the truth because then he would have to admit to his own part in rendering his family homeless.

'I see,' Lydia said at last. Her voice trembled and she did not raise her eyes from the road.

'We'll return to Dugard this fall. For David's

wedding,' Rees said, trying to cajole a smile from her. But her solemn expression did not change.

'You hope,' she said. 'I may not be able to go. Not if Farley is waiting for me.' She shook her head again, as though she could not understand what Rees had told her.

'Lydia. Sister Lydia.'

A woman's shrill voice interrupted their conversation. Rees thought her call probably penetrated to the far corners of Zion, the shout was so loud. One of the older women had come outside from the kitchen. 'I wondered where you'd gotten to. There's work to be done. Dinner will begin in only a few minutes.' She glared at Rees, as though Lydia's idleness was his fault. And he supposed it was.

'Come inside now.'

Lydia nodded at Rees as she rose awkwardly to her feet. He watched her walk up the path and vanish into the kitchen. He knew she was unhappy. She'd be unhappier still when she learned the entire truth and the part he'd played in it.

Six

Roast beef was served for noon dinner and, as Rees expected, boiled cider cake followed. He was enjoying his second piece when unexpectedly Brother Solomon rose to his feet. Rees

55

paused with the cake halfway to his mouth and stared at the Elder. Solomon nodded at him and said, 'I am very much distressed to announce that it looks as if our Brother Jabez's death may not have been an accident.'

Even now, Rees thought, the Shaker Elder sought to disguise the seriousness of the crime.

But the Family understood. A soft murmur and a rustle of clothing undulated through the room. Solomon waited until all sounds ceased.

'At this point, of course, we do not know exactly what happened. Or what vile rogue may have crept into our peaceful village and confronted Jabez. Rees,' and he inclined his head at the weaver, 'will be looking around for a day or two. If he ascertains the identity of the villain who struck down our Brother, and I am confidant the scoundrel is not one of us, he will be turned over to the constable.'

Rees put the cake back on his plate. Although the Believers would never be so rude as to turn and stare, he was aware of the furtive interest directed his way. Jonathan, his face clearly visible without his hat, was scowling. Rees couldn't see the other man's eyes, he had them fixed upon his plate, but suspected Jonathan was seething with anger. If Rees put the best construction possible on Jonathan's reaction, he would think that the Shaker Brother was just very protective of the community. But Rees suspected Jonathan simply didn't like him.

Rees glanced at Lydia. She smiled at him, but the two furrows between her brows betrayed her continuing anxiety. The children, Annie, Jerusha and Simon at least, were all grinning, aglow in reflected glory.

As the community rose from their meal, Rees gobbled the last of his cake and rose to follow. He planned to drive into Durham first thing after dinner and talk to Constable Rouge. But Rees forgot his intentions when he saw Jonathan bear down upon Simon and point. All the pleasure left Simon's face, and with his head drooping he followed the Brother from the room.

Rees began to hurry after them. Then Jerusha and the younger children wanted to hug him, and Annie wanted to offer any help she could in a breathless eager voice. 'I'll see you all tonight,' Rees promised, trying to detach himself so that he might follow Jonathan. But by the time he exited the door and stared down the path leading to the barns, Jonathan and Simon were out of sight.

Rees began walking very quickly. When he crested the slope and started down, he saw Jonathan and Simon by one of the horse troughs. Jonathan was shaking a finger at the boy, and his voice had a clearly audible hectoring tone. And Simon? Rees's heart smote him. Simon was holding his shoulders very tight as he stared at the ground. Rees broke into a trot, catching up with the boy so quickly that neither Jonathan nor Simon were aware of him until he was almost within striking distance.

'You are disobedient to your elders,' Jonathan said.

'But David says that—'

'Listen to what Mother Ann has said.

"By disobedience to the command of God, man transgressed in the beginning and thereby displeased his Creator. Thus his children, in the same state of disobedience, were in a state of darkness—'"

'Enough,' Rees said, putting his hand on Simon's shoulder. He looked down on the boy's dark head and grieved that this child, who had supported his siblings by working almost as hard as an adult would, should now be treated so poorly.

'What are you doing here?' Jonathan asked. Although he kept his voice low, Rees heard the irritation in it. He took in a deep breath, controlling the urge to punch the other man.

'This boy,' he said, 'has already had years of experience with livestock. He does not need to be instructed by you.'

'Taught by this David, no doubt,' said Jonathan sourly.

'Yes, partly,' Rees said. 'David is my oldest son. And he was taught by Levi and Deacon William.' The mention of two community members well regarded for their knowledge of livestock, particularly cattle, sent a flush of pink into Jonathan's tanned cheeks.

'Simon is disobedient to his elders,' Jonathan repeated.

Not trusting himself to reply, Rees drew Simon to him. He was determined to complain about Jonathan to Brother Solomon as soon as possible.

'When are we going home?' Simon asked, his plaintive tone inspiring both guilt and sorrow in Rees's heart. Even if he explained what had happened in Dugard, the machinations of the adult world would be obscure to a child. Even a child such as Simon.

'I see Brother Aaron in the barn,' Rees said with assumed heartiness. 'Let's go talk to him, shall we?'

'Wait,' said Jonathan. 'The boy has chores. He must go to his caretaker, Brother Daniel, and the other boys.'

Rees shot a look at the Shaker that dared him to interfere. Putting his hand on the boy's head, Rees urged Simon down the slope toward the barn.

The wiry man stopped raking when he saw Rees and the boy coming down the slope. He waited, his hands folded over the top of the handle. 'You Rees?' he asked when his visitors were in earshot.

'Yes,' Rees said, pausing as far upwind as possible while still standing close enough to hear the Brother. The stench of manure was overpowering. 'You Aaron?'

'Yes.'

'Where's Calvin?'

Brother Aaron looked around as though Calvin might be behind him. 'I don't know. That boy keeps sneaking off. Doesn't matter, though. He's useless.'

Rees wondered if he was going to have to hunt Calvin down. He'd hoped this would be easy. 'You know Brother Jabez?' he asked Aaron.

'Yeah, I knew him before he went off on that hare-brained scheme of Lucy Wright's.'

'The missionary work?'

'Yeah.' Aaron shook his head. 'That's what comes of involving women. No female should be in any high position. And the men that follows them are fools.' Shock kept Rees silent. Aaron's opinion was shared by many men but was uncommon among the Shakers, where women enjoyed equal status. 'But Brother Jabez had to follow her,' Aaron continued. 'Off he went. Didn't return for a few years.'

'And did you speak to him when he returned?' Rees asked, still trying to recover from his surprise.

'Once or twice. Arrogant as a king, he was. Not here for more than a couple of days and thought he could order us all around. He spent a lot of time closeted with the Elders. Jabez didn't look happy to be back, I can tell you that.'

'Do you have any idea why he might have been in the laundry room? Especially at that time of night.'

Aaron shrugged. 'Don't know. Maybe Mother Lucy,' his curdled tone clearly indicated his disgust, 'insisted on regular bathing. I wouldn't put it past a woman to concentrate on fripperies. But I don't know.'

'Do you have any idea who might have wanted to harm Jabez?' Rees asked without hope. Aaron spat into the dirt at his feet.

'Nope.'

Since Aaron seemed to have nothing further to contribute, Rees began to turn away. 'Wait,' said Aaron. 'Calvin. Calvin, where are you, boy?' His bellow was almost deafening.

A few seconds elapsed before a tall lanky

figure loped around the corner of the barn. Although easily as tall as Aaron, the lack of facial hair marked him as no more than twelve or thirteen. 'What?' he said in a light voice. He was a handsome boy with big brown eyes and long glossy dark-brown hair. He eyed Simon with interest.

'This gentleman here wants to ask you a few questions,' Aaron said.

'You're not helping Brother Aaron?' Rees asked, hoping to put the boy at ease.

'No. He doesn't want to,' said the boy.

'Huh?' Then Rees realized that Calvin was referring to himself.

'He's an idiot,' explained Aaron. The glance he turned on the boy was surprisingly fond. 'But there's no harm in him.'

'No harm in him,' Calvin repeated.

'I see,' Rees said, now recognizing the voice as belonging to the child who had spoken so inappropriately during breakfast. 'He's on my list of new members.'

Aaron nodded. 'He was found a few miles from here. In rags, half-starved. I think someone cared for him until he started growing. He's strong. And,' he added, 'he'll be even bigger when he reaches his full height.'

'He's strong,' Calvin agreed.

'So someone got scared. Couldn't handle him, probably. Turned him loose. Lucky for him, a Good Samaritan found him and brought him to us.' He grinned at the boy. 'We'll take care of him here. He'll be all right.'

'He'll be all right,' Calvin said with a smile.

61

Rees inspected the boy. He was already a man's height but did not look particularly strong. Of course, sometimes that lanky build disguised enormous strength. 'Any chance he could hurt someone?'

Aaron shook his head but said, 'He doesn't like to be touched. But I've never seen him be mean.'

Rees considered a scenario in which Jabez tried to touch Calvin. He supposed it was possible. But then how did Jabez, a stranger to Calvin, lure the boy into the laundry room? And at a time where most people were asleep? Unconsciously Rees shook his head. He couldn't see it.

'Well, thank you both,' he said, mentally crossing Calvin off his list of suspects. Behind him, he heard Calvin saying,

'He wants to see the horses.'

'Very well, lad. Just let me finish this last stall. We'll look at the horses before we help with the milking.'

Rees had taken no more than a few steps when he thought of something else and turned back. 'Brother Aaron,' he said. 'I understand you just returned from a selling trip.'

'Seeds, herbs, brooms, whips,' Aaron said. 'So?'

'I just wondered if you met Jabez on your travels?'

Aaron hooted with laughter. 'I never went more than ten, maybe fifteen, miles from Zion. Jabez was in western New York. Course I never saw him.'

'Who went with you?' Rees asked, knowing the Brothers usually traveled in pairs.

'Young boy. That's why we didn't go far. He got homesick,' Aaron said with a shrug.

'Oh. Well, thank you.' Rees could not understand why Daniel had suggested Aaron – unless Daniel found his fellow Shaker so difficult he wanted to annoy him. That seemed a little extreme, but then the members of any group experienced conflict. Hadn't Brother Robert alluded to 'undercurrents' here? Although Rees planned to speak with the ill Elizabeth, he did not think she would know about Aaron. Rees would have to speak to Robert again and ask him some additional questions. He, at least, was willing to talk, unlike some of the Believers, and maybe he knew why Daniel had suggested Aaron.

Rees and Simon went first to the Children's Dwelling House, but no one was there. 'Is everyone already at chores?' Rees wondered aloud.

'Maybe they're waiting for us at the schoolhouse,' Simon said and darted away. Rees watched the boy run almost straight across the village, cutting through passing Shakers apparently without noticing them. Rees shook his head, wondering at the resilience of youth. Simon had shaken off Jonathan's scolding as though it had never been.

Rees followed at a more sedate pace. School had just been dismissed for the day and the girls were still coming out. They were all ages and of differing heights and coloring, but they looked alike in their dark Shaker dresses with the berthas

63

– the capes the Sisters wore for modesty – across their shoulders. Annie was walking with another girl. Her pale, flaxen hair shone through her translucent linen cap.

'Father,' said Annie, shocking Rees into a full stop. Annie's face went through a series of contortions as she tried to ask for forgiveness and explain without speaking.

'Yes, Annie,' Rees said.

'This is my friend Deborah,' Annie said. Ah, now Rees understood. This was one of the new members. And it was important to Annie, for some as yet unexplained reason, to claim Rees as her father.

'I am pleased to meet you, Deborah,' he said, eyeing the girl. Her pale-blonde hair complemented her milk-white skin and blue eyes. Her form, only barely visible under the modest Shaker garb, hinted at an age of sixteen or so but she was much shorter and slighter than Annie, who was barely fourteen. Deborah couldn't weigh more than ninety pounds and didn't look strong enough to lift a pail of milk. Rees sighed. Another name scratched off his list of suspects. 'Thank you, Annie,' he said with a smile. 'Are you off to chores?'

'Spinning until supper,' said Deborah with a grimace.

'I'm to help in the kitchen,' said Annie, returning Rees's grin with one of her own. To Rees, she seemed more relieved than anything else. He turned to watch the girls cross the street.

'You are so lucky to know your father,' Deborah

said to Annie, her voice easily reaching Rees's ears.

She wouldn't say that, Rees thought, if she knew Annie's history. Annie's mother kept a bawdy house in Salem, and Annie had barely escaped a life there. He didn't blame Annie for choosing to hide her past.

'He is a good man,' Annie said, her voice fading as the distance between the girls and Rees grew.

'No unnecessary speech,' said a passing Brother in a stern voice. Annie and Deborah lowered their heads and continued on in silence.

Esther was waiting by the door into the small stone building. She smiled at him and held the door wide. 'Come in, Rees,' she said. 'I offered the Sisters who usually mind the children an opportunity to do other tasks.' Rees nodded his thanks. He knew Esther from his previous visits to Zion. Of all the Shakers, she seemed to remember what it was like in the World the most clearly. 'But you have only a few minutes. All of us have chores, including Nancy and Judah.' Rees nodded. Younger children worked alongside older siblings or adults, gathering eggs, collecting wood. Nancy was already beginning to learn to comb and card wool and to spin.

Esther took up a position at the door, with her back to them. Rees appreciated that small gesture of consideration.

He would have gone immediately to Lydia, who was sitting next to Simon on one of the student benches, but Nancy and the two little boys rushed to him. He knelt and hugged them all. For a few minutes all was chaos as Nancy tried to show him her slate and Judah began singing a piece of a song he'd learned, although he did not seem to know it completely as nonsense syllables filled in the gaps. In the quieter spaces, Rees could hear Simon telling Lydia about Jonathan.

Finally Rees was able to squeeze himself between the bench and desk next to his wife. Jerusha chose a seat and sat down as close as she could. She felt she was far too grown up to sit on the floor with the younger children.

'Where will David and Abigail live after their marriage?' Jerusha blurted into speech. 'Not at the Bristols', surely? Will they live with us?' Jerusha leaned forward. Although Rees knew she was asking because she feared they would move away, he cursed her curiosity. He did not want to discuss this now and possibly have to confide the whole sorry tale to Lydia before he was ready.

'I think they'll be living in the Weaver's Cottage to start,' Rees said. He could not help glancing at Lydia, but her unwavering, thoughtful expression made him so uncomfortable he quickly looked away. He wondered if she blamed him for the disaster that had befallen the family in Dugard.

'When will we go home?' Jerusha asked. 'Maybe Abby will ask me to stand up with her.'

'We will go home soon,' Lydia said, throwing a quick glance at Rees. He said nothing. He did not want to lie, but he couldn't tell the entire truth right now either.

66

Judah interrupted the conversation by pushing a desk with its attached bench across the floor. The loud scraping noise was deafening. Nancy and Joseph had to copy him and it took Esther as well as Rees and Lydia a few minutes to interfere and return the furniture to its proper place.

'It's time to go to chores,' Esther said when the room was back in order. She looked at Simon and Jerusha. Although she said nothing else, the two eldest took their younger siblings by their hands and led them out of the schoolhouse.

'There's a Union tomorrow night,' Lydia said as they followed. 'We should have time to talk then.'

Although Rees did not want to confide the story to her in public – he knew she would be upset – he nodded and tried to smile.

Seven

Rees looked up at the sky. The sun was beginning its decline to the western horizon. He thought he might have time to drive into town and still be home before supper, although with the coming of September dark came earlier and earlier. Rouge could not be involved, by order of the Shakers, but Rees wanted to bring the poker to the constable. It was the only proof Rees had that Jabez's death was something other than an accident. Besides, he believed the constable should know about the murder, even if it was just as a matter of courtesy. So, as the Brothers came in from the fields to begin evening chores, Rees went first to the Dwelling House. The poker was still where he'd left it, under the mattress. He did not think the Sisters would be very happy to see the smears of blood on the mattress, straw though it was. Then he went to the stables. It took some time to capture Hannibal, and the time was going on four before Rees finally got on the road. Fortunately, Durham was scarcely an hour distant.

The inn yard, striped with late sun, was almost empty of horses and vehicles. At least, the back door to the tavern was open. Rees stepped into the cool, shadowed room and looked around. Only a few men occupied tables. Rouge was busily wiping down the bar with a grimy rag.

'How's the constable business?' Rees asked, stepping up to the bar.

'Rees. What are you doing here? Come to fetch your family from the Shakers?'

'Eventually.' Rees wished people would stop asking him that.

'Drink?'

Rees remembered that the ale here tasted like horse piss. 'Coffee, if you've got it.'

'Yeah, I think there's some left in the pot. When're you going to start drinking a man's drink?'

Without replying, Rees found a table that was not too dirty and sat down. He put the poker on the seat beside him. Rouge disappeared in search of a barmaid, reappearing a few minutes later with several cakes clutched in his big hands. 'The girl will be along with butter and jam,' he said as he sat down across from Rees. He put the cakes on the table. 'Go on, have one.'

'I've just eaten,' Rees lied. After a dinner of roast chicken and gravy, and fresh bread to wipe the plate with, Rees was not hungry. But he wouldn't have taken a cake anyway, not off a table marked by ale and whiskey rings and scattered with crumbs.

'What's that you got there? It looks like a poker,' Rouge said.

'It is a poker. I want you to keep it safe for me.'

'Why?' Rouge asked. But before he could continue, the girl – a dark-haired beauty with at least some Indian in her, if Rees was any judge – came to the table. She put the coffee down and the hot bottom added a dark-brown scorch mark to the scars already there. She slammed the mug down in front of Rees with a thunk.

'Hey, watch it!' Rouge said in annoyance. 'Don't go breaking any more dishes. It's been three cups this week already.'

'Cream and sugar,' Rees said as the girl prepared to flounce away. 'Thank you.'

'Ah, she'll be leaving soon,' Rouge said glumly. 'I see the signs.' Since the barmaids in Rouge's tavern came and went as frequently as straw in the wind, Rees did not respond. 'So, the poker?' Rouge asked.

'There's been a murder in Zion,' Rees said. 'A man, Brother Jabez.' He paused to doctor his coffee with the sugar and cream. The maid had

69

slung it on the table with such force that the cream had slopped out of the pitcher and on to the table. 'He was struck on the head and then drowned.'

'Struck with the poker?' Rouge said, eyeing the tool with disgusted interest. Rees nodded. 'And one of that lot is guilty?'

'Don't know. But probably.' Rees thought of the list of new members he'd been given and how quickly the potential suspects had declined. Although he hadn't questioned Sister Elizabeth, he was pretty certain Sister Deborah was too small to subdue a full-grown man. And as for Calvin? Involuntarily Rees shook his head. Why, the boy had the mind of a four year old. So all he had left of the original five names were Brothers Robert and Aaron; and while both were still possible, he wasn't partial to Robert. Oh, he was strong enough. But he and his wife had been in Zion only a short while, not long enough to know Jabez. And an acquaintance of only a few days seemed too short a time to develop the kind of hatred required for murder. Rees was, in fact, beginning to wonder if the murderer was not someone new but more likely to be a Brother who'd lived in the community for a long time. 'Jabez had been away for awhile,' he said to Rouge. 'He just came back last Friday or Saturday. I'm beginning to think he left not for all the high-minded reasons I've been told but because he clashed with someone.'

'And when Jabez returned, the murderer who'd been waiting all this time saw his chance and struck.'

70

Rees nodded, blowing on his coffee to cool it. It tasted a little bit burned and was so strong he could feel his scalp prickling, but it was still better than the establishment's ale. 'It was suggested that one of the weekly visitors slipped back into Zion and murdered the man. But I don't see how that could happen,' he said.

'Course it couldn't happen. Anyone not one of them Shakers sticks out like a sore thumb. Besides, how would a stranger know where Jabez sleeps? Or where the laundry is? Or where to find a poker? No, it's got to be someone on the inside.' He paused and then added, 'So which of the holier-than-thous is guilty, do you think?'

Rees took another sip of coffee so he would not lose his temper with the other man. Rouge disliked the Shakers just because they were different. After a few moments he said, 'The Shakers are men of faith and good neighbors, no matter how odd some of their customs are.' Rouge's black brows rose.

'Really? And after you brought me a bloody poker?'

'I have no suspects as yet,' Rees said. 'So I'm keeping an open mind.' Rouge grunted.

'You always like to keep your thoughts to yourself.' Rees said nothing. 'I'll speak to the Elders myself then.'

'Elder Solomon does not want you asking questions in Zion,' Rees said.

'What?' Rouge's voice rose in volume. Somewhere in the back, a string of curses followed the clatter of falling crockery. 'I'm the

71

constable in these parts,' Rouge said, ignoring the crash behind him.

'Yes. But you are not a Shaker. And I think Solomon would prefer to believe Jabez's death is an accident or caused by a stranger. Anything that doesn't involve his community. He wasn't eager for me to investigate but agreed because I am already there. In any event, I thought I should tell you. As a courtesy. After all,' Rees added with a mocking grin, 'you are the constable.'

'I'll have to speak to them,' Rouge said, ignoring Rees's heckling.

'If you insist, tomorrow would be better. Today they are holding services for Brother Jabez after supper.' Rees said. Rouge pulled his watch from his pocket and glanced at it.

'It's almost five now.'

'I'd better hurry then,' Rees said, rising to his feet. He paused at the door and looked back, but Rouge had not moved. 'Hide the poker in your office for me. And thanks for the coffee.'

When Rouge did not respond, Rees went out into the yard to reclaim his horse and wagon. He returned to Zion with the comfortable conviction he had done his duty.

Rees joined the throng of people walking to the graveyard. Although only slightly past seven, the sky was already beginning to darken. The sun, hovering over the horizon and wreathed in red and purple, sent beams of gold to gild the cemetery. The sunlight did not reach into the dark shadows under the trees, and several of the mourners congregated there held lighted candles.

Rees was not sure what to expect. His first Shaker funeral had taken place here, in Zion. Sister Chastity had been murdered – and at first Rees himself had been a suspect. In accordance with the Elders' repudiation of all ostentation, Chastity had been wrapped in a simple shroud and buried with only a tree to mark the spot. To the World such simplicity seemed like disrespect, but Rees preferred it. He knew that other Shaker communities sometimes used coffins and gravestones, but hoped Zion had not changed their way. He had found the plainness of the Sister's funeral very moving.

When the four Brothers carried Jabez to the grave, Rees was pleased to see the body had been placed in a simple shroud. Solomon read a passage from the Bible, adding a few words ascribed to Mother Ann, and the pale form was slipped into the grave. The men planted a sapling to mark the spot. The seedling joined a sea of young trees, their leaves dancing in the soft breeze. Some of the last pale light starred the newly turned soil. Unlike Chastity's internment, there was little emotion displayed. Jabez had been away a long time, and many of the Family here did not even know him.

Rees joined the silent throng streaming away from the copse of trees and into the village. As the crowd walked down the road and past the Meetinghouse, the quiet was broken by the sound of yelling. An argument? Here? Rees left the crowd and cut across the road to the Meetinghouse, ghostly white in the increasing gloom. As soon as he went around the corner he saw that Constable Rouge had ridden into town and accosted Brother Solomon.

Rouge was doing all the shouting. Solomon, his face so still it might have been made of wax, was standing in front of the constable in silence. When Rouge paused for breath, Solomon said, 'If you wish to come into the village on Sunday and participate in the service with the other visitors, you may do so. But there is no need for you to pester my Brothers and Sisters with questions. It is my belief Brother Jabez slipped and hit his head. Nothing else. There are some mysteries about the circumstances but Will Rees, who is already installed in the Dwelling House, will surely unravel them. You are not needed, Constable.' Solomon turned and walked away.

'Wait,' Rouge shouted after him, 'I'm not finished speaking with you.' But Solomon did not turn around. Rees approached Rouge.

'I told you not to come,' he said with no sympathy. Sheriff Coulton, the previous lawman in town, had known better than to push the Elders as Rouge had done.

'The corpse was in the ground before I even got here,' Rouge grumbled. 'I never got to look at it.'

'I examined it,' Rees said. He paused. Then, shaking his head, he said, 'There's no point in applying to the Elders now, they won't speak to you. I'll tell you what I find.'

Rouge glared at Rees. He turned and stomped over to the bay waiting for him. 'You just be sure you do!' he shouted at Rees as he mounted. Rees watched the constable gallop away, the dirt spitting from beneath the horse's hooves. Then he turned and started for the Dwelling House. He was suddenly so tired he thought he might fall down. This had been a very long day.

Eight

Rees awoke with a scream and sat up. Despite the cool temperature, he was sweating hard and his heart was galloping in his chest. His mouth felt like it had been scrubbed out with sawdust. He took several quick breaths and tried to shake off the aftereffects of his nightmare. He'd been on the run from Farley and his posse – Rees remembered it exactly as it had happened, just a week ago in Dugard. In the disjointed time of his dream, Farley had caught Rees down by the river. All the trees were on fire, the orange-and-yellow flames streaming to the dark sky. And David was swinging from the noose. 'It didn't happen,' Rees told himself, trying to untangle his legs from the blanket. He still heard the echoes of David's screams. In Rees's night-mare, his arms and legs moved as though they were trapped in molasses. He couldn't reach his son to help him.

Finally, Rees managed to push himself out of bed and stand up in the cool air. All was dark and silent. He guessed it was very early in the morning, so early even the Shakers had not yet arisen. He stumbled to the table and poured water from the pitcher into the basin. Then he bathed his face again and again until finally his heartbeat slowed to normal.

He did not think he would sleep again, at least not right away. He found his candle and tinderbox by touch. As soon as the golden light of the flame sent a circle of illumination into the room Rees felt better. After all, it had only been a dream. He was safe. Lydia, secure in a room across the hall, was most likely sound asleep. Only David was out of Rees's circle of protection. Rees shuddered. He had to hope Dolly's kin were watching over the boy.

A sudden heavy footstep on the stairs outside made Rees jump. He snatched up the candle and hurried to the door. When he peered into the dark hallway outside, he saw the boy Calvin, his hand on the door latch. He wore his jacket over his shirt but his legs and feet were bare. He turned and looked at Rees.

'What the hell are you doing out here?' Rees demanded, angry from residual fear and the relief that comes afterwards.

'He wants to go see the horses,' Calvin said.

'The horses are sleeping,' Rees said.

'He wants to see the horses,' Calvin repeated.

'If I take you to see the horses, will you go back to bed?' Rees looked down at his own linen shirt and the bare hairy legs beneath the hem. Did he dare go outside like this? Others, beside Calvin, might wake.

'Yes, she will go back to bed.'

'Very well.' Rees decided to chance it. He looked around for his shoes and slipped his

76

bare feet into them. Then he joined Calvin by the door. It opened silently, with only a faint squeak. They went outside and into the dark street beyond.

A three-quarter moon shone down upon the street with a pale, silvery light. Since it was early September and fairly warm, most of the horses were still outside in the paddock. The equines began approaching the fence as soon as they saw Calvin. He fished in his jacket pockets, pulling out half-eaten apples and bits of carrots. Rees leaned against the wooden bars and held up his candle. Nickering softly, the horses tried to reach the boy. He patted each one in turn, stroking their long noses. They knew him, Rees could see that easily. They expected these nocturnal visits and the treats that went with them. Rees began to wonder just how often Calvin slipped out at night.

Some of the horses looked at Rees as well, but he shook his head at them. 'Sorry,' he said. 'I don't have anything to give you.' But he patted one or two of the animals when they neared him, enjoying the feel of their warm coats underneath his hand.

It was peaceful out here. Dark and quiet, with the smells of horses, hay and melting candle wax. Calvin was easy company. In fact, Rees wasn't sure the boy even remembered there was another person here. The tension left by the dream began to fade. Rees closed his eyes.

When all the food was gone and all the horses had been patted, Calvin turned away from the paddock, bumping into Rees as he did so. Rees opened his eyes and yawned. 'Ready to go back to bed?' he asked.

'Ready to go to bed,' Calvin agreed.

As they began walking back to the Dwelling House, Rees thought he saw a flash of white at the back of the building. He stared fixedly at the spot until his eyes began to water, but saw nothing else. Deciding it was a trick of the moonlight, Rees joined Calvin as he ascended the steps.

The hallway was still silent. Rees looked to his right, toward the women's rooms. He knew Lydia slept in one; but even if he'd known which one, he would not have dared enter it. Yawning, Rees watched Calvin go up the stairs. When the boy disappeared, Rees entered his own room. As soon as he shut the door, he felt a wave of weariness sweep over him. He thought he could fall asleep standing upright. Blowing out the candle, he kicked off his shoes. He was asleep almost as soon as his head hit the pillow.

When he awoke again, his room was brightly lit by sun streaming through the windows. Rees flopped over and looked for his clothing. He knew he had overslept, probably by several hours. The silence, which was even more pronounced than usual, and the unusual amount of sun suggested he had missed breakfast. And when he pulled his watch out of the wrinkled vest lying on the floor, he saw that he had. It was already almost eight o'clock. He dressed and went out into the hall. The Sisters were already about their work, tidying the bedchambers and the Dwelling House for the day. Their presence confirmed breakfast was over.

With a sigh – it looked like no breakfast today – he went back into the room and retrieved his reed from the loom. Might as well resolve this. The sight of the linen bag filled with heddles made him sigh again. He hoped the Shakers could repair his reed – and that he could put his loom back together when they were done.

Once outside in the street, he made his way to the red-painted workshops. Brother Jonathan stood at his post making smooth, perfectly turned oak handles for the Shaker brooms. Rees went up the steps and inside. He would have preferred asking a different Brother, but it was Jonathan who was here.

Besides Jonathan, there were a few older boys working on brooms. No one paid Rees the slightest attention. After waiting a few seconds, Rees cleared his throat and Jonathan looked up. 'Rees?'

Rees held up the reed. 'Can this be repaired?'

Jonathan took it and sighted down the length. 'It's bent.'

'Yes,' Rees said. He could see Jonathan's desire to help warring with his dislike for Rees. His urge to be of service won, and he ran his hands over the wooden frame.

'The wood is split, here and here.' He pointed out the cracks to Rees. 'We can make another frame and straighten out the reed. That should serve.'

'Thank you,' Rees said. Now that he was at the point of surrendering the piece, he wondered if he could trust Jonathan.

'It will take a day of two.' Jonathan looked up. 'What happened to it?'

'Someone . . . Well, it doesn't matter.' Rees did not want to recount the entire tale now. 'One of my family was angry with me.'

Jonathan's brows rose slightly. Although he looked as though he understood the sentiment, he said only, 'I'll let you know.'

Rees went out into the sunshine with a lift to his step. He had not realized how much the damage to the loom had weighed upon him. Now he knew it could be repaired the whole world seemed brighter.

He looked around him. The Infirmary was in a cluster of buildings to his left, cheek by jowl with the sleeping quarters for the hired men. Rees wondered again why Elizabeth had gone into this separate building. Usually the ill were cared for in their rooms. Was she contagious?

Rees crossed the street and went through the door.

The windows were covered with curtains, so the room was dim and stuffy. Although there were four beds in the space, only one was occupied. Rees walked over to the bed and looked down at the woman lying there. Untidy gray hair straggled across the pillow. She was emaciated, and Rees wondered if it was the light that gave her skin a yellow cast. She opened her eyes.

'Who are you?' she asked, struggling to breathe with each word.

'Will Rees. I met your husband.'

'Yes. Robert said . . . you might come.'

'Brother Solomon asked me to look into the death of Brother Jabez.'

'Yes.' She stopped to take a few shallow breaths.

'I'm talking to everyone who may have known him,' Rees said. He could already see this was a waste of time. Sister Elizabeth could not possibly have tipped a healthy man into a washtub.

'I did not . . . know him.' She smiled at Rees. 'It is nice . . . to have company.'

'What are you doing in here?' A heavyset Sister with dark hair trotted toward Rees.

'Just visiting with Sister Elizabeth,' Rees said, holding up his hands. He thought for a few seconds that this aggressive woman, Shaker or no, might strike him. And she looked powerful enough to hurt him if she wished. She stopped barely six inches away from him.

'You can't be in here.'

'Brother Solomon charged me with looking into Brother Jabez's death,' he said.

'Oh, and you think Sister Elizabeth might have something to do with it?' The Sister put her hands on her hips. 'This poor soul who is too weak to leave her bed? Shame on you.'

During her fierce speech, Rees cudgeled his brain for another topic that might explain his presence here and diminish the Sister's anger. 'Of course she could not be responsible for Jabez's death,' Rees said, the words rushing out. 'But she might have known him in an earlier time. She and Brother Robert were Shakers long ago. I thought they might have had a special reason for traveling all the way from New York

81

to join Zion, rather than remaining in one of the communities there.'

The Sister's fierce expression did not soften.

'We knew Brother Solomon,' said Elizabeth weakly from the bed. She stopped and panted for a moment before continuing. 'A devout man. We knew his brother too.'

'That may be,' said the Sister, unmoved, 'but Mr Rees cannot be in here, with a woman, no matter how ill she might be.'

Rees puffed out his breath in annoyance. Now he remembered how frustrating it had been during his previous investigation here when he had tried to question the Sisters. Although he did not believe Elizabeth knew anything that was relevant, he did not want to cede the field to the nursing Sister. That would feel too much like slinking away with his tail between his legs. 'Would you let me speak with Sister Elizabeth if I brought my wife?' he asked.

'Your wife?' The nurse pursed her lips. 'When one joins our company, he or she puts away the spouse. They become as brother and sister. No more, no less.'

'That may be difficult,' Rees said in a dry voice, 'since my wife is expecting our first baby.'

'Lydia,' panted Elizabeth. Despite the trouble catching her breath, she still sounded pleased. 'She has come before.' The nurse glared at Rees.

'I will have to discuss this with the Elders,' she said.

'You do that,' Rees said. He expected the Elders to give their permission, and the Sister's combative stance betrayed the fact she thought so too. He turned and smiled at Elizabeth. 'I will visit again,' he promised. Then, with a final glance at the nursing sister, he went around her and out the door into the sunshine.

He thought he would walk to the laundry shed and take another look at the tub and the floor around it. But he hadn't gone more than a few steps when his stomach growled. He looked up at the sky. He had at least another two hours until dinner, but he didn't think he could wait that long. So he made a quick left turn and walked down the path to the kitchen door. Surely Lydia would allow him a bit of bread and maybe a cup of coffee as well.

But when he tapped on the doorframe it was not Lydia who came to the door but Esther. 'Will,' she said.

'Lydia?' He craned his neck so he could look over her head.

'Lydia is not on kitchen duty this week. I think she may be in the Weaver's House.' Esther glanced behind her for confirmation. Receiving it, she met Rees's gaze once again. 'Yes, she'll be weaving this week.'

'I missed breakfast,' Rees said. He attempted to look weak and pathetic.

'Hungry, are you? Very well. Wait here.' She disappeared into the shadowy kitchen. Rees sat down upon the wooden steps to wait. A few minutes later Esther returned with a mug of coffee, light with cream, and a napkin-wrapped bundle. When he opened it, he found the heel of a loaf of bread, a hunk of cheese, and a few strips of leftover ham.

'Wonderful!' he said. 'Thank you.' He tasted the coffee just in case he had to beg a spoonful of sugar; but it was sweet, just the way he liked it. It was not very hot, but it tasted like manna from Heaven. Rees took several more sips. Then he descended the steps to the boulder nearby and ate his simple meal. When he was done, he slid the mug on to the landing outside the kitchen door and went down the path to the weaving hut.

Lydia was seated at the loom closest to the door. Although the shuttle was flying across the warp, her mouth was pinched closed and tendrils of hair curled on her moist neck and forehead. Rees knew his wife did not care for weaving. She claimed to possess ten thumbs. And already she had stopped and was peering with a dissatisfied frown at the cloth.

'Lydia!' he hissed.

She looked up. Seeing him outside, her face broke into a smile. With a quick look around at the other women, she slipped off her bench and hurried outside. 'Will! What are you doing here?'

'Just thought I would stop by.' He smiled down at her. 'I visited Elizabeth in the Infirmary. You didn't tell me you'd called on her.'

'Only once or twice. Poor woman.' Lydia shook her head sadly. 'She is very ill. The white plague, I believe.'

'I promised her we would return,' Rees said.

'You have questions to ask? I wouldn't think the poor lady would know anything to tell you.'

'I understand she hears things. Maybe she heard something that relates to Brother Jabez's death,' Rees said. 'And after seeing her, I feel sorry for her. Anyway,' he added in a burst of honesty, 'the Sister in charge of the sickroom is an unfriendly sort.'

Lydia nodded. 'Of course you can't let her tell you what to do,' she said. 'That would mean she's won!' She glanced around and, seeing that no one was watching, grabbed his arm and pulled him to the rear of the hut, where they sat on a rock below the windows placed to let in the early morning light.

'We have a few moments of solitude at present,' she said. 'Tell me what happened in Dugard.'

Rees did not speak. Faced now with the confession he'd been dreading, he couldn't think what to say. Lydia's brows drew together in apprehension. 'What is it?' she asked. 'I know Farley is still suspicious of me, still wanting to hang me for witchcraft.' She paused before adding, 'And I believe we should face him head on.' Rees did not speak. Lydia exhaled and added, 'Whatever you're hiding, it cannot be worse than that.'

'I didn't know what would happen,' Rees said. 'Caroline was threatening to take the farm. And anyway, with both of us in danger of execution . . .' His voice trailed away. Lydia did not remove her eyes from him. 'I had to protect the farm.' Rees's words sounded strangled.

Lydia nodded, looking confused. 'Yes? So? I don't understand.'

'I sold the farm to David,' Rees said. 'But it's all right—'

'You did what?' Her voice rose. Rees put his

hand on her arm to calm her. 'You sold the farm? Where will we live?'

'David offered us the use of the house, at least until they start their family—'

'And then what? Move into the Weaver's Cottage?' She uttered a short bitter laugh. 'Us and five children?'

'Don't worry. We'll find a place.'

'In one stroke you've rendered us homeless,' Lydia said, her voice trembling. 'What will we do now? We can't stay here forever. Or even for an extended period without signing the Covenant. Brother Solomon won't allow it. The only reason he has been so gracious this time is that he expects to take possession of the farm that Charles left me.' She stopped suddenly, biting her lip. Rees couldn't bear seeing the tears in her eyes.

'Maybe we can live there,' Rees said quickly. 'Just for a while.'

'I don't think so. The Shakers have already begun to work the fields.' She paused. Rees stared at her.

'There's something else, isn't there?' he asked her. She hesitated. 'Tell me,' Rees said.

'Brother Jonathan . . . Well, all the Elders . . . believe that the land belongs to the Shakers already,' Lydia said.

'But it was left to you by Charles Ellis in his will,' Rees protested.

'You don't understand. He was living here, in Zion, as a Shaker.' Lydia forced a smile. 'Even though Charles never signed the Covenant, they believe he would have signed and the farm would have gone to the community. They haven't pushed it because I intended to give them the farm anyway, but they might if I insist on living there.' Rees didn't know what to say. For a moment they sat in silence. Then Lydia said, 'You'll just have to take the farm back from David. He'll understand.'

'Yes, he might,' Rees agreed, his temper beginning to fray. 'But *you* don't understand. I don't want to move my family back to the farm and Dugard – not considering everything that happened. Especially considering the charge of witchcraft.' He looked at Lydia. 'That is still in effect. You could be hanged.'

'But surely, now that your sister Caroline . . .' Lydia's speech trailed away when she saw Rees's expression.

'It may be possible to persuade both Piggy Hanson and Constable Farley to retract their accusations, but I would rather work on that while you and the children are safe.'

'Feelings ran high,' Lydia said. 'I know that. But I'm certain that now Caroline is not stirring the pot, I'll be safe enough.'

Rees saw his wife did not fully understand how dangerous it would be for her to return. 'We can't go back,' he said in a flat tone that brooked no argument.

'It sounds like you don't want to go back,' Lydia said.

'I don't,' Rees said, stung by the truth of Lydia's statement. 'Not until the charge of witchcraft has been laid to rest.' He knew that was only partly true.

'Do you blame me for this?' Lydia asked, staring into his face.

'No. But you don't understand.' Rees made no effort to disguise his irritation.

'Why do you sound so angry?'

'I want you to listen to me,' Rees said. 'We can't return to Dugard. Not right now. It's not safe. And that's final.'

'So we truly are homeless,' Lydia said, her voice quivering. 'Five children and a sixth on the way. What would you have us do? Roam the roads?'

'Of course not. But I don't want to see you hanged either.'

Lydia pushed herself to her feet. 'I think you are exaggerating,' she said. 'Once we meet with the Magistrate—'

Rees stood up as well and grabbed her by the shoulders. 'I am not exaggerating,' he said. 'And I'm telling you, it isn't safe to return to Dugard.' Frustration compelled him to shake her with each word. He stopped only when he saw her mouth opening in shock. He quickly released her and she stepped back. Without speaking, she turned and hurried away from him.

'Lydia. Wait. I'm sorry,' he called as he pursued her. She did not respond in any way, and when Rees reached the front of the weaver's shed she was already inside and seated on the bench. He peered through the door and called to her, but she would not look up. The other Sisters began frowning at him, and finally one of the older woman spoke.

'You cannot be here. Go away.'

Rees furiously stalked back into the village.

Nine

He walked around the village several times, trying to calm down. He was so angry and frustrated he couldn't even think. As he circled the village, he saw Brother Solomon. He was striding up the main road toward the Meetinghouse. Rees recalled his intention to speak to the Elder and hurried to meet him.

'Your Jonathan is treating my son Simon cruelly,' he said as soon as Solomon came within earshot. The Brother stopped and stared at Rees.

'What are you talking about?' An unexpected irritation colored his voice. Rees, who was already upset, felt his temper rise.

'Simon is a hard worker, accustomed to dealing with livestock of all kinds. Jonathan scolds him and scolds him and scolds him. He takes his annoyance with you and puts it on Simon. It is not what I would expect from this faith.' Rees stopped talking.

'This faith, as you call it,' said Solomon, no longer sounding gentle or kind, 'relies on obedience. I've been told of your son. He behaves as though he is the adult, not a child who must be instructed.'

'Well, in that case I think it might be time for me to take my family and move out of Zion,' Rees shouted. Solomon took several steps back, eyeing Rees as though he were a dangerous animal.

'That is your choice, of course,' he said. 'Back to Dugard?'

'No. I think to the Ellis property,' Rees said, too irate to think about what he was saying. He had not wanted to show his hand but anger had mastered him. 'I own it. And I think it best if I move my family there.'

Solomon's hand clenched into a fist, so tight the knuckles were a bloodless white, and red streaks ran down the fingers. Rees adjusted his stance so as to be ready for a brawl; for a moment he thought the Elder was going to hit him. But Solomon took several deep breaths. In that space of time, Rees's fury began to die. The hasty words that had tripped so easily off his tongue now appeared intemperate and foolish.

Slowly, very slowly, Solomon relaxed his hands. 'You must do as you wish,' he said. He took off his straw hat and wiped his arm across his wet forehead. Rees could see the effort it was taking the other man to regain his equilibrium. 'Perhaps that would be best,' Solomon said. 'But I do not have the authority to approve this step. I must consult with my fellow Elders. And of course there are legal issues that must be addressed.'

Rees knew he should apologize but he couldn't force the words out. Instead he said, 'I'll talk this over with my wife. And I won't do anything until we've had an opportunity to discuss this more fully.'

'Thank you,' Solomon said with a little bow.

'Now, we have but an hour before prayers and the noon meal. Please excuse me.' Rees nodded, although he knew his permission was not necessary, and turned to watch Solomon walk the remaining distance to the Meetinghouse.

Rees returned to the Dwelling House, feeling like the lowest villain in history. First, a quarrel with Lydia. He couldn't believe he had laid violent hands upon her. He must find an opportunity to apologize. Then he'd followed up that clash by arguing quite unnecessarily with a Shaker Elder. And it was all due to his decision to give the farm to David. 'I don't know what I could have done differently,' Rees said aloud. But he still felt ashamed, especially since the Shakers had taken in his family when they'd nowhere else to go.

As he always did when disturbed, he sought solace with his loom. The Sisters had already cleaned his room. The sheets and blanket that Rees had pulled to the foot of the bed were straightened, the floor was swept, and fresh water put into the pitcher. The women would return later in the afternoon to make the bed.

Rees went to the stack of pieces that was his loom. Every time he looked at it, he saw more damage. He might have to bring other sections besides the reed to the Shaker carpenters to be repaired.

First he set up the castle, the central structure. Some of the parts had to be knocked together but they were solid wooden boards. Then he began putting on the rear beam. So far, so good.

He laid the other parts on the floor, inspecting each one as he did so. Although heavy boots had scarred the struts with dents and other marks, nothing seemed to be broken. Even the heddles, which had been jerked out of their frame, were mostly intact. Only a few were obviously bent.

A sudden knock on the doorframe made Rees jump. He started for the door but before he reached it, Brother Aaron peered into the room. 'Have you seen Calvin?'

'No,' Rees said. 'Check by the paddock. He loves the horses.'

'I did.' Aaron chewed his lower lip. 'Also the stables and the barns. It's almost time for prayers before the noon meal.'

'I'm sure he'll turn up before dinner,' Rees said.

'No doubt,' Aaron said. But he didn't sound convinced.

He closed the door behind him, and Rees returned his attention to his loom. He had to stop frequently and think; it had been a long time since he'd had to put the device together.

He was so involved in his labor he lost all track of time. But for the dinner bell, he might have missed dinner as well as breakfast. Rees looked outside. Members of the community were passing by his windows on their way to the Dining Hall. He put down the beam that he had been holding and quickly washed his hands in the ewer. Then he went out the door of the Dwelling House to join the people outside.

Dinner consisted of beef and gravy with pole beans and biscuits, but it might as well have

92

been sawdust for all Rees tasted of it. Lydia would not look at him and kept her eyes fixed on her own plate the entire time. At the close of the meal she stood quickly and sped out of the dining room before Rees even rose from his chair. As Rees turned to pursue her, Brother Aaron accosted him.

'Calvin did not come to dinner,' he said, his forehead puckered with worry. 'I'm gathering everyone to search for him. Will you help?'

Rees thought of the boy and said emphatically, 'Of course. Do you think he wandered away?'

'I don't know.' Aaron paused as another boy approached, adding with a gesture, 'Shem here shares a bedchamber with Calvin.'

'He's not there,' said the lad. He was probably about the same age as Calvin, but this boy's eyes sparkled with intelligence. He added importantly, 'It looks as though he hasn't gone back to the room either. Not since we left to go to breakfast this morning.'

'Right,' said Aaron, with a definite nod. 'We've got to search all of Zion, from end to end. Including the mill and the laundry shed, and every single field and pasture.'

Jonathan, who had not yet spoken, quickly directed each of the men to a different corner of the property. 'Esther says the Sisters will search all the buildings, including the Dwelling House and the laundry,' he said.

'Including the cottage where my wife used to live?' Rees asked. Jonathan looked surprised.

'I don't believe anyone thought of that,' he said.

93

'I'll start there,' Rees said.

'We'll meet here, in front of the Dining Hall,' Jonathan said.

Everyone separated. Aaron and the boy Shem, assigned to search the mill, walked part way down the main road with Rees until he cut off toward the smithy and the path next to it. The blacksmiths must have already joined the search, as there was no sound emanating from the smithy. Without the clanging of hammers upon the anvil, this area seemed strangely silent.

When Rees started the climb over the rocks to the cottage at the top of the slope, he could hear the Shakers calling for Calvin. Rees was frightened for the boy. Although he was gaining the height and strength of a man, Calvin's mind was still that of a child. If Calvin left the security of this Shaker community, he would be vulnerable.

Rees reached the cottage at the top of the slope. All the flowers Lydia had planted around it for the bees had gone wild. The cottage itself was almost invisible behind the thicket of bright blooms. Rees paused at the foot of the walk. The sound of buzzing was deafening, and he thought that some of Lydia's bees must have escaped from their hives. There were certainly plenty here now.

The walk was completely covered with thorny roses and stalks of purple flowers. Rees's heart sank as he looked at the overgrown path. It did not look as if anyone had come here since Lydia left, a few years before. Nonetheless, he pressed his way forward, stepping as carefully as he could around the flowers drooping across the path. When he finally reached the cottage, he knew no one was inside. The door was so swollen with moisture Rees had to throw his entire weight at it to force it open.

The inside was in better shape than he expected. But it was empty and smelled faintly of mildew; the bees had made it in here and formed a large vibrating mass over a set of empty shelves. Rees could see the waxy tops of new unfinished cells.

'Calvin?' Rees called, his voice echoing through the building. No one answered. Recalling his tentative courtship of Lydia, both of them hesitant to love again, he walked through the small space. Nothing. He peeked into the small room that had served as Lydia's bedroom. That too was empty. Finally, sighing, he went back outside and retraced his steps through the thicket of flowers and down the path to the street.

Several of the Brethren and Esther and Lydia were already waiting in front of the Dining Hall. No one looked happy. 'No luck?' Rees asked as he crossed the road. They all shook their heads. Rees looked at Lydia, willing her to meet his eyes. He wanted to apologize. But she never turned her face toward him, standing quietly beside Esther as though Rees were invisible.

Rees began to wonder what exactly they were waiting for. A question was trembling on his tongue when Jonathan, who was sitting on the steps, rose to his feet and looked south. Rees turned his head. Aaron and the boy Shem were approaching with rapid strides. 'He's not there,' Aaron said while still a distance away. 'Any sign of him?'

Again, all of them shook their heads. 'Of course, some of the Brothers are searching the most far away pastures.' But he did not sound hopeful. Rees considered Shem, who was standing next to Aaron.

'Do you have any idea where Calvin might go?' Rees asked. 'Has he ever mentioned a place?'

'I wondered, well . . .' the lad paused and ducked his head.

'Go on,' Aaron said sharply. 'This is not the time to hesitate.'

'Well. You know the farmer Reynard? His horses are out to pasture. Just across the Surry Road and down the lane. Calvin talked about seeing those horses.'

Rees could almost hear the boy saying in his light voice, 'He wants to see horses.'

'Would he cross the road?'

'No,' Aaron said. 'He was afraid of it.'

'We should check anyway,' Jonathan said.

In a group, they all walked down the road, crossed the little wooden bridge and went through the narrow strip of trees to Surry Road. Although one of the busier roads in these parts, there was no traffic there today except for an old horse and wagon heading south to Surry.

They crossed Surry Road and walked down to the narrow alley that cut through a long hilly range. The narrow lane continued west, dividing pastures on either side. They could all see the horses in the pasture on the left, mainly cobs and brown horses with rough coats. But there were a few beauties in there as well, two white horses and a couple of chestnut mares the color of roasted coffee beans. Rees's gaze was captured by a bay stallion with a cream-colored mane and tail.

Besides the horses, there was only a flock of geese congregated around the green-slicked pond. He saw no sign of the boy.

Jonathan exhaled sharply and began to turn away from the fence. 'Wait,' Shem said. He wriggled between the boards and started running. The horses jumped and scattered and the geese took flight, honking as they rose in the air. Rees didn't hesitate. He was too large to worm his way through the openings in the fence but he put his hands on the top and jumped over it. The thuds of other feet hitting the ground behind him told him that some of the other Brothers were following him.

At the far end of the field was a stone trough. As Rees approached, he saw something that looked like a shoe. 'Oh no,' he said to himself, increasing his speed. The shoe was attached to a leg, and now Rees saw a narrow patch of white shirt at the other end of the trough. Shem started crying and shouting. Rees didn't want to see this, didn't want to see the boy, but he couldn't stop his body from running toward Calvin. He went around the crib and stopped, panting.

The boy was lying face down behind the stone. His head had been covered with dry grass. Rees went down on his knees beside the boy and carefully brushed away the straw. Although only the right side of Calvin's face was visible, it was enough for Rees to see the white skin and purplish lips. A deep bloody wound depressed one side of his head.

Aaron turned away, his chest heaving as grunting sobs forced their way from him. Rees took a breath, willing the moisture in his own eyes to retreat, and looked around. A chunk of granite lay nearby, clotted blood on one face.

'This is not an accident,' Rees said, as though there was any question. 'Someone lured him here. Probably walked him across the road to see the horses. But the murderer didn't want Calvin to be discovered too soon. So he brought the boy back here and . . .'

Rees couldn't continue.

'Who would do this evil, evil act?' Jonathan said, clutching the stone side of the trough for support. 'He was just a boy. He never hurt anyone.'

'Did he have a connection with Brother Jabez?' Rees asked, glancing at the assembled faces.

Head shakes all around. Some of the Brothers were so pale and sweaty Rees hoped they did not have to be carried back to Zion.

'To my knowledge,' Jonathan said, 'Jabez didn't even know the boy existed.'

Rees nodded. So Calvin must have seen something on one of his nocturnal rambles. 'But even so, why did the murderer kill Calvin?' Rees said, not realizing he was speaking aloud. 'Calvin was no danger to anyone. Even if he did see something, he wouldn't have known it was important. He might not even have remembered what he saw.'

'I disagree,' said Jonathan. 'Calvin would remember.'

Aaron turned around, his face so contorted with grief he was almost unrecognizable. 'Calvin would remember and repeat it over and over,' Aaron said, each word trembling. 'But he didn't say anything about Brother Jabez's death. Not once. We all know. We heard him.' Several of the men nodded in agreement. 'Calvin didn't see anything . . .' Aaron broke down again. Rees looked up but, although he didn't agree with the other man, he did not speak. Calvin must have witnessed enough to know who had murdered Brother Jabez, even if he couldn't communicate it. There was no other reason to kill him.

'Someone will have to tell the others,' one of the men said. He turned and quickly walked away.

'Brother Solomon has to know,' Jonathan said.

'And we need to bring Calvin back to Zion,' Rees said.

'We can fetch a horse and wagon,' suggested Jonathan. 'It'll be easier to bring him h-home . . .' His voice broke and he turned his face aside.

'We still have to carry him across the field,' Rees said. 'I think there are enough of us . . .'

From the women who had remained outside the fence came several loud cries, followed by weeping.

Ten

The cart and its sad burden did not pull into Zion until almost five. Calvin's limp body proved too much for the small band of Shakers to carry. Some of the Brothers were unwilling to touch a corpse; and Aaron, although eager to help, was so overcome with grief he could barely keep himself upright. Fortunately the farmer and his sons arrived to see what the fuss was about, and with their aid Calvin was successfully removed to the wagon.

Rees opted to walk behind, in the company of Esther, Lydia, and a few of the Shaker Brothers. As they traveled down the lane and crossed Surry Road, he felt a hand steal into his own. He looked down to see Lydia walking beside him. 'I'm sorry,' he whispered to her.

'I am also,' she said. She smiled up at him. 'We will solve the problem of our housing together.'

'We will,' Rees agreed, his spirits lifting. 'I will never allow my family to go without a home.'

'I know.' She squeezed his hand.

Without discussing it, they walked more and more slowly than the others, allowing the Shakers to pull ahead. When the wagon disappeared into the small copse of trees fronting the road, Lydia murmured, 'Do you think Calvin's death is connected with the death of Brother Jabez?'

'I believe so,' Rees said. 'I think Calvin saw enough to know the identity of the murderer.' He looked down into her pale face. 'The boy was prone to rising at night and going out to see the horses.' His voice thickened and he had to pause for a moment to steady himself. 'The murderer sought to silence him.'

Lydia considered that for a moment. 'But Calvin never said anything. Not really.' Her eyes filled with tears. 'He was no more than a child even though he was tall and strong.'

'I know. But Calvin must have betrayed his knowledge, so the murderer felt threatened. Now Constable Rouge must be involved.' Rees would not obey the Zion Elders on this, not any longer.

By the time Rees and Lydia reached the other searchers, stopped in front of the Dwelling House, Brother Solomon had already reached the wagon. He was white with shock and horror. He clutched the wagon side for support with a trembling hand.

'Why is this happening to us?' he asked, raising a shaky hand to pull his white beard. It was the first nervous gesture Rees had seen the Elder make. 'Some villain is persecuting us, maybe some man who hates our community.'

Rees considered Solomon's words. Perhaps. He knew what it felt like to be the target of malice.

'What happened?' The second Eldress, older by some years than Esther, came down the steps from the women's side of the Dwelling House.

'Calvin will have to be taken to the icehouse,' Esther said. The walk from the farmer's field to

Zion had given her time to compose herself, and although her voice was still wobbly she had begun to think of practicalities. 'I won't be able to wash him until tomorrow morning.'

'How did he die?' The Eldress leaned forward to ask Esther. She turned to look at Jonathan, and they exchanged some silent communication.

'He was struck on the head by a rock,' Jonathan answered in the Sister's stead.

'Did he fall?'

'No, Sister,' Esther said. 'Some wicked, wicked man murdered the poor boy.' She turned her head aside to hide her tears. The older woman stepped back, one hand clutching at her throat as her mouth opened and closed soundlessly. Rees jumped forward to catch her before she fell, and lowered her to a sitting position on the ground.

'Take him,' Solomon said, waving his hand at the body. Jonathan climbed into the wagon seat, and after a few seconds two of the other Brothers joined him.

'I'll meet you there,' Esther said as the wagon began its turn. 'I'll meet you.'

'It's almost time for evening prayer,' Solomon said. 'I'll be in the Meetinghouse.' He started walking, his gait shaky and uneven. One of the younger brothers hurried to catch up and put a supporting arm under the Elder's shoulder.

'Will I see you tonight?' Rees asked, turning to Lydia. 'At the Union?'

'I doubt there'll be a Union,' she said, a shadow passing over her face. 'The Elders will not want to encourage idle conversation and speculation

102

about the recent deaths. But we can meet at the Children's Dwelling House. I usually try to visit with the children before bed. I tuck in Joseph and Judah and sing a little . . .' She tried to smile. 'I bless the Lord they are safe.'

The thud of galloping horse hooves distracted her and she looked over her shoulder. 'Who's that?' she wondered.

Rees lifted his eyes over her head. He recognized both horse and rider: Constable Rouge. 'It didn't take you long to hear the news,' Rees said sourly as the constable drew up beside him.

'The farmer's son came straight into town,' Rouge said. 'He told me there'd been another murder. The second one in as many days.'

'That's true,' Rees said.

'Where are the Elders?' Rouge looked around him. 'Where is that fellow Solomon?'

'He doesn't know anything,' Rees said. 'And Brother Jonathan is transporting the body to the icehouse. He should return soon. Tie up your horse by the stables and I'll tell you what I know.'

'What you know? Oh, I see. You were involved in the discovery of another body?'

'I'm developing a pain in my neck from looking up at you,' Rees said, refusing to be drawn. He gestured to the rails in front of the stable.

As Rouge directed his horse to the stable, Lydia touched Rees's hand and said, 'It will soon be time for dinner. Without Esther there will be too few Sisters in the kitchen, so I'll go and offer my help.'

'I'll see you at the Children's Dwelling House

103

this evening,' Rees said with a smile. She nodded, and for a moment Rees watched her walk toward the Dining Hall and the kitchen behind it. From the back, he could hardly tell she was pregnant, although she had developed a rolling walk reminiscent of a sailor. Then he turned to join the constable across the road.

Rees quickly recounted what he knew, beginning with Brother Aaron's appearance at the door of his bedchamber late in the morning, right up to the discovery of Calvin's body in the farmer's pasture. Rouge was silent for a few seconds after Rees finished. Then he asked, 'Was the boy at breakfast this morning?'

'I don't know,' Rees said. 'I overslept.' He saw Jonathan and the other Shakers come over the wooden bridge and begin to approach. 'But Jonathan will know.'

As the other Brothers and a tearful Esther continued on to the Meetinghouse for prayers, Jonathan paused and looked at Rouge. Both were dark-haired men and about the same age, but Jonathan's face was so creased and drawn with grief he looked a decade older.

'Was the boy at breakfast?' the constable asked Jonathan.

He nodded. 'Yes. But according to Brother Aaron, Calvin did not appear for his chores. Aaron did not think anything of it, not at first anyway. Calvin was easily distracted. But when several hours went by and then he didn't come to dinner . . .'

All three men lapsed into silence. Rees thought Calvin had probably already been dead by noon.

'Did anything happen at breakfast?' he asked.

'No,' Jonathan said, shaking his head. 'Nothing unusual. Of course it was always difficult keeping Calvin silent, but he didn't say anything important – "He wants to see horses", that kind of thing.' Jonathan's voice, typically schooled to sound low and calming, cracked. He looked away and swallowed several times.

Rees stared at his feet, wishing he had been there himself.

The bell for prayers suddenly sounded, rolling sonorously through the village and making both Rouge and Rees jump.

'It is time for prayers,' said Jonathan unnecessarily. 'And we need to pray today. Especially today.' Head bowed, he started for the church at the end of the street.

With a quick glance at the departing Shaker, Rees leaned toward Rouge. 'I know the Elders here would prefer to believe that Brother Jabez's death was an accident. Or caused by an outsider. But, in my mind, Calvin's murder proves otherwise. Two suspicious deaths in a community this size cannot be coincidence. I've believed all along that Jabez was murdered, and now that poor boy Calvin has been as well.'

'There's a link somehow,' Rouge agreed.

Rees nodded. 'He saw something,' he said but dared say no more. The road was growing crowded with Shakers hurrying to prayer, and he was wary of being overheard. 'I'll speak with you soon,' he said. Rouge nodded and turned to mount his horse. As the constable rode away, Rees followed Jonathan to the Meetinghouse.

He did not think there would be singing and dancing today, but he wanted to hear what the Elders said about Calvin.

Rees took a seat in the last bench of the men's side. Unlike Sundays, when the Sisters wore white and the Brothers put on indigo vests, everyone today wore their working clothes. Brother Solomon had already begun praying, blessing not only the food they were about to eat but also the labor in which each member was engaged. He reminded the congregation that they were a family and that the work they did honored God. As he moved about the floor, crossing the copper lines inlaid as boundaries for dancing, the sunlight striking from the copper blinked on and off, lulling Rees to sleep. The Elder's voice subsided to a drone. But the sudden addition of deeper tones, shaking with grief jerked the weaver awake.

'Calvin was found in farmer Reynard's pasture,' Jonathan said. 'He . . .' Jonathan stopped and swallowed. 'A nearby rock had blood on it. We can't know what had happened, whether he fell and hit his head or whether some rogue struck him down.'

Despite the prohibition on unnecessary speech, a low murmur of horror swept through the room.

Rees could hardly believe the Shakers persisted in their delusional hope these deaths were accidents. He was almost certain Jonathan knew better. But as Rees looked at the shocked and frightened faces around him, he realized that the Elders were doing their best to keep their community calm. They were frightened enough. And many of the Family did not believe this was an accident. The man across from Rees leaned over the table. 'Did the farmer murder the boy?' he asked. 'Did you question the farmer?'

'Not yet,' Rees said. 'But I will.' He did not expect it to result in anything but he would.

'Sister Esther will be preparing Calvin to go home to Mother,' Jonathan continued. With a quick glance at Solomon, who was white and trembling, Jonathan added, 'We will most likely hold services and bury our Brother later today, after the Elders have met.' Jonathan passed a hand over his sweaty forehead and stepped back. After an awkward moment of silence and since both the men seemed incapable of continuing, Esther stepped forward and began to quote the twenty-third psalm from memory.

'The Lord is my shepherd, I shall not want. He maketh me lie down . . .'

Rees rose abruptly and pushed his way past the Brothers seated beside him. He felt he couldn't breathe and needed air. He hurried outside and paused on the steps to wipe his watering eyes. He did not think he could attend Calvin's burial. The image of that boy's shrouded body sliding into the grave sent a shudder through Rees that wouldn't stop. He sat down on the steps with a thud. He had intended to investigate Jabez's death, but few had known him and fewer had liked him. Rees thought now that if he had tried harder to identify Jabez's killer maybe Calvin would not have died. In pursuing the truth about Calvin's murder, Rees swore he would never quit. Never. Not until he knew the identity of the murderer and had brought him to justice.

Eleven

With a quick look around the empty streets, Rees began walking briskly south. He wanted to question the farmer now, before one of the Brothers insisted on accompanying him and listening in. Although Rees did not expect his conversation to result in any new information, he thought the farmer might speak more freely to him than to any Shaker.

With his long rapid stride, it took Rees only twenty minutes to cover the distance through the village and across Surry Road. He did not know how far the farmer's house was, but Rees was in luck: as he started walking down the lane, he saw several men in the pasture where he had discovered Calvin's body. He jumped the fence and walked toward the group. The men had seen him now and were coming down to meet him. As they approached, the group resolved into one older man, three boys on the cusp of manhood, and a smaller boy who was probably no more than twelve. They saw Rees coming and the man stepped away from the others, moving forward to intercept Rees.

'What do you want?' he asked. He thought that this fellow, with his black eyes, black hair shot with white and skin tanned dark by the sun, would not have looked out of place on a sailing ship with a knife between his teeth.

'I discovered the . . .' Rees's throat closed up and for a few seconds he couldn't speak. 'He was a boy, only thirteen,' he managed, conscious of the horrified tremble in his voice. The farmer looked at his sons. When he looked back, his mouth had tightened into a thin line.

'None of my sons had anything to do with this,' he said. His accent told Rees that the farmer usually spoke French. Although Rees had some of that language and understood more than he spoke – there were many French people in the District of Maine – he was not at all fluent.

'Of course not,' Rees said quickly. He held out his hand. 'Will Rees. I just wondered if anyone might have seen something.'

The farmer inspected Rees's hand and finally reached out to shake it. 'Jean Reynard. I saw nothing.' He looked at his sons. The older boys shook their heads. But when Rees glanced at the twelve-year-old, he was holding himself with a certain kind of stillness. 'Did you see Calvin?' Rees asked him. 'Tall, brown hair?'

'Now wait,' the farmer began to remonstrate. But the boy nodded.

'I was in the buckwheat field,' he said. 'I saw him.' For a moment, his eyes drifted up over Rees's head and he seemed bemused. 'He stood by the fence. The horses seemed to like him, they came right over.'

'Why didn't you say something?' the farmer said in French.

'He was just looking. I didn't see anything else,' the boy replied in the same tongue.

'Was he alone?' Rees asked, returning the conversation to English. He wanted to know if someone had lured the boy to the pasture.

'No. There was a man with him.'

Rees felt a jolt of excitement shoot through him. Aaron had said Calvin was afraid to cross the road. 'What did the man look like?'

The boy gestured to the east, toward Zion. 'One of them,' he said. Confirmation, not that Rees needed it, that one of the Shaker Brethren was involved and hiding among his fellows. 'Old man.' Rees knew that 'old man' could apply to anyone over the age of twenty.

'Old like me or older?' he asked. The boy looked at Rees, who instantly felt himself aging to at least a hundred. The boy's face contorted in thought and then he shrugged.

'Older, I think,' he said finally. 'But I was too far away to see his face. And he wore a hat.' So there was no telling the color of the hair.

'Merci,' Rees said. 'Thank you.' He looked first at the farmer and then at the boy.

'This will not involve us?' the man asked. Rees shook his head.

'I don't think so.' He paused and added, 'But of course the constable knows.' Reynard nodded, unperturbed. Rees knew Monsieur Reynard had been quick to inform Rouge of Calvin's death and suspected they knew one another from the French Church nearby.

*　*　*

110

That evening, supper in Zion was a somber meal. Sniffles broke the silence, and the Sister who brought the platters of food to Rees's table had red swollen eyes. At the close of the repast, Solomon stood up and announced that Union was canceled for this evening. Rees threw a quick glance at Lydia and found her regarding him with her brows drawn together. She offered him a faint smile.

'Moreover,' Solomon continued, 'services for Brother Calvin will commence at 8:00 this evening and the burial will take place immediately thereafter.' A slight rustle rippled through the room. Rees was surprised as well. It felt as though Calvin was being hurried into the ground.

Chairs scraped across the floor as the community rose to their feet. Sisters were flying through the hall, gathering plates and scrubbing tables so as to finish by the time the services began.

Rees stood, irresolute. He wanted to fill the time this evening without attending the funeral for Calvin. He knew if he returned to his room, he would spend the time thinking about the boy. Rees needed something to distract him. After several seconds of thought, he decided to return to the hired men, the Palmer brothers, and speak to them. He was fairly certain they were innocent of anything to do with Calvin's death – they were young men, and they did not wear Shaker garb – but they might have seen something.

Accordingly, he walked the short distance from the Dwelling House, past the Infirmary, to the small structure that housed the Palmer boys. But when he peered inside he saw it was vacant. Not just empty of people, but also devoid of the Palmer's scanty possessions. They had fled. Rees looked around, hoping he might find some clue, but the young men had left nothing behind. Rees could already hear in his imagination the explanation Jonathan would offer for the Palmers' furtive disappearance. That they were guilty. But Rees wasn't convinced. The boys had already been frightened and now probably assumed they would be accused of Calvin's murder.

He sighed. Although he did not expect the young men to linger in the area, especially if they were on the run, he would ask Rouge to keep an eye out in town.

He went outside, wondering if he should tell one of the Elders the hired men were gone. Of course, Solomon and Jonathan might already know. And they would most certainly learn of it when the young men did not turn up for their chores.

After a few seconds of cogitation, Rees decided he would talk to Sister Elizabeth again, before spending some time visiting his children in the Children's Dwelling House. Knowing that Calvin would be interred, Rees felt the need to immerse himself in the boundless life and all the wonderful potential for the future evoked by children.

As he started toward the Infirmary, Lydia came out of the path from the kitchen and called, 'Will, wait.' He stopped and waited for her to cover the distance between them.

'Where are you going?'

'To call upon Sister Elizabeth. I just cannot see the body of that boy . . .'

He stopped suddenly, feeling his throat tighten.

'I know,' Lydia said, touching his wrist in sympathy. 'What's happening here?' Rees took a breath.

'That farmer, Reynard, said that it was one of the Shaker Brothers who brought Calvin over to see the horses.'

'It always seemed so safe here.' Lydia shook her head. 'Why would anyone kill a boy like Calvin?'

'I don't know. Not for sure, anyway, but I'll find out.' He reached out to take her hand. 'Calvin should have been safe here. Whoever lured him to that farmer's field had to be someone he trusted. And the same is true of Jabez, for that matter. I don't believe he went to the laundry room for a bath. Someone arranged to meet him there.' He paused and after a few seconds he added, 'How can Solomon and Jonathan still believe this is the work of an outsider?'

Lydia nodded in agreement. 'I'm frightened, Will,' she said. 'Surely even in Dugard . . .' Her voice trailed off.

'It is not safe there either,' he said. 'And now, I've got to discover the identity of the murderer. For Calvin. For all of us.' He looked down at her as he spoke. Her face contorted with a combination of reluctance and fear.

'But the children . . .' she said. 'What if you get too close? Will the murderer come after the children?'

'He wouldn't,' Rees said, although he knew that was no assurance. 'Perhaps we should move to that farm of yours, no matter the condition. I'll speak to Brother Solomon tomorrow.' Lydia was right, they had to protect the children.

113

They walked the last few yards in silence.

When they entered the infirmary, they found Elizabeth sitting up in a chair. The curtains covering the windows had been pulled back and the early evening sun streamed into the room. Despite the fresh air coming in through the open windows, Rees thought the room still smelled of sickness and death.

Elizabeth turned and smiled at them. 'I was hoping you would come,' she said. Rees thought her wheezing was not so pronounced today. 'I feel a little better.'

She paused for several breaths. 'You just missed Robert. He stopped in to tell me about the funeral for the boy.' Rees wondered what Robert had told her. Surely not that Calvin had been murdered. Elizabeth was neither shocked nor horrified. 'I've been thinking about those early days,' Elizabeth continued.

'I was wondering—' Rees began. Lydia frowned at him and moved forward.

'A time you enjoyed,' she said encouragingly.

'Oh yes. Terrifying but exciting. We were pursued from town to town. Our lives were threatened. Mother Lee was attacked more than once. But she and her brother William kept us strong in our faith.' She sighed. 'Then Robert and I realized that some of the passion we were feeling was for each other. We left and married.'

When she did not continue, Lydia said, 'You've had a happy life, though, haven't you?' She sat down beside the ill woman.

'Yes.' Something about the reply signaled a certain hesitation. Lydia put her hand on Elizabeth's

114

arm. She looked up, her eyes filling with tears. 'I have only the two children who lived. I lost so many babies. I wonder, were Robert and I wrong to leave? Was that our punishment, all those babies gone to Heaven?'

Rees tried to pretend he was invisible. He could think of nothing to say to this woman that would comfort her.

'God's ways are always mysterious,' Lydia said, choosing each word with care. 'I am sure God will understand. Isn't He the one who gave us passion? Besides, it was a long time ago. Even Mother Ann and her brother William passed on long ago.'

'That is why Robert and I chose to follow Solomon here, to Zion,' Elizabeth said, nodding her head. 'He was almost as powerful a preacher as William. I was not surprised to hear he had become an Elder.' She stopped and smiled at Rees. 'But I think you did not come to listen to my memories.'

'Of course we did,' Lydia said, throwing a stern glance at her husband.

'But I did have a question,' Rees said quickly. 'You told me when I first spoke to you that you saw Jabez and Jonathan arguing.' She nodded at him. 'I don't suppose you could hear what was being said?'

'At supper?' Lydia asked, aghast. Elizabeth nodded.

'No. And I don't think anyone else noticed. Well, except Brother Solomon. Jabez said something to Jonathan and he cut him off. But I heard Jabez arguing with someone after the meal. A

115

different Brother. I was seated on that rock outside the kitchen, resting.'

'I know it well,' Rees said. 'Could you recognize the voice?'

'No, I'm sorry. They were down the path, on the way to the icehouse and the laundry. And it was beginning to get dark, so I couldn't see who Brother Jabez was scolding, though I assumed it was Jonathan. Jabez came storming up the path past me a few minutes later. So angry.' She shook her head, coughing. Rees could see that Elizabeth was tiring. When she took her hand-kerchief away from her mouth, it was dark with blood.

'Have you noticed other quarrels?' Lydia asked in a soft voice. Elizabeth smiled.

'Brother Aaron with almost everyone,' she said. Rees laughed. 'Even Brother Solomon, who is one of the most patient men I have ever met, becomes irritated with Aaron.'

'Are you gossiping?' The nursing sister barreled through the door, her voice rising. 'No. No.'

'Please forgive us,' Lydia said. 'We were simply endeavoring to entertain Sister Elizabeth.'

'It is time for her straw tea,' the Sister said. 'Both of you should leave.'

'Please, can't they sit by me until I fall asleep?' Elizabeth pleaded. The nursing sister hesitated and Rees thought she would say no. But finally she sighed.

'Lydia can sit by you,' the Sister said at last. 'But you,' and her eyes turned to Rees, 'should wait by the door.'

That was more of a concession than Rees

expected, so he willingly took up a position by the door. The nursing sister and Lydia helped Elizabeth into bed. While the Sister prepared the opium tea, Lydia pulled up a chair and sat down. Elizabeth clutched at her hand.

'I know I'm dying,' she said, 'but I'm not afraid. I am going home to Mother. I've had a good life. And I am so grateful I met Robert.' She coughed again and couldn't stop. The awful sound went on and on, until Lydia helped raised her into a sitting position against the pillows. Finally, the hacking diminished. By then the rag in Elizabeth's hand was saturated with blood. As the Nursing Sister brought over the cup of tea, she fixed Rees with a glare. As though it were his fault, Rees thought in resentment. Lydia held Elizabeth up so she could drink from the cup. She made a face but took it all. As Lydia lay the dying woman down again, Elizabeth continued talking. 'I knew as soon as I saw Robert that the prohibition against marriage would be hard for me. He was so strong. So full of life. His hair was black as night then.'

Rees looked at the nursing sister. 'How long does she have?' he asked.

'A matter of days,' said the Sister. 'I'm surprised she's lasted as long as she has.'

'Ann and William were truly touched by God,' Elizabeth murmured, her voice barely audible. 'And Brother Solomon, a worthy successor to William. A wonderful preacher.' The breath rattled in her throat. 'I never liked his brother Abraham.' Another breath. 'I didn't like the way he looked at me.'

117

'Who?' Rees asked. 'Who looked at you?'

'Abraham. Not Solomon. He chose to abandon earthly pleasures and live celibate.'

'It is a common enough story,' the Nursing Sister said, rolling her eyes at Lydia. Something in her voice attracted Rees's attention, and he wondered what tale she might tell. Had she left a sweetheart behind? Or maybe even a husband and children?'

'The power of God . . .' Elizabeth's voice had grown quiet and slow, slurring as she drifted into sleep. '. . . changes lives. Saved Brother Aaron.'

Rees snapped to attention and turned to stare. For a second, he wished Lydia would shake Elizabeth awake and compel her to finish her sentence.

Saved Brother Aaron from what?

Twelve

'Aaron was probably a criminal,' Rees said as he and Lydia walked to the Children's Dwelling House. 'Had to be. Why else would he hide out here, in Zion?'

By now most of the Shaker community were streaming toward the Meetinghouse. Several of them turned surprised and disapproving looks upon Rees and Lydia, who were walking away from services. They glanced at one another and increased their pace.

'Maybe,' Lydia said. 'But was he a thief or a

murderer?' She paused, thinking. 'The Elders trust him. Aaron is one of the Brothers sent on selling trips. And he has always returned – with all the receipts, as well as the horses and the wagon.'

'Not a thief then. He was fond of Calvin,' Rees said, recalling the Shaker's obvious grief. 'But to my mind, Brother Aaron is a plausible killer. What is that quote you say?'

'That a man may smile and smile and smile and still be a villain,' Lydia said, with a sharp nod. 'Yes. So Aaron is crying over Calvin but still might be the murderer.'

Rees repressed a shudder. He didn't like to think someone he knew in this closed community could be so skilled at masking his true self. 'I must figure out this puzzle quickly,' he muttered. Lydia shot him a look.

'Yes,' she agreed. She shook her head, tears in her eyes. 'Oh Will, will we never be safe?'

'I thought we would be safe here,' Rees said in a grim voice.

They entered the Children's House by their separate doors and met in the front room. Except for a few chairs taken down from the hooks and a scattering of toys, the room was bare. To Rees's surprise, Annie was there, holding Joseph in her lap and tickling him. When Rees and Lydia appeared, the child squirmed out of Annie's lap and joined the children rushing to them. Rees squatted and hugged each child in turn except Simon, who wanted to shake hands like an adult. But Rees's gaze never left Annie's anxious expression.

As the evening shadows crept into the room, two Sisters came to fetch Judah, Nancy and Joseph. Jerusha and Lydia accompanied them to the bedchambers to tuck in the little ones. But Annie remained in the room with Rees. As soon as the Sisters went into the hall outside, she said in a rush, 'I'm sorry I said you were my father. It's just that Deborah, well, she came here specifically to find her father. He left the family to join the Shakers here in Zion. And I didn't want to admit that I . . .'

Tears flooded her eyes and she brushed them away with the back of her hand. And Rees, who had been a little irritated, felt sorry for her.

'I didn't mind,' he lied. 'Any man would be proud to have a daughter like you.'

She rushed forward and threw herself into his arms. He patted her back and then, as Lydia and the Sisters entered the room, released her. 'Any more news from Billy?'

She shook her head, her lips trembling. 'Not since the last letter.'

'He is probably still at sea,' Lydia said in a comforting tone. Annie nodded and began pleating her skirt with her fingers.

Simon tugged on Rees's vest. 'When are we going home?' he asked.

Rees bent down until he could look directly into Simon's face. 'We will remain here a little longer. Or at least, remain nearby,' he said. 'Mother will be having the baby soon. And now I've made a promise to find an evil man who killed two people. You understand, I must keep my promise?' Simon nodded.

'But I've been waiting for so long to see David,' he said in a wistful voice.

'We will see him sometime this fall,' Rees said. He did not know how to explain all the nuances of the accusation against Lydia, nor the fact that he had given the farm to David. 'But we may have to find another home,' he said. Simon looked at him in disbelief.

'It's time now for bed,' said the Sister. 'Come, Simon. You too, Jerusha.' She looked at the three adults pointedly.

'We're leaving now,' Lydia said. She turned to the children and offered one last hug to each. 'But I'll see you tomorrow.'

As Rees and Lydia bid the children good night, Annie went outside and waited for them. They all walked to the Dwelling House together.

Rees sat up with a scream on his lips. He was panting and sweaty, shivering now as the moisture dried in the cool night air. With the terror of the dream still upon him, he looked from side to side, expecting masked figures to menace him from the shadows. But the room was quiet. In the distance, a rooster crowed. Rees threw aside the sheet and fumbled for his tinderbox and candle. He had never been prone to nightmares, but after his experiences in Dugard the previous month he sweated through a different dream every night. And they all had the same theme: someone was chasing him and he knew they meant to kill him and his family. In the nightmare tonight, Constable Farley and Magistrate Hanson had

121

been part of the mob. Rees shuddered, recalling Hanson's laughter.

With his heart still thudding, he put on his shoes and went out of his room. The entire Dwelling House was silent and dark. Rees was glad he had not awakened the men in the rooms on either side of him, or the women across the hall. He looked up the stairs to the second level, imagining Calvin coming down on one of his nightly journeys to see the horses. Doing so suddenly seemed like a very good idea. Rees felt he couldn't stay inside any longer. He went out of the house and crossed the street to the paddock behind the stable.

All of the horses trotted to the fence. Poking their noses through the bars, they snuffled and snorted, looking for treats. Even the horses missed Calvin. 'Sorry,' Rees said to them. 'No more Calvin.' What had the boy seen that put him at risk?

Rees had slept longer this night before the dream shocked him awake. Soon the Brothers would be rising to begin the morning milking, and within the half hour after that it would be dawn. Rees looked around, thinking about Calvin and what he might have seen. Brother Jabez must have met his killer early in the morning, probably about now. The rest of the community were still asleep; they had to be, if the murder were to occur without anyone seeing. Yet Calvin would have been awake, visiting the horses. Rees knew the Dwelling House and its surroundings were visible from the paddock. Had the murderer seen Calvin as he stood by the horses? Rees walked back across the main street to the steps of the Dwelling House and stared into the darkness that was the pasture. He could see nothing. So the murderer hadn't seen Calvin. What had the boy said then that betrayed his knowledge?

The door behind him opened. Rees turned to see Jonathan and a handful of other Brothers descending the steps. Jonathan was carrying a lantern and he held it high so that the light would fall upon Rees's face. 'You're up early,' Jonathan said.

Rees nodded. 'Couldn't sleep,' he said, unwilling to admit to the nightmares that plagued him.

'Many mornings when I came out here, Calvin would come from the paddock to greet me, still in his nightshirt,' Jonathan said.

'And I'd fetch him inside,' said Aaron, his voice thickening. 'Make him wash and dress before breakfast.'

Rees rested his gaze upon Aaron. Of all the Brothers, Calvin would feel most comfortable with Aaron. Maybe Jabez knew something about Brother Aaron, who spent more time than most in the World as he sold the Shakers' products.

'We need to finish the milking before breakfast,' Jonathan said. 'With the disappearance of the hired men, we are struggling to complete all the chores. Come, Aaron.' The Brothers went down the steps and disappeared around the building, toward the barns. Rees watched them. He could think of no other Brother besides Aaron that Calvin would so willingly obey.

Rees went inside the Dwelling House to wash

and dress for the day. The Sisters who slept on the other side of the hall were leaving by way of the women's door at the back. They must be the Sisters on kitchen duty this week, Rees thought, wondering which room in this building belonged to Lydia. But he did not see her exit any of the first-floor bedchambers or descend the Sisters' staircase. Thinking about Lydia reminded him he must speak with Brother Solomon. In fact, Rees might have to meet with all the Elders about the Ellis property, but he would begin with Solomon. Like his wife, Rees no longer felt entirely comfortable here in Zion. Two murders in two days. Instead of providing refuge, the village was beginning to feel dangerous.

Rees washed and dressed by candlelight. Although the sun was rising, since his windows faced west the light did not penetrate his room. The tumbled bedding on his bed called him, reminding him he had not had a full night's sleep. But he did not dare lie down. So he sat down instead and did not move. His eyes began to close in spite of himself. The ringing of the bell for breakfast jolted him into wakefulness. He stumbled to his feet and made his way outside, feeling sluggish and dull.

Breakfast helped, especially the copious cups of coffee. By the time the community began rising from their tables, Rees felt better able to face the day. He approached Solomon and Jonathan and waited while they spoke to another man. Once his problem had been resolved, Rees approached. 'May I have a word?' he asked.

'Not more bodies, I hope,' Solomon said, sounding unhappy.

'No.' Rees darted a look at Jonathan, not wanting to complain in front of him. 'I'd like to discuss the possibility of my family moving to the farm my wife inherited, at least until the baby is born.'

'I wondered if you would pursue this,' Solomon said. Rees could see the Elder was recalling Rees's hasty words the day before. 'The farmhouse is not in good shape.'

'There is considerable doubt that your wife owns the Ellis property,' Jonathan said. 'That farm was to come to Zion with Charles Ellis.'

'But Ellis left it to Lydia in his will,' Rees argued. 'And he never signed the Covenant.'

'But his intent, clearly, was to donate the farm to the community of Zion,' Jonathan retorted.

Rees stared at the Elder in mingled frustration and dismay. 'This is why Lydia never succeeded in selling the farm to you,' he said.

'Since the farm should belong to us, I have never understood why we should offer any money for it,' Jonathan said. 'Although, of course, we might pay some small amount as a courtesy.' He said this with a quick glance at Solomon.

'Since you and your family are already staying with us now,' Solomon said to Rees in such a slow and quiet voice that he knew the Brother was angry, 'I see no reason why you shouldn't remove to the farm.' Rees glanced at Jonathan, who was staring at his fellow Elder in consternation. 'Especially now, with a new baby on the way.'

'How long would they remain?' Jonathan asked Solomon.

'That would all have to be discussed beforehand,' Solomon said peaceably.

'I see,' Rees said. He did not trust himself to say anything further. The Beast was stirring, and right now he wanted to strike someone, preferably Brother Jonathan. Although Rees perceived that there was some conflict among the Elders regarding Lydia's farm, who knew when a decision would be made? Or even what it would be? Rees had no notion of the general temper of the Elders.

'The Elders will discuss this,' Solomon said now. Jonathan nodded, with what Rees saw as a self-satisfied expression, and left.

'Jonathan is overly strict with my son,' Rees said. 'And now this. Why, he was not even here at the same time as Charles Ellis.'

'Jonathan was but recently made an Elder,' Solomon said. 'He was transferred here four or so months ago and he is very eager to demonstrate his piety and his worth. He feels it is his Gift to the Family to insure everything is done properly, as Mother Ann would have wished.'

'As *he* thinks Mother Ann would have wished,' Rees said. And he suspected most of the community here would not wish to argue against such a laudable goal. Perhaps there was another property near town that he could rent. Simon Rouge would know. Rees also thought of stopping by the lawyer Mr Golightly, or his son if the elder had passed away, to discuss Charles Ellis's will. Charles and Lydia had been married and, from

126

what Rees recalled, the provision regarding the disposition of the property was clear – it had been left to Lydia by name.

'Of course you and your family are welcome to remain here until some decision has been made,' Brother Solomon said.

'You mean until my wife gives up and surrenders the property to you for nothing,' Rees said. Solomon's mouth dropped open.

'Of course not,' he said.

'Forgive me,' Rees said as good sense prevailed. Solomon, if not Jonathan, seemed willing for Rees and his family to remove to the farm. 'That was rude.'

Rees bowed. No wonder Lydia had been so upset by Rees's news about his own farm. She must have known that taking possession of the Ellis property would not serve as a solution.

Rees pushed his way outside. Some of the Brothers, seeing his expression, hastily moved out of his way. He paused for a few seconds to take several deep breaths before continuing across the street to the stables. He intended to drive into Durham immediately.

But as he began to cross, Lydia came down the steps of the Dwelling House with an unfamiliar woman. She carried a canvas satchel that she threw into the back of the buggy. Distracted, Rees changed course, walking on a diagonal so that he might join the two women.

'I thought I saw someone I knew as a little girl,' the woman was saying to Lydia.

'Very likely,' Lydia said. 'Some of the community

here grew up in Durham. My old friend Mouse –
Hannah Moore – grew up nearby.'

'I knew some of the Moores. Isn't Hannah the
one with the harelip?'

'Yes. But you wouldn't have seen her here,
she lives in another Shaker village now.'

'Maybe it was a trick of a light,' said the other
woman, frowning in thought. 'Well, no matter.
I'll be going now, lovey.'

'Oh, Bernadette, this is my husband,' Lydia
said, touching the woman's elbow and directing
her gaze to Rees.

Rees regarded her in turn. Instead of the Shaker's
square cap, her curly blonde hair was covered by
the frilly mobcap of a married woman. A plump
woman with creamy skin and brown eyes, she
wore a striped dress that was far too colorful for
a Shaker Sister. Despite the absence of lines or
gray hair, Rees thought the woman was probably
his elder by five or so years.

'This is the midwife, Bernadette Bennett,'
Lydia said. That explained the presence of a
non-Shaker here with Lydia. The celibate Shakers
usually had no need of midwives.

'What? Is something wrong? Is the baby
coming?' The questions spilled rapidly from
Rees's mouth. The midwife chuckled.

'Oh, the baby's coming, but not just yet. Day
or two yet, I'm guessing. Sometimes the contrac-
tions begin a bit early, as a warning like.' She
smiled at Lydia and patted her hand. 'I'll drive
out again tomorrow. If the little 'un gets impatient and tries to come earlier, just send someone
for me.'

'I will,' Lydia said.

The midwife picked up her basket, and with a quick smile at Rees brushed past him and climbed into the buggy.

'When I thought the baby might be coming, the Sisters sent for the midwife,' Lydia said as the buggy drove away. She turned to look at her husband. 'You look angry.'

'Why didn't you tell me the Elders think your farm belongs to them?'

'Oh, not to them, to Zion.'

'Don't split hairs, Lydia Jane,' Rees said angrily.

'As I understand it, Jonathan believes the farm should belong to Zion. Esther thinks the Elders should abide by the terms of Charles's will. I am not certain what Solomon and the other Eldress believe.'

Rees inhaled deeply. 'At the best, then,' he said, 'it may be months before any kind of a decision is reached.' Lydia leaned over and touched his hand lightly.

'Will,' she said. Rees realized several of the passing community were staring at him.

'I'm sorry,' he said. It was an effort for him to apologize. 'I shouldn't have given the farm to David. Only I didn't know what might happen.'

'I know,' she replied, 'but what are we going to do now?'

Rees had no answer. As Lydia turned to go, Rees heaved a heavy sigh and continued on to the stables.

Thirteen

Traffic clogged the streets of Durham when Rees drove to town an hour later. Almost all of the spaces in the stables behind Rouge's tavern were filled, as well. But the ostler, recognizing Rees, promised he would find room. 'I'll squeeze your wagon in,' said the tow-headed fellow. 'And there's always the paddock for your horse. I'll make sure he's watered.'

Rees climbed down from the wagon. Slipping the ostler a tuppence for his trouble, Rees went into the tavern. Rouge was serving one of the last remaining parties – farmers by the look of them – but the room was emptier than Rees expected. Since dirty cups littered every table, though, Rees guessed that the bulk of the crowd had left to pursue other errands. The new barmaid, a lanky lass of about fourteen, was frowning as she collected the crockery.

'Well,' Rouge said to Rees, 'discovered any more bodies? It's a new day.'

'I know you think you're funny,' Rees said. 'I wanted to talk about Calvin for a bit. And I have a favor to ask.'

Rouge snorted and shouted to the girl, 'We're going in my office.'

Rees fell into step behind the constable, but not before he saw the lass make a rude gesture at Rouge's retreating back. Rees guessed this girl wouldn't last either.

Rouge went down the narrow hall and turned left at the end into a small room with windows overlooking the main street. The office held a messy desk, so piled with papers and other objects the top would not close. Ledgers were stacked under the windows, almost reaching the scarred sills. On the wall opposite the windows was a cluster of barrels and crates, some open, some not. The poker Rees had given Rouge lay in plain sight on the floor.

'Sit down,' Rouge told Rees with a gesture. Rees looked at the two chairs. Their seats were covered with bills, and a blue jacket had been dropped over the back of the nearest one. He removed the jacket, scraped the paper into one of the piles, and lowered himself to the seat. 'I spoke to the two Elders. Jonathan told me Calvin had a wound on his head.'

'Yes, he did,' Rees said. 'It looked to me—'

Rouge raised his voice. 'But Solomon told me the wound came from falling on a stone.'

'Huh,' Rees said. 'And you believe him?'

'Of course not,' Rouge said.

'Well, I'm more inclined to believe someone picked up a rock and struck Calvin on the head. I found a rock with blood and hair on it.'

'Because he saw the murderer?'

'Yes.'

'But everyone agrees that Calvin was an idiot.'

Rees thought back to his experiment the night before. 'Maybe, but he is not blind. And he was

131

prone to wandering at night. Calvin may have seen the murderer returning to the Dwelling House from the laundry.'

'If that's true, why did the murderer wait to strike the boy down?' Rouge asked.

'The killer wouldn't have seen him,' Rees said. 'Calvin must have said something that alerted the murderer. Something no one else understood.'

Rouge chewed a flap of loose skin on his thumbnail. Rees, who had to keep his hands in good shape for weaving, watched in repelled fascination as a drop of bright red blood formed on the skin. Rouge wiped it off on his shirt and said, 'Maybe he started running forward and called out a name.'

Rees grunted. That was possible but he doubted it. For one thing, he had never heard Calvin speak any names. Not even Aaron's. 'I don't think that's it,' Rees said. 'There is something, but I just don't know what it might be.'

'So, it's a second murder, just as we thought.' Rouge said. Rees nodded.

'Another thing. The hired men are missing. I doubt they're involved – the farmer said it was one of the Brothers with Calvin – but their sudden disappearance does look suspicious. Three brothers, name of Palmer.'

'You think they're in town?' Rouge shook his head. 'Not likely. With harvest, all the farms are looking for help. They've probably already found something else. Anyway, they could be anywhere by now, from Boston to Caribou.'

Rees nodded unhappily. 'Too true,' he said. 'I wish I'd had the opportunity to speak to them again. I just can't shake the feeling the youngest one knew something.'

Rouge did not look convinced. 'So, what was that favor you wanted?'

'Nothing to do with the murders,' Rees said. 'Well, in a way it is. I'm concerned about my family. I'm not sure they're safe anymore. Do you know of a house or farm I could rent?'

'What about the Ellis property?' Rouge asked. 'I thought you already owned that.'

'There is some thought – some of the Shakers think it belongs to them,' Rees said. 'My next stop will be at the lawyer's.'

Rouge grinned. 'I do know a place. Close to town and close to Zion. Do you want to see it?'

Rees eyed the constable doubtfully. There was something suspicious about Rouge's grin. 'Want to see it or not?' Rouge asked.

'Very well.' Rees hated his mother's expression 'Beggars can't be choosers', but knew it applied to him now.

'Well, get your wagon then. I'll ride with you. You can return me here, on your way to Mr Golightly's office.'

Since the ostler had shoehorned the wagon into a tiny space, it took some time shifting the vehicle into the yard so Hannibal could be hitched. But finally they were ready to go. Rees climbed up and took the reins; he didn't allow anyone else to drive his wagon. To his surprise, since he thought they would head west, Rouge directed him to turn left at the end of the inn's yard. For a brief moment, Rees wondered if they were going back to Zion. But no, they drove to the outskirts of Durham and then turned left again, so they were traveling due north. After several miles, Rouge told Rees to turn right into an overgrown lane, which he would have driven past without a second glance.

Cultivated fields lay to the left of the weathered worm fence. but the property on the right had disappeared into a forest of young birch. The rutted track over which they bumped showed evidence of some recent vehicle traffic but not much; young trees had taken root in the center. As they rode in, the road's surface became more vegetation and saplings than dirt. The road petered out in the forest within a few yards.

They climbed down from the wagon and followed what was left of the track. Large granite boulders protruded from the soil on either side of the path and it looked as though this part of the farm had never been cultivated but left as a divider between this farm and the next. Five minutes of stiff walking and they reached a stone wall with a rotting wooden gate. Once through that, they pushed their way down the slope through the saplings.

The overgrown path ended suddenly in what had once been a farm's front yard.

The house was clearly long abandoned. One side of the front porch had crumbled, and branches of all shapes and sizes lay across the roof. Rees eyed the shingles. Many were missing and he suspected rain was leaking in through the holes. Besides, parts of the roof looked soft, as though it might fall in at any moment. He turned to glare at Rouge.

'But you haven't seen the whole house yet,' Rouge said, barely able to speak through his laughter.

'I couldn't bring my family here,' Rees said, his voice rising. 'Look at it. It's safer outside.'

Rouge jumped down from the wagon. 'Come on. See the whole thing.'

'No point,' Rees said mulishly.

Rouge started toward the steps. 'This was a productive farm once,' he said. 'Come on.'

With an exasperated sigh, Rees jumped down and followed the constable.

They went up the rotting steps and into the front hall. Stairs led up to the second floor. Rees could smell damp and mold seeping down from the upstairs.

Rouge went down the narrow hall to the back. Several large rooms opened from it on the left and Rees could see polished wooden wainscoting and glass in the windows. Dry leaves had blown into the corners of the room and he distinctly saw a small furry body shoot across the floor.

He followed Rouge into the kitchen. A huge fireplace dominated the right wall. A kitchen table occupied the center of the room and cabinets lined the back wall, with a window set in the center. The glass had fallen out long ago. Charring of the floor and the cabinets spoke to a past fire. Rees stared at the black patch thoughtfully; it was nowhere near the fireplace so he wondered how the blaze might have begun.

Through the window he could see a large barn, even more dilapidated than the house, and behind it the weedy expanse of fields going wild.

'This property was quite a mystery for awhile. Although no one ever saw the farmer, his wife and children were fixtures in town. Then one day they were all gone, and the farm was abandoned.'

'Something happened here,' Rees said, turning to look at the scorch marks on the floor and cabinet. 'If I were a betting man, I'd wager that a fire was deliberately set.'

Rouge nodded. 'Exactly what I thought.' He paused and then continued. 'Sheriff Colton always suspected the wife of murdering her husband and then attempting to burn the place down to cover it up.'

'It could just as easily be the husband killing his wife,' Rees pointed out.

'True. And those scorch marks could have come from squatters. Or kids. You know, larking about.'

'Yes. This farm is in even worse shape than the Ellis property,' Rees said.

'Very funny,' he added as Rouge began laughing. But he wondered if he might be forced to bring Lydia and the children here, despite the disrepair of this house. Temporarily, of course. 'I'll just take a look upstairs,' he said.

He went down the hall and up the stairs. The treads seemed in good shape, but as soon as he entered the room at the top he saw a huge brown water stain on the ceiling. He suspected if he went up to the attic he would see sky through that part of the roof. But all the windows contained glass; someone in this house had been proud. He looked through the back window, across what had once been many acres of fields. It would take a lot of work to bring this farm back from its neglected state, and he wouldn't even have David to help. With an unhappy sigh, Rees turned and went downstairs. He hoped the lawyer could offer him some guarantees on the Ellis property.

Instead of the house with stone pillars outside of town, Hugh Golightly, son of the lawyer Rees had met previously, worked out of a neat office in town. Like his father, Mr Golightly Junior was tall and spare with bright blue eyes. His hair had already begun to go gray. 'Ah, Mr Rees,' he said as he hurried into the office on the heels of his clerk. 'I was wondering when I might see you.'

'You were expecting me?' Rees asked in surprise.

'Of course. 'Mr Golightly looked at the young man by his side. 'Will you fetch the Charles Ellis file, Mr Harrison?' As the clerk disappeared into another room, Mr Golightly turned back to Rees. 'Your wife has already been to see me, so I know about the conflict. But I felt I could not act until I'd spoken to you.'

'To me?' Rees said.

'Of course.' Mr Golightly offered a thin smile. 'When Mrs Ellis married you and became Mrs Rees, all of her property became yours.' Rees went still. He had not stopped to consider that consequence – of course, a wife's property belonged to the husband.

The young man reappeared with a sheaf of

papers tied with string. Mr Golightly untied them and began spreading them on his desk.

'Indeed.' Mr Golightly found the document he was looking for. He put on a pair of spectacles and skimmed it quickly. 'Yes, as I recalled, Charles Ellis's will was quite specific. He left the farm to Lydia Jane Farrell, his wife. Without reservation.' Taking off his spectacles, Mr Golightly went on. 'When she married you, by the laws of this state, the farm became yours, as her husband.'

'So she could not sell it to the Shakers at Zion?' Rees said.

Golightly nodded. 'Exactly. You could sell it, however, if that is your wish.'

Rees swallowed. 'Did you tell Lydia this?' He had never thought of the Ellis farm as anything but hers, to do with as she wished.

'No. I told her I needed to speak with you.' Seeing Rees's stunned expression, Mr Golightly added, 'You must understand, the Elders had just indicated that they felt the property should belong to them. Because of Mr Ellis's position inside the community.' He paused to make sure Rees understood. He nodded.

'Yes, that was explained to me.'

'I believe your wife had been intending to sell the property to Zion anyway.'

'Yes,' Rees said. 'But now we are no longer sure . . .' His voice trailed away. Mr Golightly smiled.

'It is a large property. Very valuable. If it is your wish, I will write to the Elders and indicate your desire to take possession of the farm.'

Rees hesitated. Such a letter might be considered provocative. He had too much respect for the Shaker community and was too appreciative of all the help they had offered him and his family to declare war. Besides, he didn't want the farm. He had always been willing to allow its sale. He just wanted to move his family to it for a short time, while he and Lydia considered their future.

'Not just yet,' he said at last. 'Let me discuss this with the Elders first. Maybe we can find a compromise that will serve. If we can't, then I'll return and we can go forward with a letter.'

Golightly nodded. 'Of course. As you wish.'

Rees paid the consultation fee to the clerk and went outside. During his visit to the lawyer, clouds had overspread the sky. He looked to the west and saw black boiling up from the horizon. They were in for rain. Rees hoped the storm would hold off until after he reached Zion and was inside; it would soon be time for dinner. Rees walked back to the tavern to recover his horse and wagon, returned to the yard after Rouge had taken Rees to the abandoned property nearby. 'Well, at least I won't have to move Lydia and the children to the abandoned farm,' Rees thought. He had been afraid he would be reduced to exactly that circumstance and was relieved to know it needn't happen. He would apply to the Elders as soon as he could, and hopefully Brother Solomon would speak on Rees's behalf.

A drizzle began as he started down the Surry Road. Hannibal broke into a run as thunder rumbled across the sky. The light rain was already thickening, and Rees could tell the shower would soon become a heavy downpour. They galloped into Zion but were forced to stop, as the Shakers were hurrying to the Meetinghouse for prayers. Already soaked to the skin, Rees jumped down and took hold of Hannibal's bridle. They threaded their way through the crowd to the stable, where Rees unhitched the horse and put him in one of the stalls. Then, leaving the wagon parked outside the stable, Rees ran across the road to the Dwelling House and went into his bedchamber.

Rees found a newly laundered towel by the ewer and dried his hair and face. Every article of clothing on his body needed to be changed; he was fortunate that his other set of clothing had been washed and was neatly folded in the bureau. Rees hung his wet clothing – shirt, breeches, vest and stockings – over every available surface. He hoped no one came in to see it; the arrangement of clothing on the furniture would upset the Shaker notions of order and simplicity.

He was struggling to tie his damp hair into a neat ponytail when the noon bell began to ring. Rees hastily used his hands to smooth his hair back over his ears and pushed his feet into his wet and muddy shoes. He clapped his hat on his head and went outside, joining the flood of people hurrying to the Dining Hall. The Brothers crammed into the antechamber; no one wanted to wait outside today. The odors of wet wool and livestock overlay the faint aroma of pastry seeping in from the kitchen.

140

Solomon and Jonathan entered. Rees lowered his eyes to the floor and fixed them on the scarred wood. Right now he was very glad of the prohibition on speech. He didn't know what he would say to these men about the Ellis farm, and anyway he wanted to speak with Lydia first. When the doors opened and they went in, Rees chose a table as far away from the Elders as he could. When he thought about his behavior, he realized that anger was simmering just below the surface, ready to burst out at the slightest provocation. Again he wondered why he was so tetchy. He had a temper; everyone knew that, but this level of irritability was recent.

As the Sisters began bringing in roast chicken, squash and green beans, Rees forced his thoughts away from the Elders, especially Jonathan, and thought instead about the Ellis property. He had not seen it for two years and hoped it was not in as poor a condition as the abandoned Johnson farm. How much work would the house need to make it livable? And the fields? They had already been overgrown when he saw them last. Was there a room with good light in the house? Rees would need that to weave. It would be best to drive over to the property and take a look at it. In fact, depending upon its condition, it might be better to sell it and purchase something in town. Rees began to wonder if there were any weavers in Durham and the environs; if not, he might be able to support his family just by weaving.

But first he had to finish the repairs on his loom and make sure he could use it, before he began building castles in the air.

Blueberry pie and thick cream finished the meal. Rees looked around the room as he scraped his plate, but he did not see Lydia. The children – all of them, not only his – were being herded from the room. No doubt they had all begun talking and otherwise misbehaving. But of Lydia he saw no sign, and he wondered if she had gone to help the Sisters in the kitchen.

Rees did not speak to anyone after dinner, but hurried through the rain to his room. If there was any possibility of remaining here in Durham, he wanted to have his loom set up and ready to go. He would need to find a place for his warping board as well.

He'd pieced most of the loom together before Aaron interrupted him the previous day. For a moment Rees remembered why Aaron had come calling: that was the beginning of the search for Calvin. Rees's throat tightened. The poor boy. As he considered Calvin, Rees became even more determined to remove his family to a safer location. With that decision spurring him on, he bent over the remaining pieces and began fitting them together.

Fourteen

He'd been at it for barely an hour when he was once again interrupted by a knock. This time when he opened the door he found Brother Jonathan outside, a cloth wrapped bundle in his hand. Rees regarded him through the narrow crack.

'May I come in?' Jonathan said. Rees hesitated but finally took his hand away from the door. Jonathan stepped inside. Although he looked at the clothing hanging from the back of the chair and across the table, he did not comment. 'I have your reed,' he said instead. 'And I see you are setting up the loom.' Rees nodded. Jonathan held out the bundle.

'Thank you.' The words stuck in Rees's throat. The loom would be of little use without a home to work from.

'I wanted to tell you . . .' Jonathan stopped and looked at Rees with a frown. 'You must know that Sister Esther and Solomon do not agree with me about the Ellis property.'

'No.' Rees paused. 'I spoke with Mr Golightly this morning. Now Lydia and I are wed, the property is mine. I am not willing to give it to Zion, not right now anyway. Not until my situation is more settled.'

'I don't understand.' Jonathan scowled. 'We were promised the Ellis farm. It should be ours. Besides, you and your family are living here. Why do you want to remove yourselves to that property?'

Now Rees found himself in a quandary. Should he confess he feared for the safety of his family? Or find a convenient half-truth that would serve? 'We wish to live as a family,' he said at last. 'That is not possible here, in Zion, living with this Family of Believers. I promise you, the Ellis farm will come to you eventually.'

143

'Brother Charles was living in Zion as one of us,' Jonathan argued. 'All his property should have been given freely to the community.'

'Charles Ellis should not have married Lydia,' Rees said. 'But he did.'

'Choosing celibacy and living communally as we do is a serious decision,' Jonathan said. 'Many of our community find it difficult to commit fully. Charles Ellis struggled with his decision.'

'I understand that.' Rees tried to suppress his irritation. 'But Ellis chose to marry Lydia. And his will clearly left that property to her.'

'While he was living here, as one of the Brethren,' Jonathan said. 'If the Elders who were guiding Zion then had known of the marriage, Charles would have been told to choose – either repudiate his wife or leave.'

Rees nodded, experiencing an unexpected flash of pity for the beleaguered Charles. It must have be an impossible position to be in: the desire to serve God in this community warring with the love of a woman and the siren call of home and family. 'There must be others who struggle with that choice,' he said.

'It is even more difficult when one spouse wishes to join and the other does not,' Jonathan said. Rubbing his eyes, he turned his face away. 'Husbands tossing a wife's Shaker cap into the fire. Or an ugly divorce where the custody of the children is contested.' Rees eyed the other man, wondering what personal experience Jonathan spoke from. Rees did not quite have the courage to ask. 'Still,' Jonathan said in a more cheerful voice, 'we do receive regular conversions. And, of course, it is gratifying to see those, like Brother Robert and Sister Elizabeth, who were once of our community return.'

Rees did not speak. He thought that Robert and Elizabeth had rejoined more for the care of the ill Elizabeth than for any other reason, but did not want to sound so cynical.

'Anyway,' Jonathan said, 'I hope the reed works.'

'I'll try it,' Rees said. 'The loom is almost ready for the reed.' He glanced over his shoulder. 'I have no yarn though,' he said to himself.

Jonathan smiled. 'I'll ask Sister Esther to collect some of the ends from the Weaving Shed.'

'Thank you,' Rees said.

It was not until Jonathan withdrew that Rees realized the Brother had repaired the reed as a peace offering. And offered yarn besides. Now Rees felt both guilty and ashamed that he had not been more appreciative.

Rees turned to look at the remaining loom pieces – the treadles and the heddles – on the floor. He still had to find a place on the wall to hang the warping board. He brought the repaired reed to the loom. With only a little bit of sticking, the comb-like part slipped into place. Rees expelled the breath he had not realized he was holding. The knowledge that he would continue to have the ability to support his family took such a weight from him that he began to whistle softly as he placed the treadles underneath the loom. Perhaps he could borrow a few nails.

With the loom together and finally workable,

Rees decided to go visit the children at the schoolhouse. Taking the sheet of oilcloth he usually used to cover the loom in bad weather from his pack, Rees threw it over his soggy straw hat and went out into the rain.

The Sisters in the classroom were surprised and not very pleased by Rees's unexpected arrival. He saw their frowns but forgot them in the surprise of seeing Simon. The boy was sitting in the corner of the room, in a chair, with his arms folded across his chest and a glower on his face. Rees absently hugged Jerusha and Nancy while he turned a questioning look upon the caretaker Sister. By Rees's estimate, she was in her late teens or early twenties.

'Apparently there have been some issues with obedience,' the Sister said. 'And since he does not even know his alphabet, it was thought . . .' Her voice trailed off under the censure in Rees's expression.

'So you humiliated him?' he asked, crossing the room.

'Jonathan brought him,' she said in a stiff voice.

'I should be with the other boys,' Simon said in a loud voice. 'I can help with the livestock. I can learn to mend tack.'

'I'm afraid he has been something of a problem,' the Sister said, directing a stern glance at the boy. Simon crossed his arms even more tightly and contorted his face into a ferocious scowl. Rees regarded Simon, seeing the boy's determined effort not to cry. Recalling the resolute little boy who had worked so hard to support his siblings, Rees turned such an angry glare upon the Sister she took a step back.

'Come, Simon,' Rees said, detaching Nancy's clinging arms from his legs. He scooped up the boy and took him to the porch outside, despite the rain, which blew in every now and again. Simon's long legs hung off Rees's lap; the boy was really too old to be comforted in such a manner, but he leaned into Rees's chest and clung to his damp shirt with both hands.

'What's the matter?' Rees asked. 'You've always been so brave.'

The boy had been expecting anger, not gentleness, and tears welled up in his eyes. 'They sent me here, to the girls,' he said in a thick voice. 'The Brother said if I argued . . .'

He stopped and began chewing his lower lip.

'And you did?'

'No. But I saw him do something wrong.'

'Who was it?' Rees asked. 'Aaron? Jonathan?'

'No. Someone else. I am respectful to my elders, I really am. But he was offering a sick horse oats, and Brother Aaron said not to.' Tears stood out in Simon's silvery eyes. 'And when I tried to explain, no one would listen and I got sent here.' He sniffed and Rees could feel the boy's body tense as he tried to hold in the sobs.

'I know you don't want to be with the girls.' Rees paused. He was shocked that the Shakers had done this since they were so careful to keep the sexes separated. 'But it is important to have book learning. David knows how to read and write. And do figuring. They're important for a farmer.'

147

'They are?' Simon wiped a dirty hand across his eyes. 'My mother always said such book learning was only for the rich.'

Not for the first time, Rees wished he could shake Simon's mother, deceased though she was. 'That's not true. Let's say you have five bags of grain. How do you know which grains are inside if you can't read the tags? How will you know if someone is cheating you if you can't figure out the weights? 'He had planned to go on, but he could see Simon was thinking. Finally he nodded, as though what Rees had said made sense to him.

'But the Sister put me with the babies,' Simon said. 'With Nancy and Judah. I'm not a baby.'

'Of course not,' Rees agreed, his throat tightening in sympathy. He paused and thought about what he should say. 'Maybe the Sister thought you could help them.' Simon shook his head.

'Nancy already knows her letters,' he said in such a soft voice Rees could barely hear him. 'She knows more than me.' He burst into tears. Rees rocked him awkwardly, wishing anyone – Lydia, David, someone more experienced with this kind of thing – was here.

Rees wondered how many times David had wept like Simon was crying now and Rees had not been there to comfort him. Rees swallowed several times. He would have to return to Dugard and check on David. If only the accusation against Lydia had been resolved, they could all go home. Although Rees wasn't sure he wanted to, not after the cruelty and betrayals of the summer.

Rees allowed several seconds to pass before saying, 'I know you can learn your letters. Would you feel better if you could sit next to Jerusha?' Simon inhaled and his face lit up.

'Yes,' he said, nodding. 'Yes.'

'And maybe Jerusha and Annie and Mother can help you catch up in the evenings?'

'Yes. Oh, yes.'

Rees held the boy for a few more moments. Then he put Simon down and rose to his feet. 'Are you ready to go back inside?' he asked. Simon used his shirt to wipe his eyes and nodded. Together they went back inside the schoolroom.

'I'd like to speak to you,' Rees said to the Sister. She appeared reluctant to leave the security of the children clustered around her. 'He doesn't want to sit with the babies,' Rees said when the Sister did not approach him.

'Because he has spent most of the summer outside with the Brothers, Simon knows less than Nancy and Judah,' the Sister said, her lips a thin line. 'I don't want to put him with the girls. At least, Judah still wears dresses.'

'Simon has been the man of his family for a very long time,' Rees said. 'You shouldn't put him with the younger children. Why can't he sit with Jerusha?'

'A girl?' The Sister looked horrified. 'It is difficult enough to include the little boys in the classroom.'

'She's his sister! He's a bright boy, and I know he'll learn quickly.' Rees looked down at Simon and smiled. 'Jerusha seems to have an aptitude for schoolwork and she can help Simon.' The

Sister exhaled in exasperation. 'And she can teach him at other times, so he doesn't forget.' Rees looked at Jerusha, and she nodded with an air of importance.

'Very well,' said the Sister. 'For now.' She did not sound happy, but Rees did not care. He looked down at Simon and smiled in triumph.

'Go sit by your sister,' Rees said to Simon.

As the boy squeezed on to the bench next to Jerusha, Rees caught the Sister's frown. She probably wished Rees had never come to visit and that he would leave immediately. Rees had not appreciated how much time he'd spent with his children at the farm in Dugard until now, when he was so restricted.

He nodded his farewells to the children and went back out into the rain, walking across the street to the Dwelling House. Although he felt a sense of accomplishment – the problem with Simon had been solved – he was now more certain than ever that he needed to move his family to a home of their own. He valued the safety Zion had offered when his family required it. But that security had proved to be an illusion. Besides, the Shaker customs were not conducive to family life. He had told Jonathan the truth, although he had not meant to. He wanted to live with Lydia and the children, all together, not sleep across the hall from her or in another building apart from his children.

When Rees went into the Dwelling House, he found a large canvas sack tucked by the door. When he opened the bag, he saw it was full of balls of yarns. Although some were dyed indigo

150

blue or rose madder, most of them were the cream color of undyed wool. His spirits rising, Rees went inside to set up the warping board.

Fifteen

Panting, Rees ran full speed through the forest. Farley and his posse were behind him and closing. He could hear the shouts and knew with sickening certainty that they would hang him if they caught him. He had seen the rope, coiling through Farley's hands like a living thing. But Lydia was screaming. Her frantic, terrified cry ripped through the trees. Rees turned toward the sound and tried to force his way through the close-growing tree trunks and thick understory. He was practically weeping himself with terror.

Another scream ripped through the forest. But the footsteps thudded behind him, closer and closer, a fusillade of loud, booming steps . . .

Rees sat up in bed with a shout. The first light of dawn colored his windows with gray. He was trembling and his feet were tied up in the sheets. Perspiration coated him in a second skin. But the screaming wasn't just in his dream: another cry sounded through the Dwelling House. And someone was pounding on his door.

'Rees. Rees.' A soft call penetrated the thick wooden door of his room. Rees swung his feet to the floor and pulled on his breeches. Barefooted, he padded across the boards and opened the door.

151

Esther stood outside, her square linen cap askew on her head. 'Lydia's in labor,' she said, lifting a quivering hand to wipe her forehead. 'Go fetch the midwife.'

All the wisps of sleep and the terror left from his nightmare disappeared in an instant. Rees was flooded with fear of another sort. Gulping, he nodded and slammed the door. He dressed although his hands were shaking so much he could barely pull his stockings over his toes. He put his hat on his uncombed hair and ran out of his room.

His shirt flapping, he raced across the road to the stable and paddock. He'd forgotten to light a candle or bring his tinderbox, and the inside of the building was almost too dark to see. Fortunately, he remembered where he had left his wagon. He ran to the gate leading into the paddock and whistled for Hannibal. It seemed to take forever for the gelding to respond, and even longer to put on the leather traces. But finally Hannibal was harnessed to the wagon and Rees could climb into the seat and start for town. When he looked east, he saw the pink light streaking upwards, into the sky. Cursing – it had taken him far too long to get on the road – Rees slapped the reins down upon Hannibal's back. 'Faster!' he shouted. 'Faster!' Oh God, what if something happened to Lydia? He knew how many women died in childbirth. Every time a woman was brought to bed, there was the possibility she could die.

By the time he reached the town, the sun had risen. The streets were still quiet; none of the shops were open yet and their proprietors were most likely still eating breakfast. That's when Rees realized he had no idea where the midwife Bernadette lived. Swearing even louder and almost weeping with desperation, Rees thought frantically. What should he do? Simon Rouge would know. And he lived above his tavern.

Rees slapped the reins down once again, drove into the town, and made the turn into the tavern yard on two wheels. He jumped out of the wagon, ran to the back door, and pounded on it with furious intensity. Rouge, wearing a towel over one shoulder, opened it almost immediately, leaving Rees standing there with his fist raised.

'What in hell are you doing?' Rouge asked.

'You're up?' Rees said.

'Of course. The first stage to Boston leaves at half past seven, and all of those passengers will want to eat something before they leave. Then there are the shopkeepers. Most of them will have eaten, but they'll want their ale or cider. What are you doing in town so early?'

'My wife is in labor,' Rees gasped. 'I don't know where the midwife lives. Do you? Oh God!'

'I see,' Rouge said reaching out to turn Rees's hat around. 'You have it back to front. That's better.' He turned to toss the towel on a table inside. 'The midwife lives just around the corner. Come on, we can cut through the inn yard. I'll show you.'

'Don't break any more plates or cups,' he said to someone inside. 'I vow, you are clumsier than the last girl. And being my niece won't save you.'

As he stepped on to the porch, the unmistakable sound of crockery shattering on the closing door reverberated through the wood. Rees wondered if the girl inside had thrown something on purpose, and judging by Rouge's furious expression Rouge thought the same. 'My brother's daughter,' he said in explanation. But he didn't turn back. Moving at a rapid trot, he started through the yard.

'I hoped you would know,' Rees said, striding after the constable.

'Of course I know,' Rouge said, turning a mocking grin on Rees. 'Bernadette is my sister.'

'Of course,' Rees thought. Bernadette would be related; that's the way these small towns were. Everyone was related to everyone else. Why, Dolly was connected by blood or marriage to half the farmers in Dugard. Rees recalled his dream and shuddered.

'Bernadette began helping my mother as a child,' Rouge was continuing, 'and now her daughter is assisting her. When Bernadette is too old to deliver babies anymore, I expect her daughter will step in.' He reached the fence and, putting his hands on the top bar, hoisted himself over and into the next yard.

'Why don't you put in a gate?' Rees panted as he followed.

'We aren't that close. Come on!' Rouge began trotting through the weedy back yard, shouting 'Bernadette! Get up, you lazy female!'

Rees doubted anyone would respond to that command. But as he circled the small house and ran up the steps to the front yard, the weathered front door popped open and Bernadette appeared in the doorway. She was already dressed, and behind her Rees could see a fire burning in the fireplace.

'Why didn't you answer me?' Rouge asked in annoyance. His sister's lips tightened.

'I was out all night. Just returned a little while ago, in fact,' she said. 'Forgive me if I wanted to sit down for a moment with a cup of tea. 'She shook her head at her brother. 'You seem to think you can order me around like you do those poor girls that work for you. Well, you can't. Especially not when I've had barely two hours sleep.'

Turning to Rees, she added, 'Go on home. I'll follow in the buggy. Don't worry, I'll be there shortly.'

Rees nodded. 'Please hurry.'

'Don't worry.' Bernadette smiled at him. 'Babies usually take their own sweet time. We'll arrive with hours to spare.' She closed the door.

Rees declined to clamber over the fence again, choosing instead to walk around the corner and down the block to the tavern's front door. He thought he saw Ned Palmer ducking down an alley. But when he turned, the young man, whoever he was, had vanished. And Rees was certainly not going to pursue a will-o-wisp now.

Rouge, who had gone over the fence, was waiting for him. 'Do you want some breakfast?' he asked. 'I've already got a pot of coffee on.'

Rees put his hand over his belly. Right now his guts were in such turmoil he doubted he could force anything down. 'Thank you, no,' he said. 'My stomach is too upset.'

He passed through the tavern, from front door to back and out into the yard. The ostler was wiping down Hannibal and faced Rees will a scowl. 'You left this poor beast hot and sweating . . .

'I'm taking him home now,' Rees said. 'I had to come for the midwife . . .' He snatched the reins from the fellow and climbed into his seat. His legs were trembling and he was suddenly afraid Lydia had had the baby already without him there. He turned the wagon, almost running into the ostler without noticing, and galloped back into the road.

He parked in front of the Dwelling House and pounded on the Sisters' door. After several minutes, Esther opened it. 'Is the midwife coming?' she asked.

'Yes,' Rees said. 'She should be here soon. How is Lydia?' He tried to look over her head, as if he could see not only into the hall but around the corner into Lydia's room as well. 'Can I see her?'

'Of course not. Not now. The very idea.'

'But she's my wife.' Rees was tempted to push past her and barrel his way down the hall until he found her room.

'She doesn't want to see you. Not now, anyway. And that's besides the fact this is the Sisters' side. You need to be patient.' Esther shut the door firmly in Rees's face. He knocked again, but she didn't answer and the door remained closed. In the end, he drove his wagon across the street to the stable, where he unhitched Hannibal and spent some time walking him around and around. Then he rubbed the horse down with a rag before releasing him in the paddock. The entire time, Rees kept his eyes trained on the door to the Dwelling House.

Finally the midwife, or midwives since Bernadette's daughter accompanied her, arrived. They parked their buggy in front of the Dwelling House and went up the steps. Rees raced across the road. The two women paused on the stoop. 'Don't worry, Mr Rees,' Bernadette said, looking down at him with some sympathy. 'I'll send my daughter out to speak with you as soon as I know how your wife is doing.' She knocked on the door, a much daintier sound than Rees's hammering. The door promptly swung wide and Esther gestured the two women inside.

Rees collapsed upon the step and dropped his head into his hands with an anger born of fear and frustration.

The Brethren began gathering for breakfast. Rees watched the first few as they silently disappeared through the Dining Hall doors. He still wasn't sure he could eat anything, but sitting on the steps for the next few hours seemed foolish. He couldn't do anything to help; in fact, he would not be allowed to assist. And if something happened, well, Esther would make sure he knew. He crossed to the stable, where he washed his face and hands in the trough and tried to slick down his hair. Then he joined the other males in the small waiting room. He intercepted several sympathetic glances, but no one said anything.

Afterwards, Rees did not remember what he

ate or even if he ate anything. His entire consciousness remained focused on the Dwelling House and Lydia inside. As soon as he could leave, he returned to the street outside and took up his position on the steps.

He'd only been there for a little while when the door opened and Bernadette looked out. A scream followed her through the opening, and Rees jumped instantly to his feet. 'Don't you worry now,' the midwife said. 'It won't be much longer. As soon as the baby is born I'll send my daughter out to tell you.'

'Will Lydia be all right?' Rees asked, a lump forming in his throat.

The midwife came through the door and patted Rees's shoulder. 'Don't worry. I've birthed some babies in my time.' Her smile invited him to join her amusement. 'Your wife will be fine, and the baby too. Your wife is strong and everything is going well.' She regarded him in silence for several seconds. 'Usually I see this intense anxiety at the first child. But I understand you have others?' She paused delicately.

'Yes, an older son from my first marriage. And my wife and I adopted several children last winter. But this is *our* first child.'

Bernadette's mouth made a round 'O' of under-standing. 'I see, Will Rees the weaver.' She looked at him once again. 'Lydia tells me you're something of a sheriff or constable?'

'Not exactly,' Rees said. 'It's just that, well, I keep stumbling into unexplained deaths.'

'Yes, my brother told me there've been two murders this past week. And here, in Zion too.'

She tsked. 'Such a quiet community. They don't even have a jail.'

'I know,' Rees said. 'This community doesn't need one. Not usually. As for the two murders . . . I can't see a connection between them.'

Bernadette nodded gravely. 'I was born in Durham,' she said. 'And so were my children. I know everyone in town, sometimes more than I would like. But here in Zion, outside of a few members that came from the neighboring farms, everyone is from away. There are new people all the time. How can one possibly know everyone? How can someone know that the person to whom you are speaking is not lying to you about his past?' She leaned forward to peer into Rees's face. 'Do you know, this is the very first time I have been called here to deliver a child?'

'Is that why you came? To see this place?' Rees asked. He was not so fond of knowing everyone in his hometown, or having everyone know him. For one thing, a reputation gained at the age of ten could follow a man all his life, no matter whether he changed or not.

'Partly,' Bernadette admitted. 'I do believe my daughter could have brought your child into the world without my help. But I wanted a chance to look around.' She smiled at Rees. 'Do you feel calmer?' Rees realized he did. The midwife patted his hand. 'I should see how the birth is progressing,' she said as she climbed the steps.

Just before she closed the heavy wooden door behind her, Rees clearly heard another scream of pain and jumped up once again. No longer calm and far too worried to sit, he began to pace. What if something happened to Lydia? The fear bubbled up inside until he felt as if his whole body was vibrating with it. He'd thought of his first wife infrequently these past few years, but now he remembered his feelings at her death as sharply and clearly as if she had died yesterday. Although he'd become fond of her, their marriage had been one of convenience and he had not loved Dolly as he did Lydia. How would he go on if something happened to Lydia?

The front steps of the Dwelling House went from gray granite to gold in the rays of the rising sun. The morning disappeared and the members of the community began to gather at the Dining Hall for noon dinner. But nobody – not Esther, not Bernadette, not Bernadette's daughter – appeared. Rees began chewing his thumbnail.

Solomon passed by on his way from the Meetinghouse to the Dining Hall. He paused in front of Rees and ran his fingers through his beard.

'Mr Rees,' he said. 'Come inside for dinner.' His tone was gentle. 'I know how terrible the waiting is, I was married once. But you can't help anything sitting on these steps.' Rees sucked in his breath as he looked over his shoulder. The Sisters' door remained stubbornly closed. 'I'm sure Esther will send word if something happens,' Solomon continued. Rees exhaled and managed a half nod. Together, he and Solomon walked to the Dining Hall.

Although Rees should have been very hungry, he could barely choke down the food. Every sound brought him to attention, but Esther did not come. Finally, as the Sisters were distributing apple pie, Esther appeared and hurried across the room to Solomon's side. She bent over and whispered something, her eyes searching the faces all the while. She found Rees and her gaze locked upon his.

'Will Rees,' Solomon said. The unexpected sound of loud speech reverberated through the silent room. Almost everyone turned to stare as Rees leaped to his feet and hurried toward Esther. Jerusha gathered up Simon, Judah and Nancy, and they joined Esther and Rees as well. The Sisters tried to recapture the children, but Simon and Jerusha became very loud and very difficult.

'Let them be,' Rees said as Jerusha's hand stole into his.

They followed Esther out of the women's door, Rees not even realizing they had done so until he was in the street outside. He did not think Esther had noticed either; she was ahead of him and almost running. 'You'll be permitted entry into the Sister's side this time,' she said over her shoulder. 'This one time only. Just to see your baby.'

'Us too?' Simon asked.

'Of course,' Rees said, shooting a stern look at Esther and daring her to protest.

They followed Esther up the steps and into the Dwelling House. The hall was identical to the one on the Brother's side. When Rees looked across, to the other side of the staircase rising to the second floor, he could see the door to his room. They walked all the way to the back to the two sets of open doors in the rear. Light streamed through to shine on the wooden floor. Esther gestured Rees into the last bedchamber on the right.

He saw that this room looked exactly the same as the chamber in which he was staying on the other side of the house, and then all of his attention was focused on Lydia. She had been propped up in a sitting position with the aid of several pillows. Although very pale and with dark smudges of fatigue under her eyes, she was holding a blanket-wrapped bundle and smiling.

'Come and meet your daughter, Will,' she said.

'Are you all right?' Rees asked, aware that his voice was trembling. He took several deep breaths and tried to steady himself. He could see she was fine, so why was he on the verge of tears?

'Of course.' She looked down at the bundle and Rees thought he had never seen her so happy. 'Come over Will, come over children, and meet your baby sister.'

Staggering a little on his unsteady legs, Rees hastened to cover the few paces necessary to reach the bed. Lydia held up the bundle, but before he took it Rees bent and kissed Lydia's forehead. He wanted to snatch her into his arms but didn't dare. What if he hurt her? Instead he took the small, solid warmth of the baby. 'She's a good size,' Bernadette said. 'Sturdy and strong.'

She did not feel sturdy or a good size to Rees, but as tiny and as fragile as a baby chick. He looked down into her face. Her skin was still flushed red and her face slightly swollen from her birth. But the sparse hair on her head glinted red-gold; and when she yawned and opened her newborn milky-blue eyes, she seemed to look straight at him.

Rees felt tears rush into his eyes. He tried to hold them back, but they began streaming uncontrollably down his cheeks. And he knew he would do anything, anything and everything, to protect her and keep her safe.

Sixteen

'We must talk about a name,' Lydia said after a few seconds. Rees nodded, fighting to contain his emotions. He had not expected to react so powerfully.

'Can I hold her? I want to hold her,' Jerusha said, stretching out her arms. Rees turned his new daughter upright and brushed his lips across her soft, fine hair, unwilling to relinquish her. Lydia frowned at him. Exhaling with annoyed reluctance, he put the baby into Jerusha's arms. She bent over the child, crooning wordlessly.

'Come and sit by me,' Lydia said to Rees, looking up at him and beaming. He lifted a chair down from the wall and pushed it up close. 'I wanted to know if you've discovered anything new about Calvin,' Lydia said, dropping her voice to a soft murmur. 'I feel for that poor boy.' Her voice thickened and she passed a hand over

163

her eyes. 'I'm sorry, I seem to cry so readily right now.'

'That is entirely normal,' Bernadette said as she washed her hands in the basin. She turned a warm smile on the new mother. 'And it will last for a while, maybe even as much as a month or more.' Lydia acknowledged the midwife with a nod and looked back at Rees.

He shook his head. 'Nothing so far,' he admitted.

'I wonder if you shouldn't speak to Brother Aaron again?' Lydia said. 'He knew Calvin best. I know it seems unbelievable, but Aaron treated the boy with kindness and patience. Maybe Calvin said or did something that Aaron doesn't realize is important, but . . .' Her voice trailed away as she looked at Rees.

'I'll do that,' he said. 'I find myself at a standstill. And while I can conceive of any number of reasons for the murder of a man, I can hardly imagine what kind of threat a disabled fourteen-year-old boy could offer. Even if he saw something, he could barely communicate.' The burn of anger Rees always experienced when he thought of Calvin's death swept through him. Calvin was an innocent.

'I want to hold her.' Simon's voice rose into a shout. 'I want a turn.'

'Now, children,' Rees said, jumping to his feet so hastily the chair fell over. He did not want to chance seeing the new baby dropped. But Bernadette had the situation well in hand. She pressed Simon into a chair and moved the baby from Jerusha's arms to Simon's.

'She's heavy,' he remarked.

'A good seven or eight pounds,' Bernadette said, as proudly as though the child was her own.

'I want another turn,' Jerusha said.

'You'll have plenty of time to hold her,' Esther said, speaking for the first time. She had pressed herself against the wall.

'It's time for all of you to leave and let your mother rest,' Bernadette said.

'Let them stay a few minutes longer,' Lydia said. 'I won't see much of them for a day or two.'

'Longer than that. Not until you're strong enough to walk outside,' Esther said. Her eyes went to Rees. 'I doubt he will be given permission to visit again, and anyway he'll have to leave when the Sisters begin returning.'

'But this is my wife and new baby,' Rees objected, although he knew that would not be considered important. Esther nodded, her face creasing with sympathy.

'I know. But you have been among us often enough to know our ways. And although you have not signed the Covenant, while you are here we expect you to live as we do.' Rees did not reply, but when he returned the chair to its peg he threw it so hard it landed with a loud clatter.

'I'll return tomorrow, just to check on you,' Bernadette said, patting Lydia's wrist.

'I'll deliver the children to the schoolroom,' Esther said, plucking the new baby from Simon's arms and returning her to Lydia.

'I'm supposed to be in the buckwheat field,'

Simon said, his voice diminishing in volume as Esther pushed all the kids into the hall outside. Bernadette smiled at both Rees and Lydia and quickly followed Esther outside the door.

Understanding that the women had given him a gift, Rees quickly bent over his wife and kissed her. 'I'll find a way to visit,' he promised.

'Our baby has been born,' Lydia said, looking up at him with anxious eyes. 'I'll recover my strength quickly. Now I hope we can return to a home of our own. Whether it is Dugard or the Ellis property.'

Rees sighed, kissed her once again, and followed the others out.

He crossed the hall quickly, not wanting to be found on the women's side, and went out the front door. Bernadette had handed her leather bag to her daughter, seated in the passenger seat of her buggy, but she turned when she heard his footsteps behind her. 'Good luck, Mr Rees. I expect I'll see you again.' Rees followed the midwife around the buggy and assisted her into the seat.

'Isn't your husband concerned that you drive around alone?' he asked. 'Or with only your daughter for company?' Just this past summer, Lydia had driven into Dugard with David and had still been attacked. But of course that had been something different.

'I'm a widow, so I have no husband to tell me what to do,' Bernadette said, lifting up the reins. She grinned at Rees. 'Besides, I'm as safe as I can be. I know everyone hereabout and they know me. They know my brother is the constable.

And anyway, if the wives and girlfriends and in some cases the mothers are to survive, then their menfolk will allow me to pass unmolested.' She slapped the reins down and the buggy accelerated in a cloud of dust. Rees watched it for a moment, heading north to the junction with the Surry Road, and then he started east, toward the barns and Brother Aaron.

Rees did not find Aaron at the barns. When he asked the Brothers working nearby, they said they were not sure where he was today. 'Try the broom workshop,' suggested one man. 'I believe Jonathan is there. He'll know.'

So Rees walked back to the center of the small village in the hot sun. At least his hat was drying out, although the straw had lost its shape and the brim drooped over his eyes. Rees was thankful he had brought his tricorn. An old hat, and long out of fashion, but still serviceable.

The workshops were on the main street, north of the Meetinghouse. When Rees went up the steps and inside, he did not see Jonathan. But Brother Aaron was smoothing broom handles. The wood was almost white and the air smelled pungently of fresh wood. Aaron, his hands stopping the up and down motion, stared at Rees like a rabbit confronted by a wolf. 'May I speak to you outside?' Rees asked. Despite his polite tone, Aaron looked alarmed and angry. He glanced quickly from side to side, as though hoping someone would come to his aid. But, although the two other Brothers paused in their work, they did not join him.

'I won't hurt you,' Rees said. 'I just want to ask a few questions.' And then, just in case Aaron had forgotten or was considering ignoring Rees's request, he added, 'This is part of the investigation approved by the Elders.'

Aaron threw down the glass paper he was using and followed Rees to the street.

'I'm curious,' Rees said. 'You expressed much emotion at Calvin's death. More than I would have expected. Were you Calvin's father?'

'No,' Aaron said. 'But I am – or was – a father.' He stopped. Rees waited, hoping the Brother would elaborate. 'My son is about the age of Calvin,' Aaron said finally. 'But Calvin, although he had almost a man's growth, his mind was still that of a little child.' He looked down at the ground, but Rees saw the sheen of tears in the other man's brown eyes.

'I am so, so sorry,' Rees said, his own voice growing hoarse. The birth of his little daughter had scraped his emotions raw, and understanding and compassion hit him like a bath of cold water. 'I have a son.' David was approaching seventeen, a man in every way. He would marry in the fall, becoming a husband and probably a father himself in the not too distant future. But Rees had missed David's birth and most of his childhood and, although he and David had contrived to bridge the anger and regret separating them, Rees knew he would never recover those years.

'I know your children,' Aaron said.

Rees nodded, although he had not meant the children here. In a way, he'd been trying to recapture some of the experiences he'd missed with David by raising those five adopted children. He vowed now that he would do his very best to avoid making those same mistakes with his little daughter. He would be there during her childhood, that was a promise.

With Calvin, Aaron had been doing exactly the same as Rees, trying to grasp those fleeting precious moments. Rees wondered if Aaron had missed them because he'd left his family to join the Shakers, or if his son had died.

'Calvin was so defenseless,' Aaron said. 'He trusted me. And I watched out for him.'

'I know,' Rees said. One thing was certain. Unlike Rees, who had married and could have other children, Aaron would not have that kind of chance again. Not as long as he remained a member of the Shakers. So he had found a way to relive his son's childhood. And because of Calvin's disability, Aaron could have maintained his connection to a child for many years. If Calvin had lived. 'I cannot conceive of anyone wishing to harm such an innocent,' Rees said. 'Do you have any thoughts?'

Aaron's mouth opened and he stared at Rees. 'Calvin should see justice at least,' Rees added. He knew with absolute certainty that Aaron did have some suspicion. But before he could speak, Jonathan and Solomon came out of a nearby workshop. Aaron turned to look at them and his mouth shut into a thin line. Although frustration swept through Rees, he was more interested in the look Aaron shot at the Elders, a glare of anger and determination.

'Go back to work,' Jonathan said in a quiet

169

voice. Aaron obeyed without glancing at Rees. 'Do you think he is guilty of the deaths?' Jonathan asked as soon as Aaron had disappeared up the steps.

And Rees, who would have sworn these men were completely trustworthy, was suddenly no longer so sure. In fact, he eyed Jonathan with reservation as he spoke. 'No, I don't think so. But he is grieving for Calvin.'

'He is indeed,' Solomon said. 'I am worried about him. He was far more attached to the boy than I realized.' An inverted V formed between his brows. 'After what happened to his family . . .' His voice trailed away when he saw Rees regarding him with intense interest. 'But that is all in the past and of no interest to anyone anymore.'

'You can be assured,' Jonathan said to Rees, 'that Brother Aaron would never harm Calvin. I think you need to look further afield. At the farmer in whose pasture the boy was found, for example.'

'I still think someone is coming in from the outside and attacking our Brothers,' Solomon said. He acknowledged Rees with a nod and began to draw Jonathan away. 'I say again that I think we should forbid observers from attending our services. Just for a space of time, until the culprit behind these murders is identified.'

'But some of those observers become members,' Jonathan objected, his voice fading as the two men went inside the shop. The argument sounded well-worn, as though it had been repeated with variations several times. Rees turned away and

170

began walking back into the village. Whether onlookers should be permitted at the services remained a perennial question for the community, one that Rees had no interest in discussing. He did wish, however, that the Elders had not interrupted his conversation with Aaron. He was within a hairbreadth of confiding something, and Rees was not the only one who suspected Aaron was hugging something important close to his chest. The Shaker Brothers thought so, too.

At least I'll see him at supper, Rees thought. As soon as the meal was done, he would corner Brother Aaron and press him hard until he answered.

As Rees approached the Infirmary, the nursing sister came down the front steps and turned down the path toward the kitchens. Rees suddenly saw his chance; he could speak to Elizabeth once again. He was through the door and inside before he even really thought about it.

Elizabeth was not sitting up this time. She was lying in the granny cradle in front of the window, her gaze fixed upon the sky. She turned her head as Rees's footsteps sounded on the floor. Rees saw with sorrow that even that simple movement was an effort for her. 'Mr Rees,' she said.

'I won't stay long,' Rees said. 'I don't want to tire you.'

She smiled. 'It's nice to have company.' Her gaze went back to the blue sky outside. 'Soon I will . . . go home to Mother.' Rees nodded. He hesitated asking his query of a dying woman. But Elizabeth looked back at him, her eyebrows rising inquiringly. 'Ask your questions.'

171

'When I asked you about the undercurrents you sensed in this community, you mentioned friction between Jonathan and Jabez. Do you know why? I think this may be important. Especially now, after the death of the boy Calvin.'

Elizabeth did not respond at first. She kept her eyes fixed upon the sky outside. A flock of birds cut through the sky in a sharp arrow-headed V. 'It will be fall soon,' she murmured. Rees did not reply. He did not think Elizabeth would see the fall, for all that the solstice was only two and a half weeks away. He grieved for Elizabeth who was dying, but even more for Robert. Rees knew how empty he would feel if he lost Lydia.

'No. But both of them are – were – passionate about their faith. And Jabez was arrogant.'

'Is there anyone else with whom Jonathan quarrels?' Rees asked.

'Brother Aaron. But he fights with everyone.'

Rees sighed. That was what he expected her to say. 'Do you know why they argue?' he asked. Elizabeth shook her head and smiled. Rees thought again how beautiful she must have been as a young woman. Although waxy pale with illness, her eyes were still a bright blue and the bones of her face well defined.

'Aaron is difficult, isn't he?' She coughed and clutched her chest. Despite the prohibition on physical contact between the genders, Rees supported Elizabeth into a sitting position so she could breathe more easily. After a moment, her coughing ceased. Rees could hear the wind whistling in and out of her lungs. 'He doesn't like the Sisters.'

'But he was married once,' Rees said.

'Was he?' Elizabeth tried to push her pillow behind her back but her wasted limbs were too weak. Rees held her with one arm while with the other he dragged the bedding behind her. 'Thank you,' she whispered. 'But that is not uncommon here.' She breathed for a few moments. 'Many of the members were married once. And some of the wives and husbands came too.' She panted and Rees could see she was tiring. 'But some were left behind, to fend for themselves and their children as best they could.' She took a breath. 'Sometimes Jonathan quarrels with Solomon.'

'What do you think you're doing here?' The nursing sister came through the door yelling. Rees looked at her red face, a vein pulsing in her neck, and stepped quickly away from the cradle. Rees thought anyone who believed the Shakers to be soft and gentle should see this Sister. 'Bothering a dying woman, Mr Rees? And in a woman's bedchamber besides?'

Rees looked at Elizabeth. 'Lydia had the baby,' he said quickly,' else she would be here visiting you.'

'What . . . was it?'

'A little girl.' Despite the nursing sister glaring at him, Rees touched the pale shriveled hand. 'We will call on you as soon as we're able.'

'Get out, get out now,' the Sister shouted.

'Do you need help removing Elizabeth to the bed?' Rees asked.

'I said get out.'

Rees looked at her, realizing that she was just

seconds away from grabbing him and doing her best to drag him out by force. With one last smile at the ill woman, Rees headed for the door. The Sister followed on his heels all the way.

Seventeen

Rees searched for Aaron at supper, but the Shaker Brother was not in attendance. Rees's stomach began to grind with apprehension. He did not want to find another dead body. As soon as the meal ended, he looked for one of the Deacons. 'Daniel,' Rees called, attracting several disapproving glares. Daniel paused and looked at Rees.

'Unnecessary speech!' Daniel said, wagging his finger.

'Where's Aaron? I want to speak with him.'

'Aaron has left,' Jonathan said, coming up behind Rees.

'Left? Left where?' Rees said, reluctantly turning to face the Elder. He had not wanted to speak to either Jonathan or Solomon.

'Brother Aaron finds your questions both intrusive and frightening,' Jonathan said.

'Frightening?' Rees repeated. 'Does he have something to hide?'

'He requested an opportunity to take out a wagon of brooms and whips and other supplies and sell them.' Solomon said as he approached, raising his voice to speak over Rees.

'But Aaron may be the murderer,' Rees said, trying to keep his own voice from rising into a shout. 'Or, at the very least, he might suspect who the killer is.' He sounded as though he were growling.

'Of course he isn't the murderer,' Solomon said, dismissing the suggestion without hesitation. 'I have said from the beginning, from the death of Brother Jabez, that if these are murders and not simply regrettable accidents, then the murderer must be someone from outside the community. And Aaron would know nothing of anyone from the World.'

Rees looked at Jonathan. He had folded his hands in front of him and was staring at the floor. Rees sensed that Jonathan did not entirely agree with his companion, a feeling that was strengthened when he spoke.

'Brother Aaron would never harm Calvin. And your interrogation of our members and brooding presence here in Zion are disruptive. Why, you've even pushed your way to the bedside of a dying woman. A Sister.'

So, the nursing sister had complained. Rees felt his temper fraying. 'I see. And my inquiries, my disruptive questions? It's more important to keep things peaceful than find a murderer hiding in your midst?' The impulse to grab Jonathan and shake him was so overwhelming Rees raised his arm. But the shock and disbelief on both Brothers' faces halted him, and after an awkward few seconds he dropped his hand and turned away.

He walked out of the Dining Hall very quickly, panting and muttering to himself.

He had been willing to consider the possibility that Brother Jabez's death was an accident, but Calvin's murder had persuasively argued otherwise. And after speaking to the farmer, Rees was certain – not that he had required much convincing – that the murderer was here in Zion and a member of the community. Solomon and Jonathan just did not want to admit it. 'And how,' Rees said aloud, 'am I supposed to determine the identity of the murderer if I can't talk to people?' He scowled at the Brothers on either side of him. They shied away from him. Rees knew he probably looked ferocious but he didn't care.

He returned to his room and in the golden rays of the late afternoon sun continued winding his warp. Gradually, his heartbeat slowed to normal and he began to calm. The arguments in his head lost their power, and by the time the light failed he was no longer thinking of Solomon and Jonathan at all.

The long tree branches clutched at Rees, holding him back. He could hear Lydia ahead. Oh no, they were putting the noose around her neck, 'Lydia!' he cried. 'Lydia!' But he could not force his way through the tree branches. The leafy twigs grabbed at him, clinging and pulling him back. Someone was crying hard.
'Will. Will.'

Rees came up out of sleep with a gasp. Perspiration coated him in a clammy film and he was shivering. All of the bedding lay on the floor, thrown off the bed by his flailing limbs. Lydia bent over him, her face almost

176

unrecognizable in the candlelight. Although her chin was brightly lit, her eyes were dark hollows and Rees thought for a second he was still caught in his nightmare. Lydia put the candle on the table.

'You were calling me,' she said. 'I heard you from across the hall.'

Rees looked around. His room was completely dark, outside the small circle of light provided by the candle flame. 'Bad dream,' he muttered. 'Did I wake anyone else?'

'Probably,' Lydia said. 'But no one came into the hall.'

'What time is it?' Rees asked, passing his hand over his sweaty face.

'I don't know. Early. I was already awake. I was feeding the baby.'

Now Rees realized Lydia was clad only in a thin night shift with a shawl thrown over her shoulders. 'I'm fine,' he said although he was still panting hard. The memory of the dream sent an involuntary, convulsive shudder through him. Lydia sat down beside him.

'No, you're not,' she said. 'What's wrong?' Rees did not respond. 'You've been like a bear with a sore head since your arrival from Dugard. Irritable, snapping at everyone, losing your temper at the least provocation. Something is bothering you. What is it?'

Rees felt his mouth open; he thought he'd been behaving just as usual. Although his face and body were damp with sweat, his mouth felt as though it were filled with cotton. 'Water, please,' he said.

177

Lydia rose and poured him a beaker of water. When she brought it over to him, he drank it in one long draft then she took the beaker and set it on the floor as she sat down beside him. 'What happened last month in Dugard?' she asked.

'I told you,' he muttered.

'You told me you solved the murders,' Lydia said, frustration lending a sharpness to her voice, 'and that you gave the farm to David because of the accusation of witchcraft laid against me. But there is something else. I know it.'

Rees regarded his wife for several seconds. She was only slightly visible in the dim candle-light. 'It sounds so simple, so bare, the way you've described it,' he said.

'And it isn't?'

Images crowded Rees's head. The rope carried by Farley's son, the sight of Mac's body in the mill, the frantic flight by the river, and the end to that journey – the fire that consumed the shed, sending orange light across the water where Rees had taken refuge. Then his terrifying escape from the town, and the continued search for him by Farley and his deputies. Rees had almost been caught several times. And finally his identification of the murderer, someone he had never suspected. Rees felt he would never recover from the betrayal. It ached like an open wound.

'Oh Will, tell me what happened,' Lydia said. The gentleness in her voice unmanned him and he felt a lump harden in his throat. He turned his head away from her and tried to push the terror and grief away. Lydia reached out and pulled him into her arms. He felt the roughness

178

of the knitted wool of her shawl against his cheek. It smelled faintly of sheep and milk and lavender. 'Tell me,' she repeated.

'Well, you know most of it,' Rees said, intending to shield her from the worst of the experience. But this time once he started talking it seemed he couldn't stop. He told her everything, not just the bare facts of the murders but what Thomas McIntyre looked like strung up in the mill and the effort to frame Lydia herself for the murder. He described the expression on Farley's face when he came to the farm to arrest Lydia, and the rope carried by the constable's son. Finally, his voice hoarse with talking, he recounted his frantic flight from the farm and his search for a refuge from which to search for the murderer.

By the time he finished, the cacophony of chirping birds outside the window heralded the coming dawn. Nervous – would Lydia scorn his weakness? – Rees pulled back and looked at her. Her face was shiny with tears.

'Oh Will, I didn't know. You never said.'

'I wanted to protect you,' Rees said, touching the scar on her forehead with his finger. 'And Farley is still constable. Although I am no longer a suspect in the murders, the charge of witchcraft against you has not been suspended.'

'I wish I *were* a witch,' she said, her voice low but trembling with rage. 'I would make them all sorry. That Farley – no amulet would save him!'

'When I gave the farm to David,' Rees said, reaching across and taking her hand, 'I wasn't sure what would happen. We might both have

179

been hanged. I wanted to safeguard the farm for David and the children.'

'All of them might have been orphaned!' said Lydia. Except for scarlet slashes across the cheekbones, her face was white. 'I could kill that Farley! How could the magistrate allow this to happen?'

Rees was prepared to remind her that Piggy Hanson had always disliked him, but the thud of footsteps overhead distracted him. 'Everyone will be up soon,' he said. He had talked a long time, far longer than he expected, and when he looked at the windows he saw the first faint streaks of light.

Lydia nodded. 'I'd better return to my own room. If they find me here . . .'

Rees nodded. 'I've already been told I'm disruptive. As much as I want you to stay, we shouldn't risk it. Right now we have nowhere else to go.' Lydia nodded, her mouth trembling. She inhaled, and manufactured a smile.

'The baby will need to be fed soon, anyway.' She pushed her way off the bed and started toward the door. 'We still have to think of a name,' she added, attempting a light tone. As she opened the door, a faint mewling cry wafted inside. 'Oh.' She clutched at her chest. 'I have to feed her.' The door closed behind her with a click.

Spent, Rees lay back against the pillow. At the moment he felt too tired to even contemplate the knot in which he found himself. But he couldn't return to sleep and, after a few minutes of listening to footsteps clattering down the stairs and disappearing into the early morning outside, he got up. It would not have been light enough to weave, even if he had warped the loom, but he could continue winding the yarn around the pegs on the warping board. He washed in the tepid water, thinking longingly of the big tub in the laundry. He didn't dare use it without permission, and anyway the Sisters would be rising from their beds as well. For all Rees knew, some of the women were already there, starting the fires underneath the kettles of water. He made sure his hands were clean before he touched the yarn. Because these were ends from other projects, there were knots everywhere. Well, he thought with a lift of his spirits, the baby would need diapers. And his little red-headed daughter wouldn't mind the knots, as long as they didn't irritate her delicate skin. That would be three in diapers: Joseph, Judah and the newborn.

Rees knotted a new strand on to the length hanging from the board and began winding. He felt washed out, as if everything inside him had been drained away. Everything, including the grief and terror of the nightmare. Rees's thoughts turned to his current puzzle. There was no doubt, he thought with a definite nod of his head, that Aaron's departure was significant. But how? Was Aaron the murderer? Although Rees could believe Brother Aaron was guilty of Jabez's murder, Calvin's would be harder to explain. Aaron's shocked grief at Calvin's death had seemed genuine. So did that mean there were two murderers? Rees paused, with the hand clutching the yarn still elevated. He shook his head doubtfully, two murderers in *this* community? And wouldn't that also imply that at least some of the Shakers were protecting a murderer? Unwillingly, Rees's thoughts turned to Jonathan. But Solomon and Daniel too were reluctant to accuse Aaron. So what was Rees missing?

There were no answers here. Frustrated, he uttered a curse and threw the strand of wool at the warping board.

The knock on his door and a Shaker Brother's voice announcing breakfast came as welcome relief to Rees's thoughts.

Eighteen

On the surface, breakfast seemed the same as any other meal. But as Rees tucked in, devouring bacon and eggs, he began to sense something, a certain tone, shuddering through the Dining Hall. He paused, his knife held halfway to his mouth and looked around. Few of the men seemed aware of something amiss. But when Rees glanced over to the Sisters' side, he recognized the signs of distress, for all that no one was speaking. Many of the women were looking around, their expressions drawn into frowns. He caught several glances directed at him, and began to wonder if someone had seen Lydia entering or leaving his room. Even married couples were expected to live as brother and sister, and without physical contact. He did not doubt that the crying of his new daughter kept many of the women awake and if Lydia had been seen – he gulped and peeked nervously at Elders Jonathan and Solomon. To Rees's relief they were eating stolidly, without demonstrating any interest in him at all.

Still, he thought it wise to leave the village for a few hours. This might be a good time to inspect the Ellis property. After the deaths of Brothers Jabez and Calvin, Rees was eager to take his family somewhere safe. As soon as the meal was done, he joined the flood of Brothers leaving the Dining Hall. As they turned to go to the fields he crossed the road to the stable, whistling for Hannibal as he did so.

The Ellis property lay northwest of Zion, in the foothills of the mountains, a few miles north of the turn-off to Durham. Rees passed the turn toward town. Although the property to his left was wooded, neat fields continued on his right. The flat Shaker straw hats rose and fell as the Brothers moved among the rows. Rees eyed the men in some surprise. These fields had once belonged to the Doucette family, not to Zion.

It took almost an hour to reach the small lane that led to the Ellis property. As Rees drove along it, he was astonished to see tidy fields on either side. A small orchard, its trees just big enough to bear fruit, had been planted next to the drive leading to the house. Rees pulled Hannibal to a stop and stared at the trees with a mixture of incredulity and anger. He now knew why Jonathan was so eager to keep the farm: the Shakers had already begun to work the land.

And of course, having done the work, they were not eager to hand the farm to someone else. Shaking his head, Rees picked up the reins and slapped them down. In his opinion, the use of these fields shaded perilously close to theft. He was going to have to talk to the Elders.

He followed the lane to the farmhouse.

Chest-high weeds fringed the dilapidated barn. When Rees looked down the track leading to the paddock behind the barn, he saw a worm fence surrounding a field of weeds. The top bar had fallen down, and the lower half was completely invisible in the high grass. It was clear that no one had used that paddock for a very long time.

Rees turned to the house, recalling his visits to this place. Shaking off the memories of a previous case that had come to fruition here, Rees approached the building. The front porch had been mended with fresh boards, but when Rees went up the steps he found the front door was still nailed shut. He walked around toward the kitchen, looking up at the roof as he circled the house. From the lighter patches, it looked as though fresh wooden shingles and tar had been installed some time recently. Probably by the Shakers, Rees thought. They wouldn't want to see damage to a property that soon might be theirs.

A path had been hacked through the weeds leading to the back door. Previously Rees had been able to climb through one of the smaller windows. But a board had been tacked up across that entry point. Shutters had been nailed across the window next to the door. The door itself was weathered gray, and the wood was splintering from the onslaught of rain and sun. Rees tried to open it. Although it too had been nailed shut, he saw only a few of the square-headed nails. And with the condition of the door, he guessed a good sharp shove would break it open.

He really wanted to get inside. From out here, the house appeared in good enough shape to live in. After a moment's hesitation, Rees threw his weight against the door. The old wood shattered, leaving fresh white scars, and the door flew open. Rees stepped into the shadowy interior. The window over the sink, although not shuttered, let in a pale greenish light. The bush outside had grown up to cover the glass with leafy branches.

Rees walked into the dining room, still occupied by a long table flanked with benches. It would need serious scrubbing but it was useable. Rees began to feel a little more optimistic about moving his family into this house.

The front room looked exactly the same as he remembered except the upholstered chairs were even more ragged. Bits of shredded stuffing drifted across the floor and a nest of leaves and fluff occupied one shadowy corner. Rees looked up at the ceiling. He couldn't see any water stains or other damage. The first floor seemed weathertight.

The big question was the roof. Rees ran up the staircase to the second floor. Here, under the roof, the air was hot and still. He performed a hasty examination of the bedrooms. Although mouse droppings were plentiful, he saw no holes in the wooden walls. One of the bedrooms had even been plastered. Rees thought the cracks could be easily plastered over. Although the shutters were missing from several of the windows, all the glass in the frames was intact. Sunshine streamed brightly into every room. And the few brown blemishes left on the ceiling appeared to be from old leaks.

Now all he had to do was persuade – or compel – the Shakers to allow his family to move here. If his own arguments failed, he would involve the lawyer. In fact, maybe he should speak to Mr Golightly first. Immediately. Today. Since it was fast approaching mid-morning, the lawyer would most likely be in his office.

Rees closed the kitchen door as tightly as he could and climbed into his wagon. He drove south on the Surry Road toward the turn-off, but had not gone very far when he realized something was different, something was wrong. He stared around him, trying to understand what his senses were telling him. Then he knew. No one was in the fields. Not one man. Where had the Shaker Brothers gone?

With a sudden prickle of unease, Rees urged Hannibal into a trot. Maybe he would stop by Zion first, before going into town.

When he reached the center of the village, Rees found several Brothers in front of the Dwelling House. Although Solomon and Brother Robert were seated in a buggy, most of the men stood in a crowd with both Eldresses. Men and women standing in such close physical proximity was so unusual in the community that Rees slowed down. When all of the Shakers turned as one to stare, Rees pulled Hannibal to a stop and jumped down from the wagon.

'Where have you been?' Esther demanded, rounding on him with a fierce scowl. Rees threw her a look, surprised by her tone, but he replied readily enough.

'At the Ellis property.'

'The Ellis property?' Solomon repeated. 'Why?'

'I wanted to see what kind of shape the farmhouse was in,' Rees said. He kept his eyes fixed upon the Elder, daring him to protest. But Solomon, his graying brows drawing together until they almost met over his nose, shook his head.

'I don't suppose you saw a young girl there?'

'I didn't see anyone,' Rees said, his irritation rapidly fading into apprehension. 'What happened?'

'Deborah has disappeared.'

'Who?'

'You may not know her,' Esther said, inserting herself into the conversation. 'She's about fourteen.'

A memory of a girl with pale-blonde hair walking with Annie popped into Rees's mind. 'Pretty girl with flaxen hair?'

'Have you seen her?' Jonathan asked, leaning forward in excitement.

'Not for several days.' Rees turned to Esther. 'She's gone?'

'Her bed wasn't slept in last night.' The Sister rubbed her hand across her red-rimmed eyes.

'Perhaps she walked into town or something,'

187

suggested the older Eldress. 'Decided this life wasn't for her.'

'She didn't take anything with her,' Esther said in a brusque tone. 'Nothing. Not even a cloak.' She turned to Rees and her eyes began to fill. 'Please, you must find her.'

'You're sure there was no one at the Ellis property?' Jonathan asked, the hope in his voice fading as Rees shook his head. 'You're absolutely certain?'

'I didn't search the barns,' said Rees. 'Or the stables.' He doubted she would be found there. He'd seen no signs of anyone, but supposed it was possible.

'I think we should take another look,' Solomon said. 'Just in case she's hiding.' He reached up to tug at his beard. When his cuff fell back, Rees saw swollen red marks all over his wrist and the back of his hand. The blotches made the Elder seem human and vulnerable. 'We have to be sure,' Solomon added, meeting Rees's eyes.

'Of course,' Rees said. 'I wish I had seen her. What about . . .?' He gestured to the buildings around him.

'We've searched everywhere,' Esther said, her voice trembling with panic.

'Even the foundry,' Jonathan added. 'And the icehouse. Places a little girl would have no reason to be.'

Solomon picked up the reins. With a nod all around, he slapped them down upon the horse's rump and the buggy drove away in a spurt of dust. Rees watched the vehicle and the Shakers disappear in the direction from which he had just come. He knew they feared, as he did, that they would find another body. Another dead body. 'I'll help you look,' he said.

'We aren't sure where else to go,' Jonathan said in desperation, his gaze rising to the sky as if the answer might present itself there.

Rees tried to think. Deborah had not run away, that much seemed clear. And if she was not hidden here, in Zion, she was most likely hidden close by. As Calvin had been. Rees shut that thought off immediately, not wanting to remember the boy or imagine the death of another child. 'Well,' he said. 'If Brother Solomon is searching the Ellis property, why don't we look at that abandoned farm on the way into town?' He kept a sharp eye on Jonathan in case he looked self-conscious or tried to persuade Rees against such a course. But the Brother only appeared confused.

'What abandoned farm?' he asked in surprise.

'Constable Rouge showed it to me. As the crow flies, it lies about halfway between Zion and Durham. The house and barn are half falling down, but it is private.' He stopped abruptly, trying to avoid imagining what activities might require privacy.

'I cannot conceive why she would want to go to a derelict farm,' Jonathan said, sounding both angry and frightened. Then he shot a terrified glance toward Rees, who nodded in understanding. 'I suppose we had better take a look,' Jonathan said. 'Just in case.' He swallowed as though it hurt him.

'You will want to wear boots,' Rees said, his eyes traveling from the Shaker's straw hat to the clogs on his feet. 'The terrain is rough and we'll have to hike in.'

Jonathan looked down at his feet and the muddy clogs that encased them. 'Very well.'

As the Brothers hastened up the steps into the Dwelling House, Rees turned to Esther. 'Will you tell Lydia where I've gone?'

'Of course.' She forced a smile. 'Although I don't want to tell her of Deborah's disappearance, I don't want to worry her. Not now. Women are delicate after a birth.'

Rees expelled a breath. 'I know. Tell her instead I've gone into town to see the lawyer about the Ellis farm.' That would be partly true. He had to move his family, had to. He hadn't been here for an entire week and yet during that time two people had been murdered, and now a third was missing. There was no safety in Zion. Rees shivered. So much for his dreams of refuge. Maybe, once he got his family away from the village, he could successfully protect them. 'Watch over them for me,' he said, meeting Esther's eyes.

'Of course. I thought once I came here all the cruelty and wickedness I saw in Georgia . . .' Her voice trailed away and she shook her head. 'I hoped this place at least would be different.' She looked around and added in a hasty undertone. 'You should know – Lydia and the baby will soon be moved to the Children's Dwelling House. I won't be able to watch over them then.' Before she could say anything else, Jonathan clattered down the steps in his heavy boots.

Rees waited for Jonathan and his fellows to

hitch up another wagon, a matter of twenty minutes or so. By the time they'd finished, Rees was practically screaming with impatience and frustration; the Shakers' movements were so deliberate and slow. He wanted to shout at them and remind them that a girl's life was at stake, and if they wanted to find Deborah alive they needed to hurry.

When they were finally ready to go, Rees climbed into his wagon seat and urged Hannibal forward at a rapid trot.

Nineteen

Rees feared he would miss the turn-off to the lane, but as he led the other buggy north from Durham he easily spotted the rail fence that separated the cultivated fields from the rutted lane. It seemed in even worse condition than Rees remembered. He had a bad moment when they climbed down from their vehicles and walked into the lane: at first, he didn't see the stone wall. But then, as they crested a rise, the wall appeared and he knew the farmhouse couldn't be far.

'Who owns this place?' Jonathan asked as he scaled the tumbled stones of the collapsed wall.

'I don't know,' Rees said. 'But maybe Zion wants to purchase it.' He grinned provocatively at the Brother.

'It's so overgrown,' Jonathan said. 'Bringing it back to farmland would be difficult.' Nonetheless, he continued glancing around as though inspecting the farm for purchase, and Rees suspected the Brother was laying out the fields in his head.

The farmhouse was just as Rees remembered it from his earlier visit: a crumbling structure hemmed in by trees.

'It has been many years since anyone lived here,' Jonathan remarked, threading his way through the saplings to try the pump handle. It creaked and groaned but nothing came out. 'This needs priming.'

'I'll go round to the barn,' Rees said. Jonathan nodded and turned to the rotting steps. 'Be careful,' Rees warned. 'There's a hole in the roof, and Rouge told me there'd been a fire in the kitchen. Much of the structure is weak.'

He walked around the house. Wild roses and head-high thistles caught at his clothing as he muscled his way through them. By the time he'd fought his way to the back he was bleeding from a score of scratches. Black flies had come down upon his ears, and he could feel the bloody welts rising below the hairline. The passage through would have been much harder but for the granite intermittently protruding through the soil. Nothing but lichens grew on the stone, and Rees was able to move easily across it.

The barn was even more dilapidated than the house. A portion of the roof had fallen in and the slender white trunk of a birch tree stretched up toward the sky. Rees stepped through the broken door and into the gloom. More than just the birch tree had taken root in the left side, under the opening. A patch of forest shrouded the shingles and shattered boards in green. The space smelled moist; of forest and old hay and, almost imperceptibly, of cattle.

Rees ducked under a collapsed rafter, being very careful not to touch it. Who knew what would happen? Why, the entire building might come down around him. But he saw no sign that anyone had been here recently.

He went through the opposite door. While the ground to his right fell precipitately to a narrow valley, the descent in front and to his left was more gradual. The thickets of shrubs told Rees that these had once been cultivated fields. They could be again – but the work required would be almost as great as if this was virgin forest. No one had been here for many years.

Rees turned around and retraced his steps. He pushed his way through the back and into what had once been the kitchen garden. The fence rails were all on the ground and the interior was a jungle. But he saw some vegetables that had reseeded themselves: lamb's quarters and purslane. There was even squash, the vines tumbling over the ground and climbing up the fence posts, their bright-yellow flowers nodding rakishly over the weathered wood.

Rees looked at the back of the house. The door to the kitchen was still firmly closed. The glass of the window had fallen out and he could see the telltale sparkle of shards glittering in the grass. Through the opening he could hear the Shakers tramping through the upstairs and hoped no one would fall through the floor to the level below.

Sighing with frustration, he examined the remainder of the yard.

At the distant back was a shed, perhaps what remained of a pigsty, and an outhouse. As Rees began pressing his way through the vegetation, he realized the ground sloped upward. It was a gentle incline but he found himself beginning to pant. Once he reached the outhouse – the door was hanging from one hinge – he saw that the building had been positioned in such a way that the back protruded over the edge of the gully. Rees guessed that moving water filled the ravine for at least some of the year. Someone had been thinking: the waste would be swept away from the house and the well at the front. He squeezed his way through the fir trees and the other shrubbery that had grown up around the structure and peered over the edge. The incline grew slightly steeper as it dropped toward the overgrown fields at the back. And yes, water trickled down the narrow crack, even now, in the dry part of the year.

Rees swept his eyes over the gully, from the bottom up to the top where heavy rains had cut their own channels. Once, without the heavy vegetation and perhaps with a path that led to the edge, this stream could have provided water for the animals. Rees began tramping beside the stream back to the house. But he had not gone very far when he saw something white on the other side, just under a flat granite boulder. Half-buried by stones and mud, an ivory knob protruded from the rocks, the light color shining like a beacon. Rees stared at it, a horrible suspicion growing in his mind. Once the thought had taken root, he couldn't stop gnawing at it. And he couldn't look away from the round white object caught in the rocks and thick tree roots.

Rees hesitated, swallowing. Surely, that white thing could not be a bone. It couldn't be! But he had to investigate, had to be sure. He began to hurry, trampling everything in his path as he followed the lip of the gully. Although he was not more than thirty feet from the back door, the overgrowth was so thick and so high he could barely see the roof of the house.

He had to step into the water to cross to the other side. Although September was a dry month, the recent rain had combined with the flow from an underground spring to create a shallow but fast moving stream. From the flat boulder Rees lowered himself into the gully, clutching at the thick roots for balance. Some of the roots stretched almost a foot from the ground, a clear indication of the severe erosion that had washed the soil away. With his feet skidding over the muddy stones, Rees made his way to the white ball. He did not have to be very close before he recognized it for what it was: a human skull.

He thought at first that the skull had been snared by a basket of intertwined roots and stones, but when he brushed away the leaves and twigs he saw the ivory gleam of other bones. A collarbone, maybe. Or a breastbone. And below that the rounded curve of a rib, rising above a heap of gravel.

'Dear God in Heaven!' Rees muttered. He began hauling himself back up to the top by way of the

195

wrist-thick stems. He would need the help of the Shaker Brothers to recover the remains.

As he thrashed through the thicket separating the house from the ravine, he heard a shout. Moments later, Jonathan called Rees's name. He sounded both panicked and horrified. Rees tried to hurry, but speed was impossible in this thick underbrush.

Finally he made it through to the house. Jonathan waited by the back door to the kitchen. 'Where have you been?' he asked, brushing a dirty hand over his tanned cheeks, leaving a streak behind. Without waiting for Rees's response, Jonathan continued. 'Something terrible happened here! Come inside.'

Rees peered into the kitchen. It looked just as he remembered with the large kitchen table in the center and scorch marks running across the floor. 'You need to come in,' Jonathan said, pulling Rees by the sleeve. Rees was too surprised by Jonathan touching him to protest.

Rees stepped inside. The two other Brothers moved aside as Jonathan urged Rees to walk around the table. The wooden floorboards on the other side were stained a dark rusty brown. Rees spat on his handkerchief and went down on one knee to draw the cloth across the stain. It had been there a long time, so it was unlikely to leave a mark on the linen, but Rees already knew what it was. Blood. A lot of it.

'That looks like . . .' Jonathan stopped, standing well away from the dried pool. 'Not the girl, surely?' But his voice lifted in despair.

'No, not Deborah,' Rees said. 'This blood has

been here too long.' The youngest Brother retched and fled from the room. Rees could hear him vomiting outside.

Rees looked around him. From this lower vantage point, he could see splashes all over the lower cabinets. Someone had been kneeling here or crouching as they were beaten to death. The killer had probably hoped the fire would take hold and hide the crime.

'I found some bones. I'll need help pulling them out of the stream.' He looked up at Jonathan. Although the Brother's mouth tightened, he nodded.

'Very well. Do you think . . .?' He gestured at the blood. 'Murder?'

'Probably.' Rees supposed the bones in the gully belonged to the woman who had once lived here. Her husband had probably killed her, then set the fire and fled. Maybe the Shakers and their belief in celibacy, unnatural though it seemed, was the more honorable way of living. The Sisters were not only unlikely to die in such a way but also had a say in the governance of their community.

Rees swept his gaze all around him again. This time he noticed a bit of white cloth, kicked to the other side of the kitchen and lying under the cupboard. He stood up, went around the table, and bent over to retrieve it. It was not a handkerchief, as he'd thought, but one of the linen caps worn by the Shaker Sisters. He held it up.

'Deborah was here,' Jonathan whispered, his eyes huge.

Twenty

The Believers followed Rees through the under-brush to the stream. The youngest of the three Brothers, skinny and light as a young boy, came last. Rees could see he would be of no help; most likely he would be swept off his feet by the stream of water going down the gully. When they gathered on the flat rock, he turned a funny greenish white as soon as saw the bones, and then backed up so hastily he tripped and fell on his backside.

'We should send for the constable,' Rees said, turning to look at Jonathan.

'Yes,' he said, swallowing. 'Who . . .? Who do you think it is?'

'I don't know. The bones have been here a long time. Probably at least a few years.' He moved aside several rocks and extracted an arm bone. It was not an ivory color like the skull, but blotched with deep tea-brown stains. 'From the leaves,' said Rees, looking at the bones faintly visible among the rocks. 'We can send the boy to fetch the constable,' Rees continued. 'He'd be of no use, anyway.'

Jonathan turned and looked behind him at the boy, still sprawled upon the ground. 'Yes,' he agreed. 'He'll be fastest. Go! Take the buggy and ride into town for Rouge.'

The young man scrambled to his feet with

alacrity and disappeared into the thicket. As the sound of his thrashing through the underbrush faded, Jonathan said, 'I suppose this poor soul is fortunate. The roots caught him. Otherwise, he'd never have been found and given a proper burial.'

'Fortunate *she* was found, maybe,' said Rees. He was convinced this was the remains of a woman. 'Yesterday's rains washed away some of the debris. But she wasn't captured by the roots.'

'What do you mean?' Jonathan glanced into the ravine, his mouth tightening as he looked at the curve of a rib protruding over the stones. 'You think . . .?' He stopped.

'Look at the way the stones are piled around the rib cage.' Rees pointed. 'They were put there purposely. The murderer did his very best to conceal his crime.' He paused, waiting for Jonathan to speak. But he did not protest. The blood on the floor of the kitchen and now these bones were too persuasive.

Rees lowered himself into the gully and made his way to the cairn. 'Some of these bones are broken, too.' He began moving the heavy stones away. Although he did not hear Jonathan give a command, the third Brother jumped into the ravine with Rees and began to help.

It took them two hours of struggle to free the bones from their nest of rocks and roots. Jonathan took possession of the bones as they were handed up to him, laying them out upon the flat granite shelf to dry. Rees and his helper, by now wet and coated with mud, conducted a final search for the smaller bones. Most of them were missing, carried away by small animals or the action of the moving water. Finally, the two men climbed to higher ground. Rees put his back against a pine tree, and for a few seconds just breathed.

Jonathan had laid out the bones in a rough approximation of a body. Rees found his eyes drawn to them. He did not want to think of this woman's last moments: the fear and pain and the awful realization that no one would come to her aid. But as his gaze focused upon the skeleton, something began to gnaw at him. Something about the bones did not fit with his assumptions. What was he seeing and not understanding? Finally, unable to bear the itch of curiosity, he rose to his feet and crossed the short space of dirt to the boulder. Bending down, he examined the wide breastbone. Would a woman be so broad through the shoulders? Rees picked up a femur and held it against his thigh. The bone was only slightly shorter. Unable to believe this result, Rees did it again. But the bone did not appear any smaller. And it was solid too, with some weight to it. Not at all delicate.

'What's the matter?' Jonathan asked.

'I'm not sure,' Rees said. He guessed a woman could be almost six feet tall, though it would be very unusual. Could a woman have beaten her husband to death?

'Rees. Will Rees,' Rouge called from the bank by the house. Rees dropped the femur and looked up, but the constable was still hidden behind the thick vegetation.

'Here,' he shouted. 'Over here.'

Rouge's face appeared through the screen of greenery.

'What is it this time? The boy said you found a body?'

'We did. Come over here.'

Rouge's nose wrinkled as he took in Rees's appearance. 'What have you been doing, bathing in the mud with the pigs?'

'We had to retrieve the bones,' Rees said, gesturing to the skeleton reposing at his feet. Rouge's eyes widened. Without another word, he tramped across the top of the gully and picked his way through the undergrowth until he stood beside Rees.

'You think the blood inside the house belongs to this poor devil?' Rouge asked. 'The boy showed me. No one could survive losing that much blood.'

'Some of the bones are broken,' Rees said. 'And the murderer went out of his way to ensure the body would stay undiscovered.' He gestured to the now empty cairn.

'But who is it?' Rouge asked.

'I was hoping you could tell me,' Rees said.

'Not likely,' Rouge muttered. 'Mon Dieu! It's been years since anyone lived here. I hardly remember the wife, I wasn't even constable then.' Brow furrowed in thought, he chewed his lower lip. 'But my sister might. Especially if there were children born here.'

'I'll ask her,' Rees said, relief sweeping over him. A name. That was all he wanted, the name of the owner of these bones.

'How did you know the bones were there?' Rouge turned his sharp black eyes upon Rees

'I was searching for Deborah. Did the boy tell you she is missing?'

'Yes.' Rouge grinned, flashing his brown teeth at Rees. 'Seems like Zion is losing quite a few of its members.'

'I saw the skull from the bank,' Rees continued. 'Saw something white, anyway,' he corrected himself, 'and went to see what it was.' He paused and then added, 'After what happened to Calvin, I . . .' Rouge heard the emotion in Rees's voice and nodded in sympathy.

'I know. You wanted to search everywhere. Has she been found?'

'No. Not so far.' Rees heard his voice crack with worry and stopped speaking. Rouge clapped Rees on the shoulder.

'Let's get these bones out of here, shall we? Give them a decent burial.' Then he looked down at his vest and breeches, liberally spotted with grease but so far untouched by mud. He shot an inquiring look at Rees.

'Very well,' he said. 'I'll bring the bones over.' Then he realized he had no sack.

'Use your shirt,' Jonathan said. 'Why is everything always so complicated with you? Problems seem to stick to you as persistently as that mud.' He gestured to the brown spots that covered Rees almost to his chin.

Ignoring Jonathan, Rees said to Rouge, 'The bones have been here for so long I doubt we will ever identify the murderer.' He shrugged out of his shirt.

'It's been awhile,' Rouge agreed. 'But the killer might be a local farmer or someone from hereabouts, anyway. Could still be around.'

Rees paused and then nodded. 'Maybe so. I'll try to identify the victim. Put a name on the tombstone. And once we have his – or her – name, we might know the identity of the murderer.' Suddenly aware that Jonathan was staring at him, Rees turned. 'What?'

'You shame me,' Jonathan said. 'You have such a passion for justice.'

Rees, his face growing hot, bent his head over the shirt and began tying the sleeves together. With the sack completed, he began picking up the bones. Once they were all contained within the linen, Rouge took possession. He held it daintily by the cuffs, so no mud would transfer to him.

By now, the passage of many feet had crushed the vegetation down and created something of a path at the top of the ravine. Rees made his way across the gully to the other side. New wet mud was added to the dried layer on his shoes and now they felt as heavy as bricks. He clomped after the other men, leaving a trail of mud clots behind him.

Once they got to the lane and out of the heavy shade, Rees was surprised to see how high the sun had risen in the sky. It was almost time for the noon meal. And after his morning's labors, Rees's stomach was growling in a demanding manner. He was very hungry and, by the speed with which Jonathan and the other Brothers jumped into the buggy, they were as well.

Panting, Rouge lifted the sack of bones into his wagon. 'They get heavy after awhile,' he told Rees. 'I'll turn them over to the doctor.'

Rees nodded. He really wanted to follow Rouge into the village, but knew he couldn't. He was shirtless, for one thing, and completely covered with mud and sweat for another. 'I'll come by later this afternoon,' he said. Rouge's eyes went from the top of Rees's head to his feet and back again.

'It would be a good idea to clean up first,' he advised with a grunt. He climbed into his wagon, and a few seconds later Rees was alone.

His hands were stiff and scraped raw. After his efforts of the morning and then the hike back to the road, he ached. Groaning, he climbed into his own wagon and turned toward Zion.

When Rees drove into the village, Brother Solomon and both Eldresses were gathered around Jonathan's buggy. Rees pulled Hannibal to a stop and with slow, stiff movements climbed down.

'I see Sister Deborah is not with you,' Solomon said. 'What took you so long? And why,' he added, eyeing Rees's bare chest in disgust, 'are you so dirty?'

'We didn't find Deborah,' Jonathan said. 'But we did find something.' He looked at Rees. Rees hesitated, caught in indecision. He hadn't wanted to mention the bones.

'We found a skeleton,' he said at last as the pause became uncomfortable. All the blood drained from Solomon's cheeks, and his eyebrows shot to his hairline.

'A skeleton?' Esther repeated, pressing her hands to her chest.

'Not Deborah's. An old skeleton,' Rees said. 'Long buried.'

'Where did you find the bones?' Esther asked, grimacing with horror.

'At an abandoned farm between the Ellis property and town,' Rees said.

'Any idea to whom the bones belong?' Solomon asked in a hushed voice. He had gone pale. Rees shook his head.

'No. Rouge didn't even remember the name of the family who once lived there.'

'The constable was there?' Solomon asked, his voice rising.

Rees nodded, yawning. 'It looked like murder,' he said. 'We had to summon the constable. Don't worry. There is no doubt that the bones have nothing to do with the Zion community.' He did not want to think about the hostility between Solomon and Rouge right now. Hungry, dirty and tired, Rees wanted to wash and eat in that order.

'It will soon be time for prayers,' Jonathan said, throwing a sympathetic glance at Rees. 'And we still have to unhitch our vehicles and take care of the horses.'

Although Solomon was frowning, he acknowledged Jonathan's words with a jerk of his head.

'But the bones?' Esther protested.

'Not important now,' Jonathan said. 'Prayers,' he added, gesturing pointedly at the Meetinghouse. After a few seconds, Esther obeyed the implied command and she and the other Eldress began walking to the imposing white building at the end of the street. Solomon shot a sharp glance at Rees but said nothing before following the Sisters.

Rees and Jonathan drove their vehicles to the stables and unhitched their horses. Jonathan handed his horse to one of the hired men before hurrying to the Meetinghouse himself. After several minutes of walking Hannibal to cool him, Rees asked the young man if he would mind caring for Hannibal at the same time as the other horse. The boy nodded in silence, and Rees gave up the reins.

Although he tried to knock the rest of the mud off his shoes before going into the Dwelling House, the leather still wore a film of dirt. Rees left them outside the door before entering his room. He changed quickly, leaving his filthy breeches and vest by the door. Soon the Shakers would be gathering for dinner and Rees did not want to be late. But when he stepped outside his room, all was silent. He opened the door of the Dwelling House. No Shakers were in the street outside. Rees glanced at the Meetinghouse. No one was exiting the building; the Shakers were still inside at prayers. Making his decision in an instant, Rees padded silently across the hall and into Lydia's room.

Twenty-One

Lydia jumped, startled, when he entered. She was out of bed and fully dressed, although she had not replaced the bertha around her shoulders. Rees thought she had just finished feeding his new daughter. Lydia pulled a light blanket over the child, who lay asleep in the cradle, and turned to look at her husband. 'What if someone sees you?'

'They're still at prayers,' Rees said, putting his arms around her and kissing her. She returned his embrace at first but then she pulled away, with a nervous glance at the door. 'What happened to you? You smell of wet leaves. What have you been doing?'

Rees hesitated. Should he tell his wife about Deborah's disappearance? Lydia looked so happy. 'Something's happened,' Lydia said, shaking Rees's arm. 'I can see that. Don't try to shield me. It's demeaning and I won't have it.' Rees looked down into her face. She frowned at him. 'Tell me.'

'You've just had a baby,' he said, rubbing his hands over her shoulders.

'And that means my ability to think is now impaired?' Lydia pulled away, her mouth set in an angry line.

'I didn't mean that,' Rees began. But he did not complete his protest. She was right. He was attempting to protect her from harsh news as though she were a delicate flower and not the strong and intelligent woman he knew her to be. Besides, any effort to spare her would be met with fierce resistance and was already doomed to failure. 'One of the young girls is missing. Deborah.' Rees said.

'Deborah,' Lydia repeated. 'I know her. I mean I've met her. She shares a room with Annie.' She paused, her face creased with worry. 'I wondered why Esther was so anxious. Have you spoken to Annie?'

Rees shook his head. 'Not yet.' In truth, he had not thought to do so.

'I will then, the next time Annie calls in to see the baby. She might know something. Probably does, in fact.' She paused, eyeing Rees with dread. 'But that doesn't explain why you smell of moss and mud.' She paled. 'Oh no! You didn't find Deborah's body, did you?'

'No,' Rees said. 'We didn't find any sign of her. All of Zion has been searched, as well as the Ellis property. Brother Solomon – and I – looked there. It's not in a terrible condition, by the way, and I think we could move our family to it.'

'I would like that,' Lydia said. 'At least as a temporary measure. But that still doesn't answer my question.'

'Constable Rouge had shown me an abandoned farm, so I thought it wise to look there.' Lydia's hand crept up to cover her mouth. 'We found signs of a struggle in the kitchen, and a skeleton half-buried in a stream. Old bones,' he emphasized.

As he spoke, Lydia relaxed. 'So you had to climb down to retrieve the bones,' she guessed when he finished speaking. Rees nodded, feeling like a guilty schoolboy. 'But you didn't find the girl?'

'No.' Rees thought of the linen cap. 'But I think she was there.'

'Oh dear!' Lydia reached out and put a hand on her daughter's soft head. The baby sighed in her sleep. 'I hope she has just run away, perhaps to join a sweetheart,' Lydia continued. 'Although if it was my child . . .' Tears flooded her eyes. Rees knew what she was thinking and understood. A young girl was so vulnerable. But he was more afraid that Deborah, like Calvin, was no longer alive.

He did not want to think of that. Eager to see the white-faced terror fade from Lydia's face, he said, 'We still haven't named our daughter,' he said. 'What shall we call her, this new child of ours?'

Some of the color returned to Lydia's cheeks and she uttered a shaky laugh. 'I thought Ann, after Mother Ann Lee,' she replied.

'No,' Rees said flatly, in a tone that brooked no argument.

'But Mother Ann was a great woman,' Lydia argued.

'For a second name, perhaps,' Rees said.

Lydia did not seem too surprised by his refusal. Sitting gingerly upon the bed, she said, 'Well, then maybe Sharon? It means His song. Sharon Ann.' Rees rolled the name around in his mouth for a few seconds, and then he glanced at the bundle sleeping in the cradle. Against the white bedding, the baby's thin hair shone like a halo of bright red-gold. 'Sharon. It seems a big name for such a little baby,' he said.

'She won't be little forever,' Lydia said with a smile.

The sound of a female voice outside brought Rees upright, with his hand on the door. 'I'd better go,' he whispered. Lydia nodded. But as he eased his way into the hall outside she said quickly, 'Talk to Elizabeth again. I'm persuaded she knows something. She's worried. I'm not sure why. It may be something she doesn't even know she knows. But see if you can encourage her to talk.'

Rees acknowledged her suggestion with a quick nod, before shutting the door behind him. He hurried to the other side of the hall. When one of the sisters came through the women's entrance, he was putting on his shoes by the men's door. He went out and joined the men walking to the Dining Hall.

Today's dinner was boiled beef – the excess calves were being slaughtered – with a side of beets. It took Rees back to his childhood and his mother's dinners. He'd thought of her only fleetingly these past few years, but now he missed her with a sudden fierce pang. Carried away by a fever when David was a baby, she had never known her grandson. Rees wondered now how she would have reacted to her new little granddaughter. Thrilled probably. He would send a note to his sister Phoebe to let her know about Sharon. Rees couldn't decide whether to include Caroline, who now lived with Phoebe, in his notice or not. His feelings were still so conflicted about her. Her malice and resentment had put his whole family in danger. Still, she had paid a very heavy price for her behavior. He felt sorry for that. Rees shook his head, attempting to shake away his memories and the emotions that plagued him, and told himself that Caroline had made her bed and now she must lie in it.

The Brother seated at the table with Rees frowned at him for fidgeting and he dropped his eyes to his plate. The morning's work had been hard on him and for a moment he considered returning to his room for a nap. His shoulders and back ached, and his fingers were so tired from moving rocks he could barely hold his knife. A score of scrapes and cuts marked his skin and Rees hoped they would not make weaving difficult. But sleeping in the middle of the day? It seemed the height of laziness. Besides, Rees had several tasks: driving into town for a conversation with Rouge for one and speaking to Elizabeth for another.

At the conclusion of the midday meal, Rees took up a position on the steps of the Dwelling House and watched for the nursing sister. Only a few minutes later, he saw her come out of the Infirmary. She carried a tray of dishes, most of them untouched, and went straight to the kitchen. Knowing he had only a short window of opportunity in which to visit Elizabeth, he set off at a rapid trot. But when he entered the room, he

211

thought his efforts had been in vain. It seemed Elizabeth was asleep.

He tiptoed to her bed. She looked so frail and pale against the pillow. She opened her eyes and stared at him, so suddenly Rees took a step backward. 'I was just thinking,' she said, every word separated by a labored breath, 'of Mother Ann Lee. Her conviction and her passion.' Her voice was a rough painful rasp. Rees realized she had been dosed with opium; her pupils were such tiny pinpoints that her irises seemed very large and blue.

'Don't try to talk,' Rees said, abandoning his attempt to question her. Even if she knew anything, he would get little sense from her now.

'I know the craftiness of evil spirits . . .' she said. 'I know the temptations . . .'

Rees realized she was rambling and confused. He hesitated, torn between the urge to leave and the desire to offer what comfort he could to a dying woman. Elizabeth moved her pale hand to grasp his large freckled paw. 'Mother Ann, I denied your holy teachings and turned my back on the Light of God . . .' Her voice trailed off and she tossed her head restlessly on the pillow. 'All my dead children . . . Only the eldest two survived.' Her eyes filled with tears. 'Was that my punishment for succumbing to earthly pleasures, oh Lord?'

She looked up at Rees as though he could answer. He flushed hot with discomfort. 'I'm sure no one blames you,' Rees said, feeling both clumsy and helpless. 'Mother Ann would surely forgive you.'

Moistening her dry cracked lips with her tongue, Elizabeth shook her head. 'No, no, she would not. She believed in mortifying the flesh to still the desires. Forgive me, Lord, I was too weak to sacrifice all earthly pleasure. You understand, Abraham.'

'Maybe Elder Solomon will speak with you,' Rees said, staring wildly around for someone to come to his aid. 'He will offer you forgiveness and comfort.'

'A true cross-bearer forsakes his desires,' said Elizabeth in a perfectly lucid tone. 'But I have seen, Oh Lord, a wolf come down among the sheep.'

'Uh, good,' Rees said, trying to remove his hand from her clinging fingers.

'Too weak, too weak to curb earthly temptation,' Elizabeth murmured. 'Still, perhaps you were the honest man.'

Rees heard voices outside. He lifted his head and listened. The speakers were still far away and their conversation was too faint to decipher the words. But he could tell they were approaching and he knew he had to leave. 'I must go.'

Elizabeth looked straight at Rees and tightened her grip. 'Please, keep Robert safe.' Rees thought she was incoherent despite the intent stare she had fixed upon him, but then she said, 'You will, won't you, Mr Rees?'

'Certainly,' he said although he thought Robert was well able to care for himself.

'He has not been to see me since his injury.'

'What injury?' Rees said sharply. But Elizabeth's eyes were beginning to close.

213

'Farewell,' she said. 'The Holy Mother is sounding her trumpet for me.' She turned her head restlessly on the pillow. 'Soon. Soon I will take flight to thee.'

Rees pulled his hand free and lay her limp limb upon the counterpane. Then he went as quietly as he could to the door. When he peeked out, he saw the nursing sister in conversation with Elder Solomon. 'I would like to speak with her before she goes home to Mother,' he said.

'I gave her laudanum,' the Sister said. 'I'm certain she's sleeping by now.'

Rees realized there was no way for him to slip out without being seen and certainly no place to hide unless he crawled under the bed. So, to put on as good a face as possible, he walked out of the Infirmary with his shoulders back and his head high.

Both Shakers turned to stare at him.

'I thought I would look in upon her,' he said, turning his gaze toward Solomon. 'But she is almost asleep. She asked for you.' Maybe the Elder could extend some comfort to the dying woman.

Hoping he would find another opportunity to speak with Elizabeth, Rees continued on his journey into the village center. He felt as though the eyes of both Solomon and the Sister were burning a hole into the back of his head.

Twenty-Two

Although Rees had intended to drive straight into town, he revised his plans and went instead into the Dwelling House. Since Robert was not in the Infirmary, he had to be convalescing in his bedchamber.

The door into Rees's room was closed, but all the others were open and he was able to peer into them. No Robert on the first floor. Rees went up the stairs and continued his search, finding Robert's chamber at the end of a long hall. He was seated in a chair, his back to the wall and his face turned toward the door. Bandages circled his head and padded his right shoulder. When he saw Rees, Robert forced a smile. Rees thought the other man looked terrible: white and shaky, his eyes huge.

'What happened?' Rees asked, his voice loud with alarm.

'Hush,' said a Shaker Brother, moving into Rees's sight. Rees stepped across the threshold and into the room. As well as the man who had spoken there was another Brother, in the corner.

'It was an accident,' Robert said, throwing a fleeting glance at the two Shakers. Rees thought Robert looked nervous, almost frightened.

'What happened?' Rees asked again. Robert swallowed, his Adam's apple rising and falling convulsively.

'A piece of metal fell on me in the smithy.'

'From the loft?' Rees asked in surprise. When he visualized the interior of the blacksmith's building, he recalled the stored items as being pushed well back from the edge. Besides, they were lined up in neat rows, with nothing out of place.

'Yes.' Robert nodded. 'I was alone. It came hurtling down.' He gulped. 'I was fortunate. I heard it.' He paused and Rees knew Robert had intended to use another word and thought better of it. 'I got out of the way. Almost. One of the Brothers heard me scream and came in.'

'It was an accident,' said one of the Brothers. 'When I found him lying on the floor he was raving, claiming someone had tried to kill him.'

Rees turned to Robert. Raving? Rees doubted that. 'Did you search the smithy?' he asked.

'I did,' said the other Shaker. 'No one was in the loft.' Rees nodded, but couldn't help thinking Robert's attacker might have jumped through the back window to the hillside beyond.

'It was an accident,' Robert said again. His eyes shifted to the two Shaker Brothers and then returned to Rees. Protestations to the contrary, Robert looked frightened. Rees did not dare question him further, not while under the scrutiny of these men.

'Will you be all right?' Rees asked, leaning forward.

'Yes,' Robert said. 'I think so. Someone will always be with me until I feel better.'

Rees nodded to show he understood. 'I'll visit you again,' he promised. He didn't blame Robert for not wanting to confide the truth in front of the two Shakers. He probably didn't know whom he could trust.

Rees left the bedchamber and hurried down the stairs, wondering who had tried to kill Robert. But as he crossed the street to the stable he realized he was asking the wrong question. Right now it was more important to know *why* Robert had been targeted. Did he have some secret? Or had he too seen something that identified the murderer?

Rees felt badly for taking Hannibal out again so soon after this morning's excursion. 'I know you're tired,' he crooned to the gelding as he slipped the bridle over the horse's nose. 'A bag of oats when we return. But I've got to speak with both the constable and Mr Golightly. And look at those bones again.'

'Mr Rees.' Jonathan's voice spun Rees around to face not only Jonathan but Solomon as well. Jonathan had changed from his muddy boots into clean shoes. Rees looked at Solomon. He stood with his hands clasped together and his eyes cast down, his pose clearly indicating his reluctance to be there. 'You can't continue to visit Sister Elizabeth,' Jonathan said. 'It isn't seemly. Besides, she is dying. Let her spend her last days in peace.'

'I just looked in on her,' Rees began. Then he stopped, realizing that any response from him would make him appear a child with a litany of excuses.

'Brother Robert does not visit her as often as you do,' Jonathan said.

'That's a pity.' Rees couldn't help the tactless words that sprang from his lips. 'Of course he can't now. He's been injured.'

'Surely you aren't suggesting someone here hurt him?' Solomon said, lifting his head to stare at Rees.

'Of course not,' he said.

Jonathan frowned at him. 'You are too much of the World, Rees,' he said. 'And your behavior mocks our ways.'

'I do not mock your ways,' Rees protested.

'We took your wife and family in when they came to us for refuge,' Jonathan continued, raising his voice over Rees's. 'But you do not show respect.'

'I do,' Rees said, biting off each word. 'But I also respect the dead, those members who lived among you who have been murdered. Don't you care about them? Their lives were cruelly cut short, years before natural death. And now Deborah is missing.' He stopped short of mentioning Robert. After all, what proof did Rees have that Robert had been attacked? Only the injured man's fearful expression. He had said that he'd been hurt in an accident.

'Surely you don't believe Elizabeth is guilty?' Solomon said in disbelief. 'She is bedridden and too weak to feed herself.'

'Of course not,' Rees said. He did not want to admit the truth – that he thought she might be more willing to confide in him than some of the other members of the community. 'I seek only to comfort her.'

'I fail to see how you might achieve that,'

218

Solomon said. 'You are a stranger to her. And she is already shuffling off this mortal coil.'

'That is so,' Rees agreed. 'She speaks only of the past.'

'Besides, comforting her is not your responsibility,' Jonathan said, his mouth pressed into a severe line. 'Leave her alone and let her find her way home to Mother in her own way.'

'I think it best if I move my wife and children out of the community,' Rees blurted out. 'To the Ellis property since that was deeded to my wife and now belongs to me.' He stared at the men defiantly. Should he remind them again that Charles Ellis had never signed the Covenant? He took a deep breath and decided to be courteous instead. 'I know we are a distraction for everyone here.'

'It would not be so if you were more respectful of our customs,' Jonathan said, his voice shaking. Solomon put his hand on his companion's sleeve.

'Why are you so eager to leave us?' he asked in his soft voice.

'I appreciate all you've done for me and my family,' Rees said, looking only at him. 'But I want the comfort of my own hearth with my family all about me. I respect your ways, I do, but they are not for me. I don't want to surrender my family.' To his surprise, Elder Solomon nodded.

'I understand.' He threw a quick glance at his fellow Elder. 'It is a difficult sacrifice to give up one's home and family. Perhaps it would be best if you do remove to the Ellis property for now.

Just until you return to your home.' Jonathan turned an outraged glare upon his fellow. 'But, until you move, will you promise not to call upon Sister Elizabeth again?'

'I can't do that,' Rees said. Both of the Brothers stared at Rees. Obedience was a cornerstone of the Shakers' beliefs, and Rees's flagrant refusal to yield to their wishes left them momentarily speechless. 'Look,' he continued. 'You asked me to look into the murder of Brother Jabez. Since then Calvin has been murdered, and now the girl Deborah is missing. I will not stop until I find the person, or persons,' he swept his gaze over the Brothers, 'responsible.'

'You can't possibly suspect anyone here,' Jonathan said, his voice rising in disbelief. 'Look to the hired men who fled just after Calvin's death.'

When Rees said nothing, Solomon sighed. 'Of course we must identify the murderer. Killing another person is an offense against God as well as against Man. And if the murderer is among us, we must discover him: "If thine own eye offends thee, pluck it out." I do not want you to cease your labors, Rees. But I also agree that you and your wife and children have proven to be a disturbance to our peace. I hope you can continue your search from the other farm.'

'Only after Mr Rees arrived did things begin happening,' Jonathan muttered. 'Before that everything was fine.'

'We will discuss this further at another time,' Solomon said, turning and looking at his partner. The younger man's lips twitched, and he looked as though he was just managing not to argue.

Rees watched the interchange with interest. The Elders, in fact all the Shakers, usually presented a united front. They did not allow any sign of a disagreement to disturb the serenity they projected, and the fact that Rees witnessed any difference of opinion at all told him how deep this dispute went.

'Gentlemen,' he said, inclining his head and turning back to his horse. Rees did not intend to allow anything to sway him from his purpose – from ensuring the safety of his family and his new baby daughter – and he didn't want to be lulled again into confessing his intentions. He would move his family, Shakers or no.

By the time Rees reached Durham, the sun had begun to sink in the sky. The Shaker Brothers and all the other farmers hereabouts would soon be starting their evening milking. How was David managing without Rees's help? But then, Rees thought with a mixture of shame and regret, David was used to working without his father's help. Rees hoped David was having no trouble with his neighbors or with Magistrate Hanson. Rees swallowed and shook his head. He couldn't keep thinking about his son and worrying. Maybe, even though it had been less than a week, Rees would send him a letter. It would be faster to drive there but he didn't dare leave Lydia and the children, not even for David. Not right now, anyway. Rees thought that as long as he was here, nothing terrible would happen to anyone, especially his new baby girl. But he still could not help worrying

221

about David, whom he had left so hastily and so alone.

Rees pulled into the inn yard and walked into the tavern. Knowing Rouge, he still had the bones gathered in Rees's shirt. He wanted to examine them once again before going on to speak to Mr Golightly.

At this time of the day the taproom was almost empty. Rouge was poring over a large blue ledger and frowning. Ink spotted his fingers and streaked his shirt.

'Ah, Rees,' he said, looking up. 'A new shirt and breeches. You look better than when I last saw you. But your shoes!'

'I wouldn't criticize if I were you,' Rees said, waving a hand at Rouge's shirt. The constable looked down at the ink stains and gasped. 'I want to take another look at the bones,' Rees said. 'Did you take them to the coroner yet?'

'No,' Rouge said, 'they're still in my office.' He gestured with his head in the direction of the hall. 'I've been busy, but I'll send a message to my sister as well.'

'I can talk to her later,' Rees said, walking to the hall. 'I want to consult with Mr Golightly this afternoon.'

'Wait,' Rouge shouted after him. 'I have news . . .' But Rees, paying no heed to him, went down the hall and into the office.

The bones, still bundled in Rees's shirt, had been dropped casually on the top of a stack of ledgers. Rees thought he could save the shirt. Except for several mud stains, the linen was undamaged. He saw no rips or tears, and mud

222

was much easier to remove than blood. He undid a few buttons and took out one of the thighbones. Once again he held it up to his own leg, and again he remarked its length. Would a woman be so tall? Rees slid the femur back into its holder. He knew he shouldn't be wasting time on these old bones, despite the likelihood that the owner had been murdered. Rees had much newer cases to consider: the murders of both Jabez and Calvin and now the disappearance of Deborah. But this skeleton, so carefully buried under a cairn of rocks in a stream, caught his interest.

A footfall behind Rees turned him around. 'I'm glad you came in to town,' Rouge said. 'I found one of the hired men you were looking for. The young one. You remember?'

Rees nodded. With Jonathan's accusation against the Palmer boys still ringing in his ears, Rees said, 'I want to talk to him. Are the rest of his brothers here?'

'He said they left town. And that's all he would say,' Rouge said.

'You asked him about Calvin?'

Rouge nodded. 'And he refused to answer me. Now, with that Shaker girl missing, well, I threw him into jail. I told him he could rot there until you spoke to him.'

'I don't know if I have time today,' Rees said. 'It is extremely important I consult with Mr Golightly about another matter.'

'The boy is in jail,' Rouge said. 'So whenever you—'

'You wanted to see me?' Rouge's sister,

223

Bernadette, stood just outside the office door. Her hair had been hastily pinned up in a messy knot, and her bodice buttoned wrong.

'What's the matter?' Rees asked, looking at her closely and noticing the shadows under eyes. 'You look . . . tired.' Bernadette nodded.

'I am.' She yawned widely, covering her mouth with her hand. 'I had a difficult birth last night.' She turned her eyes to her brother. 'The Fitches.'

'What happened?' Rouge asked.

'The baby wouldn't turn.'

'Did he survive?'

'Yes. But his mother didn't.' Tears rushed into her eyes. 'I tried so hard but I couldn't stop the bleeding. And what will Mr Fitch do, with three older children and now the baby?'

Rees knew there were some men who buried three or four wives. He thought of Lydia, his throat closing up, and was overcome with gratitude that both his wife and baby girl had survived the birth.

'It was terrible,' Bernadette continued. 'Mrs Fitch was in labor over thirty hours.'

'Rees has a question for you,' Rouge said, nodding at the other man.

'It could have waited,' Rees said, scowling at the constable in annoyance. 'I did not mean to rouse you from your bed,' he added, sending an apologetic smile at Bernadette.

'I'm here now,' she said with another yawn. 'Ask your question.'

'We found some old bones,' Rees began.

'At the abandoned farm that adjoins the Fitch property,' Rouge put in helpfully.

'Do you know who lived there?' Rees asked.

'I thought you might have delivered a baby or two,' Rouge said.

Bernadette closed her eyes for a second or two. 'I did deliver a baby there about ten years ago,' she said slowly. 'A little boy. There was already a little girl of about three or four.'

Rees exchanged an excited glance with Rouge. 'What was the name of that family?'

'I don't remember.' Bernadette looked from Rees to Rouge. 'Something common. The mother's name was Catherine, I think, but I never met the father. He was a traveling preacher, I believe.'

Rees felt himself deflating with disappointment. 'I thought we could at least bury the poor soul under the proper name,' he said.

'Are the bones . . . Do you think they belong to Catherine?' Bernadette asked. 'The family disappeared so suddenly.'

'I thought they might,' Rees said, meeting her gaze. They both had seen some of the worst conditions marriage offered. 'But I'm not so certain anymore. Was Catherine tall? Heavily built?'

'Not at all. She was a tiny thing. I worried about her ability to bear a child, she was so small.'

'Then these bones cannot belong to her,' Rees said.

'There was a hired girl,' Bernadette said, thinking out loud. 'She was taller and quite strong, if I remember correctly.'

'How tall?' Rees asked. 'Almost my height?'

225

'No,' said Bernadette with an involuntary laugh. 'That would be a terrible height for a girl. More mine.' Rees mentally reassessed the length of the thighbone, looking at the woman who stood before him. If the bones had belonged to a woman Bernadette's height, her legs would have reached almost to her breastbone. He shook his head.

'The bones belong to a man, in that case. Perhaps Catherine's husband?'

Bernadette yawned again. 'I'm sorry, I can't help you there.' She turned to go.

'If you remember anything,' Rees said to her back, 'let me know.'

'Of course,' she said and walked away.

'Do you want to question the hired man?' Rouge asked as his sister's footsteps disappeared down the hall.

Rees pondered. The jail lay some distance from the tavern and the center of town, closer in fact to the field where market was held every Saturday. And Rees guessed the time must be approaching five. 'No,' he said. 'He'll keep. I want to reach Mr Golightly before six, when he closes his office. I'll return here for my horse and wagon afterward.'

Twenty-Three

'I'm afraid I have no news for you,' Mr Golightly said when Rees sat down across from him. Rees could tell by the neatness of the lawyer's desk

– only a few documents lay upon it – that he had been preparing to leave. Rees having walked down the street from the tavern, had been shown in most reluctantly by Mr Golightly's secretary. 'Have you spoken to the Zion Elders yet?'

'Not formally, no. There is some difference of opinion among them,' Rees said.

'I cannot progress until the issue is fully discussed between the two parties,' said Mr Golightly,

Rees exhaled in frustration. 'You should know that I am planning to move my family to the property immediately. How will the Shakers resolve the issue then?'

Golightly's eyes widened and he fiddled with his cuffs. 'Oh, I don't think that is a wise course of action at all. Why, the Governors might turn you over to Constable Rouge.'

'I have been threatened with expulsion from Zion,' Rees said, 'because my family and I are distractions. So, this is not entirely by my choice. My children need a safe place to live. Besides the five adopted children for whom I am responsible, my wife has just had a new baby girl.'

'You must have tried the Elders' patience,' said Mr Golightly with a stiff smile. 'I have never heard of them expelling anyone.'

'Oh, it happens,' Rees said, thinking of his wife. She had been expelled when she'd borne Charles Ellis's baby. 'They haven't sent us away yet. But I know there is something going on. Something ugly. And I intend to remove my family from it.'

Mr Golightly picked up his quill pen and ran

his fingers down the feather. He set it back into the ink well and took it out again. 'This time I shall write a formal letter to the Elders then,' he said. 'And I will do my utmost to press them. What about your farm – in Dugard, isn't it?' Rees shook his head.

'I cannot return there at present.'

'Hmmm. I just think that the Zion community has grown rather used to treating the Ellis property as their own. I'll see what I can do.'

'Thank you,' Rees said. Mr Golightly replaced the pen in the ink well and fixed his spectacles on his nose. He turned his attention upon the papers lying before him. He looked up a moment later to see Rees still sitting before him.

'Was there something else?'

'I just wondered . . .' Rees paused. How much should he tell the lawyer? 'Do you know the abandoned property adjacent to the Fitch farm?'

'What abandoned property?' Mr Golightly removed his spectacles and reluctantly raised his eyes from the documents on the desk before him. Although he met Rees's gaze, Mr Golightly continued to look distant and distracted.

'Constable Rouge showed me the property,' Rees said. And when Golightly shook his head, Rees leaned across the desk and put his hands on the documents so the lawyer could not read them. 'I pulled the bones of a dead man out of that stream five hours ago. Who owns the property?'

Now completely aware of Rees and his inquiry, Golightly said, 'Where is this property?'

'We went in by way of the lane between the

Fitch farm and the abandoned farm. But I think at one time there was probably an entrance from the main road.'

Golightly considered the question. After a few seconds he nodded. 'Been abandoned for ten years or more, I fancy.' Rees nodded.

'Yes, that's the one.'

'I don't know if I ever knew the family who lived there.'

'Well, somebody owned it at some time.'

Golightly sighed. He took his spectacles from his pocket and polished the lenses with careful deliberation. 'Very well, Mr Rees. I'll see what I can find. Someone must be paying the taxes. Come back tomorrow.' He turned a pointed gaze on Rees's hands, still pressed flat upon the documents. Rees took them away, and when Mr Golightly did not speak again Rees turned and went out.

By the golden light of the declining sun, Rees guessed the time to be about five. He hesitated on the step of the lawyer's office; he was much closer to the jail from this end of town than he would be at the tavern. After a few seconds of indecision, he turned down the lane separating Mr Golightly's office from the building beside it. There were several horses stabled in the mews behind and a groom lying on a pile of hay asleep. Rees went up the slope to the side of the stable and down again to the road. If he turned right and followed the dirt surface into town, he would soon reach the midwife's house. But instead Rees crossed the road. The jail was sandwiched into a corner between the churchyard, with its gravestones, and the brick wall surrounding a wealthy merchant's property across the road.

Rees peered through the grate. Ned Palmer was lying on the stone bench with his eyes closed. Rees thought again that he was little more than a boy, probably no more than two or three years older than David. Most of Rees's attention had been focused on Ned's brothers. This boy had said very little when Rees had spoken to them, allowing his older brothers to do the talking.

'Ned Palmer,' he said. He could see by the fluttering eyelids that the boy heard him and was trying to decide whether to acknowledge his presence or continue pretending to be asleep. 'Besides the murder of Brother Jabez,' Rees said in a conversational tone, 'there has been another murder. That of a boy. Calvin.'

'I didn't do anything.' The young man leaped up from his prone position and hurried to the window. 'I didn't. You can't prove I did.' Rees eyed Ned thoughtfully. He was younger than Rees had first thought, just barely old enough to shave. The whiskers on his chin were more of a shadow than a beard, and a scattering of pimples dotted his cheeks.

Rees still had not found even the hint of a reason why this fellow, or any of the men hired to help the Shaker Brothers, would want to murder Jabez. Or Calvin, for that matter. Since Ned's brothers had left town shortly after Calvin's murder, Jonathan assumed they were guilty. Rees was not so sure. For the first time, he wondered why this young man had not left with them.

Unless . . . Rees suddenly had an inspiration. Ned was just a few years older than Deborah and handsome enough.

'A young Sister is missing,' he said. You wouldn't know anything about that, would you?'

'No,' the boy said, after just a beat too long, 'I don't know anything about Deborah.' He turned his back on Rees and lay down again on the stone ledge.

'How did you know her name?' Rees asked. 'I didn't mention it.' Ned remained stubbornly silent. Finally, Rees turned away in disgust. He would try again tomorrow, after meeting with Mr Golightly again.

By keeping Hannibal moving at a steady trot, Rees arrived back at Zion just before supper. By the time he'd unhitched Hannibal and released him into the paddock, the meal had already begun. He walked into the Dining Hall late, expecting to be the focus of all eyes. But no one paid him the slightest attention. Every single person in the room had turned to face the table where Brother Solomon was standing. Rees paused in the door.

'Our Sister Elizabeth, whom many of you know, has been taken home to Mother.' Solomon's cheeks were flushed and he paused to wipe his eyes with his handkerchief. For a few seconds he could not speak. 'I found her when I called upon her a little while ago. I remember our Sister from the early days. She too was a believer in Mother Ann's visions. And when her life turned around again she and her husband rejoined our faith, coming home at last.' His voice wavered and he stopped again. Rees felt his own eyes pricking. But rather than surrender to emotion, he blinked hard and looked around. Jonathan's mouth was turned down and he stared at his hands, clasped in his lap. He looked very serious, but then he usually did. Esther's caramel-colored cheeks were shiny with tears. She had put an arm around the nursing Sister who was weeping noisily. But most of the other Shakers, although sad, appeared composed. Rees thought they must not have known Elizabeth very well. She had gone into the sickroom so soon after her arrival.

Rees looked around the large chamber once again, realizing that he did not see Brother Robert. He had not looked too severely injured to eat with the rest of the Family, so perhaps he was sitting with his wife's body for a final goodbye. Very quietly Rees withdrew, stepping backward into the lobby. He wanted to pay his final respects to the woman, although Elizabeth's death was so sudden he could hardly credit it, and offer his condolences to Brother Robert. The visit would make Rees late for supper and the Elders would scold him, but he didn't care.

When Rees entered the Infirmary, he found Brother Robert seated by Elizabeth's body, just as he expected. She could almost have been asleep. Rees put his hand upon Robert's uninjured shoulder. He turned his tear-streaked face up to meet Rees's gaze. 'It was so sudden,' Robert said. 'I know she felt poorly, but . . .' His words trailed away as he stifled a sob. Underneath the bandage circling his head, his right eye and cheek were swollen and purple with bruising.

'I can hardly believe it, either,' said Rees. 'I just visited with her a few hours ago. But sometimes our loved ones are carried away far faster than we expect.'

'I was aware that she would not improve,' Robert said in a shaky voice. 'I should rejoice that she has gone home. But I can't.'

Rees remembered all too clearly his confusion and pain at his first wife's death. 'I understand,' he said. 'But know this. The grief does become easier to bear. You don't ever forget it, but it fades a little.'

Robert nodded and scrubbed his face with his sleeve, his handkerchief now too sodden to use. 'They'll bury her tomorrow,' he said.

Something in Robert's tone caught Rees's attention. 'And then what?' he asked, staring at Robert. 'You sound . . . determined. As though you've made a decision.' Robert passed his hand over his eyes, but Rees suspected it was more to gain time than because he needed to wipe away his tears. 'Are you leaving the Shakers?' Rees asked.

Robert hesitated and then nodded. 'Yes. I'm going home to my children and my farm.' Although Rees did not speak, Robert burst out, 'This was always Elizabeth's dream.' He sounded defensive and Rees hastened to say, 'I am not judging you. I plan to remove my family from Zion also.'

Robert's shoulders slumped. 'We were married only a few years when Elizabeth began to feel

233

guilty. We lost several babies, you know, and she thought God was punishing her for leaving the Believers to marry.' Rees nodded in understanding. 'But something is wrong here.' He touched the white linen binding his head. 'I don't belong here anymore . . .' His voice trailed away, and for a moment the two men stood in silence.

'I never had the chance to question her,' Rees said at last. Robert heaved a sigh.

'I know she was worried about something. She heard things, you know. But she did not gossip.'

Rees turned to regard the dead woman, wondering what she might have suspected. 'A wolf among the sheep,' he muttered. Robert turned to look at him in surprise.

'What?'

'Nothing. Just something your wife said to me.' Rees returned his gaze to Robert. 'What happened to you in the smithy?'

Robert hesitated a moment and then sighed. 'It could have been an accident,' he said. 'But I heard something, Rees. I'm not sure what it was, but I looked up and saw the old hammer coming down and I jumped aside as quickly as I could.'

Rees thought, but did not say, that the murderer expected Robert to be harder of hearing than he was. There could be little doubt that if Robert had been deafer the hammer would have struck him squarely on the head and killed him.

'You were fortunate,' Rees said. Robert nodded solemnly.

'God was looking over me that day,' he said.

'Why kill *you*?' Rees asked. 'Why you?'

'I don't know,' Robert said. 'I've cudgeled my

brain but can think of nothing. I have not heard or seen anything.' He looked at Rees in bewilderment. 'There is no reason.' Rees did not know what answer he could offer, and for a few seconds the two men again stood in silence. Then Robert lifted his right hand, to shake Rees's, but as a spasm of pain crossed his face he dropped it again and held up his left instead. 'Thank you, Mr Rees. And thank your wife as well. I know Elizabeth appreciated your visits.'

'Best of luck to you,' Rees said, grasping Robert's hand and giving it a firm shake. Robert started for the door. 'Are you going to supper?' Rees spoke to Robert's back and he turned to reply.

'No. I think it best I leave immediately. I know it seems uncaring not to wait and attend the funeral and burial, but Elizabeth would understand. I don't want to be kept here.'

'On the contrary, I think you are wise to leave,' Rees said.

As Robert disappeared through the door, Rees turned back to the body lying on the bed. He and Robert had not discussed the possibility that Elizabeth had been helped along, but it was clear they both suspected it. It would have been an easy thing to put a pillow over the dying woman's face and hold it until her breathing stopped. Already weak, she could not have fought back. And with her poor lungs, her death would have occurred quickly. Rees took up a candle and held it over Elizabeth's face. He pried open an eyelid. The white was speckled with red dots. He'd seen this before in men who'd been hung or strangled.

He straightened up, so distracted he did not realize his candle was dripping wax upon the sheet.

He had only considered it a possibility before, but now he knew. Elizabeth had been murdered.

What had she and Robert known?

Twenty-Four

Rees walked into the Dining Hall almost half an hour late. This time he attracted some attention, and both Solomon and Jonathan turned and frowned. Rees quickly found a seat at one of the tables nearest the door. Most of the Brothers there had already almost finished eating. Rees cut himself a piece of bread with his knife and buttered it. He was not very hungry. The discovery of another murder, this time of a woman so ill she was expected to die within days, had rattled him. Why would anyone murder a woman on the brink of death? Unlike Calvin, Elizabeth could not have seen anything. Unless . . . Rees paused with the bread halfway to his mouth. Perhaps someone had told her something. But few had visited her. Rees chewed and swallowed without even realizing he was doing so. And whatever she knew, so did Robert. There was no other explanation for his attempted murder.

Rees jumped when one of the Sisters slid a plate in front of him. Beans cooked with thick bacon, and a side of greens. But Rees did not begin eating immediately. Instead, he allowed his eyes to roam from one Brothers' table to another. Everyone looked peaceful and innocent, just as always. No Robert – he had left immediately as promised. For the first time Rees entertained the possibility Robert had smothered his wife. He would have wished to prevent further suffering – Rees understood that feeling – and her death would free him to leave Zion. But, although both explanations were plausible, Rees just didn't see Robert as capable of such a heinous act. And it seemed unlikely that Robert had hit himself in the head with a hammer.

At the close of the meal, most of the men returned to their chores. Rees fell into step behind the Brothers streaming from the room, but he did not succeed in escaping before being intercepted by Solomon. 'You were late to dinner.'

Rees ducked his head in assent. 'I stopped in to . . .' He jerked his head toward the Infirmary.

'To see Sister Elizabeth?' Solomon asked, plucking nervously at the gray hairs in his beard.

'To pay my respects. I heard you say she'd passed away. I saw Robert.' Realizing he was babbling, Rees closed his mouth.

'Even after we asked you not to visit her,' Jonathan said, approaching Rees.

'I wasn't visiting her exactly,' Rees said.

'What did Robert say?' Solomon asked.

Now Rees found himself in a quandary. Should he confide all that Robert had told him? 'He was grief stricken,' Rees said, carefully choosing every word.

'He did not come to supper,' Solomon said.

'No,' Rees agreed. He did not want to tell them Robert had elected to leave, and steeled himself for the next question. But when it came, it startled him.

'Did you learn anything new in town?' Solomon asked.

'Yes. I expect I'll learn the identity of the owner of that abandoned farm tomorrow,' Rees said, surprised into honesty. Should he admit that Ned Palmer had been found and put in jail? No, he decided. Knowing he was looking at one of the hired men would only encourage the Shakers in their conviction that the Palmers were guilty.

Jonathan fixed a steady gaze upon Rees, almost as though he sensed all of the information Rees was holding back. But, after several seconds of this accusatory regard, Jonathan looked back at his fellow Elder. 'We must discuss arrangements for our departed Sister,' he said.

As the Shakers moved away, Rees heaved a sigh of relief and quickly left the room. But again he was stopped, this time as he reached the road outside.

'Mr Rees?'

He turned. 'Yes, Annie.' In her time with the Shakers she had lost her hunted expression, but now her forehead was wrinkled with worry. Biting her lip, she darted an anxious glance at him before fixing her gaze upon her tightly clasped hands.

'Lydia asked me to tell you . . .' She stopped, took in a deep breath and started again. 'Deborah was sneaking out at night. But I thought she was meeting a boy.' Annie shot an apologetic glance at Rees. 'She swore me to secrecy.'

Rees thought of the young man currently incarcerated in the Durham jail and nodded. 'The youngest of the hired men, I expect,' he said.

'You knew?' Annie let out her breath. 'Yes, I think so. She never said. And she usually sneaked out when I was sleeping.'

'Did she go out before midnight or after?' Rees asked.

'Both, I think. It varied. She and the hired man had some way of communicating.' Annie's lip curled and she added in an aggrieved tone, 'I wouldn't have found out except that I woke up one night just as Deborah was leaving. She must have been doing it for awhile – she didn't even take a candle. She knew her way in the dark.'

Rees nodded. He remembered the flash of white he'd seen from the corner of his eye when he'd been standing at the horse pen with Calvin. Deborah's nightgown, he guessed now.

So, what did Ned know? And where had he put Deborah? 'Thank you, Annie,' Rees said. 'That is helpful.' She nodded and hurried away. But Rees stood for a minute longer, staring blindly at the Meetinghouse and wondering how Deborah fitted in with Calvin and Elizabeth and Robert. And Jabez, for that matter.

As he lingered in the street, Esther came down the steps from the Dwelling House. She started across the street to be met by Solomon and Jonathan. They had fetched a cart that they dragged up outside the Infirmary. Rees watched as the two Brothers disappeared into the building. A few minutes later they reappeared, carrying a wasted form shrouded in a sheet. By now the body seemed quite stiff, and when they laid it in the cart it resembled a piece of wood. It would be stored in the icehouse on the sawdust-covered blocks until the following day.

As the cart and its burden passed by, Jonathan sent a ferocious glare Rees's way. He wondered if he was being blamed for Elizabeth's death.

Rees watched the Elders take the body to the icehouse. The corpse sat up, the thin sheet falling away from the waxy features. It was Lydia. Oh no! Rees felt a scream building at the back of his throat. She pointed a long thin finger, white as bone, at him. 'Think,' she said.

'Do not suffer a witch to live,' said Farley, holding up a rope. When Rees looked at his wife, he saw the rope, and the red weal left by it on her throat.

'No!' Rees shouted, propelled into an upright position by the nightmare. He sat still for a moment, gasping for breath. Lydia was safe, at least for the time being. He knew that, so why did the fear still haunt him? Rees wiped his sweaty face with the sheet. When he slid out of bed he stood for a moment in the cool night air, allowing the perspiration to dry. He lit a candle and in its flickering light poured some water from the jug into the ewer and splashed it on his face. He had hoped these nightmares would cease now that he had been here in Zion for a week. But they hadn't. Was it because the Shaker community had proved almost as dangerous as the World?

But now he thought about this most recent dream, it seemed different. It had not taken place at home in Dugard. True, Farley had made an appearance. But the action had happened here, in Zion. Rees considered that for several seconds. Did that mean he was recovering from his experiences in Dugard? Or was he just transferring his fear to Zion? He couldn't decide.

What he did know was that he had to assure himself of Lydia's continued health. On bare feet, he silently tiptoed out of his bedchamber, hurried down the hall, and darted behind the staircase to the only lighted room on the floor.

Lydia was sitting in the chair, nursing the baby. She looked up as Rees slipped in and smiled. He quietly closed the door behind him. With the shadow of the dream still lying upon him, he felt an overwhelming relief at seeing both of them alive and doing well. He knelt beside the chair and put his arms around them.

'Another nightmare?' Lydia asked. Rees nodded and pressed his head against her arm. 'We're all safe,' she murmured.

So far, Rees thought.

'Has something else happened?' Lydia asked, turning to look at him.

Rees sat back on his haunches. 'Elizabeth died.'

'Oh no.' Tears flooded Lydia's eyes. 'I should be happy she's no longer suffering, but I'm not. I'm sorry. Oh, poor Robert.'

'She was murdered,' Rees said. He instantly

241

regretted speaking so baldly when Lydia pressed her fingers to her mouth.

'Oh no! How terrible!'

'And Robert has left Zion. Gone home.'

Lydia turned so she could better face him. 'Do you think Robert had something to do with her death?'

Rees thought back to his visit in the sick room. 'Possibly,' he said. 'Although I doubt it.'

'Why?' Lydia's gaze sharpened. 'Because you like Robert? Or because you think he's innocent?'

Rees did not reply immediately. He had been so hurried when rushing to see Elizabeth. Now he paused and formulated his thoughts. 'I believe he's innocent,' he said. 'Think about it. If Robert did smother his wife, would that mean he murdered Jabez and Calvin too? Why? He didn't even know Jabez. And would that also indicate he abducted Deborah? Or are all these just a coincidence and there are two killers here? It's possible – but considering the small size of this community and the attack on Robert himself, I don't believe he had anything to do with his wife's death.'

Nodding, Lydia shifted the child to the other side and adjusted her white bertha for modesty. 'Then Elizabeth must have known something. And I would guess that Robert knows it too. Elizabeth surely confided in her husband. I know I would.'

Rees smiled and leaned over to kiss her. A few minutes elapsed before Rees reluctantly drew back. 'Yes,' he said, 'that makes sense. But why wouldn't Robert tell me?'

'It must be because he doesn't know he knows it.' Lydia looked at Rees, her mouth rounding. 'That's why, I'm certain of it.' Rees nodded slowly.

'But the murderer believes Elizabeth knew something and told Robert. That's why Robert was attacked and Elizabeth smothered.'

'Elizabeth was worried about something. I could tell that,' Lydia said.

Rees scarcely heard her, he was thinking hard. 'A wolf in the sheepcote,' he muttered. What was it that Elizabeth and Robert knew? 'I should have pressed her,' Rees said now. 'I should have pushed until she told me what was worrying her.'

'Maybe somebody thought you did,' Lydia said. She stopped, suddenly conscious of how thoughtless her comment had been. 'Oh Will, I am so sorry! It's not your fault.'

But Rees nodded at her. 'Yes, it is. I visited Elizabeth several times, and the murderer knows I visited her. I didn't hide it.' He looked at Lydia. 'And he or she,' he added, thinking of the belligerent nurse, 'probably thought Elizabeth told me whatever it was she knew. But she didn't tell me anything.'

Lydia met his gaze and reached over with her left hand to touch his arm.

'This wasn't your fault, Will.'

'Yes, it was,' he said. Why hadn't he been faster at identifying the killer, he thought? Elizabeth should have died on God's terms, not the murderer's.

'No, it wasn't. For all we know, he would have killed her anyway, without anyone caring or wondering how she died. But Elizabeth does deserve justice, just as much as Calvin, for all that she was old and sick.'

She stared at him. 'Isn't that so, Will?'

Rees met her gaze and nodded. 'Yes. I will obtain that for her at least.'

'I have better news,' Lydia said.

'Oh yes?' Rees attempted to smile despite his heavy heart.

'Sharon and I will be moved to the Children's Dwelling on Monday. That should make your visits easier.' Lydia's smile invited Rees to smile as well. He tried. But instead he thought that his wife and child might now be reached even more easily by someone who wanted to harm them.

'I will be speaking to Mr Golightly about the Ellis property again tomorrow. Uh, later today,' he said. It was already Saturday. 'I hope and expect that we will all remove to that farm soon.'

'A farm without David,' Lydia said teasingly. 'Are you sure you can manage?'

'I'll have to,' Rees said. 'At least for a little while.' He had not farmed that property all summer, so he would have no grain, no food, put by for the winter. No livestock either. Dear God, what would they do? He pushed the thought aside. 'We will be together and safe, I think. Simon will be happier. To the Brothers, he is only a disobedient child.'

'I know,' Lydia agreed. 'He sees himself as an adult.' She hesitated for a few seconds and then said, 'It sounds as if you suspect someone here, in Zion, of the murders?' She turned to look at him, her forehead furrowed. Rees lifted one shoulder in reluctant agreement.

'All of the victims had a connection to this community,' he said.

'Except the bones,' Lydia put in.

'Except the bones,' Rees agreed. 'But Brother Jabez, Calvin, Sister Elizabeth, Robert, even Deborah, were all members here. As far as I can tell, the only connection among them is this community of Zion.'

The skin around Lydia's eyes puckered in distress, but she nodded. 'Someone new then?' she murmured.

'Perhaps,' Rees said, stopping short of identifying anyone by name. It could be someone new like Jonathan, who had been here less than a year. Or someone like Aaron. At least Aaron had to be innocent of Elizabeth's murder, as he had been out in the World selling. Then Rees realized he didn't know that for certain. Nor did he know where Aaron might be. The Brother could be hiding nearby, could have crept back into the community with no one noticing.

Rees sighed and, dropping a kiss lightly on the cap over Lydia's hair, he slipped from her room.

Twenty-Five

Rees did not go back to bed. Instead he paced his shadowy room, fretting alternately about his family's safety, about the Ellis farm and about the recent murders and Deborah's disappearance. He heard the Brothers rise and leave the Dwelling House for early chores. When they began to return, he joined them in the Dining Hall for breakfast. But he did not linger after the meal. Instead, he harnessed Hannibal to his wagon and drove into town. Tomorrow was Sunday; only a week had passed since his arrival in Zion. Yet, during that time several murders had occurred. Rees wondered if he'd done the right thing bringing his family here. Although he didn't see what else he could have done, he was now afraid he'd put his family at risk.

Although he started out for Durham early, he found the roads already congested with wagons, buggies and other vehicles. All the local farmers were flooding into town for Saturday's market. He'd forgotten it was market day. Rees tried to accommodate himself to accepting a slow and lengthy trip, but without success. He grumbled and complained under his breath the entire journey. Some of the farmers in the wagons near to Rees's heard him and turned to stare.

To add to his irritation, Rouge's inn yard was crammed with vehicles. Rees slowed down and tried to peer through the side window. The interior of the tavern, at least as much of it as he could see through the grimy panes, appeared equally thronged. With a muttered epithet, he continued driving west. The main road became only more congested as it neared the field where the market was held. Rees turned off as soon as he could, joining other conveyances trying other, hopefully less crowded, routes. But when he turned right, they turned left and he was able to reach the jail without any further difficulty.

The Palmer boy was still asleep, but he woke up quickly enough when Rees called his name. 'Ned. Ned Palmer.' Although the lad's head turned so he could look at the door, he did not move from the stone ledge. 'I think we should try again at obtaining some answers,' Rees said. 'I have a witness who saw you meeting young Deborah. Now, where is she?'

'Do you have anything to eat?' Ned asked. 'I'm so hungry.'

'Isn't the constable feeding you?' Rees asked.

'No. Well, hardly at all since I've been here. Nor water, either.'

Of course not. Rees cursed under his breath. Any monies expended would come out of Rouge's own pocket and he was not a generous man. 'I'll get you something,' he said. Ned crossed his arms, his posture indicating an unwillingness to speak at all until he was fed. 'I'll return,' Rees said.

He left the wagon where it was and headed back to the tavern. Although the streets were crowded with farmers' wives, Rees was able to push his way through at a rapid pace. He cut across the midwife's front porch and clambered over the fence that divided her house from the inn yard. He reached the tavern much sooner than if he'd been driving. He pushed his way through the crowd at the bar and said, interrupting a farmer who had been ordering beer, 'I want something for the boy in jail. How could you let him lie there without any food or water?'

'I've been feeding him. If it were up to him, he'd beggar me with his appetite.'

'Come on, Rouge,' Rees said. The other man shrugged.

'He's guilty, ain't he, of that Shaker girl's disappearance? He probably killed her.'

'We don't know that,' Rees said through gritted teeth. 'And I can tell you this, he's not going to be much good at answering questions if he's dead from hunger.' Rouge leaned over the bar, ready to argue, but the sight of all these customers reminded him he was busy. Rouge called for the girl.

'Get some bread and cheese for Mr Rees here. And a jug of ale as well.' He bared his teeth. 'You're paying, of course.'

Rees scowled but threw a few pennies on the wood. After all he'd done to help Rouge with his investigations too!

The girl wrapped the food up in a rag, clean but worn thin, and Rees made sure to thank her with a farthing. Then he walked back to the jail.

Ned drank half the ale in a few swallows and devoured the bread and cheese with huge bites. When he had finished, and wiped his mouth and fingers on the rag, Rees said, 'Now, let's talk. Where's Deborah?'

'I don't know,' Ned said. 'She's too young to live like those Shakers, with no prospect of a husband and children of her own. Ain't natural. We've been meeting, that's true. But she didn't show up last time.'

'Meeting at the abandoned farm?' Rees asked. Ned shook his head.

'No. We met at the farm once or twice. She knew of it, I don't know how. But mostly we met at the laundry.' Ned wiped the back of his hand across his mouth. Then he clutched at the bars and leaned forward as far as he could, so that his face pressed against the rusty iron. 'I haven't seen her. I told you, she didn't show up. I waited and waited.' Rees regarded the boy thoughtfully. His story sounded plausible, but still . . .

'I'm telling the truth,' Ned said angrily. 'Do you think I'd be hanging around this town if I'd done something to her? We was planning to run away but she wanted to speak to her father first.'

'You were planning to run away?' said Rees. 'She's still a child.'

Ned shrugged. 'I don't know what to say to that.'

Rees began to pace, thinking. Ned couldn't have murdered Elizabeth or attacked Robert, he'd been locked inside the jail these last few days. 'Did you ever see anyone else wandering around Zion when you were meeting Deborah?' Rees asked. 'Especially anyone who didn't belong there.'

'No. Well, only that idiot boy,' Ned replied. 'He came out every night I was there and went to the stables.' Rees frowned at Ned. Poor Calvin.

'Did you see anyone at the laundry?' Rees asked. 'Brother Jabez, for example?'

'No. We – Deborah and me – always tried to be back in our rooms by four, because my brothers woke up at four thirty and by then some of the Shaker men would be going to the barns to start the milking.' Ned paused. 'I really didn't see anyone. I wish I had.' He sounded mournful.

Rees didn't think he could go without that much sleep and still function. Maybe when he'd been as young and lusty as Ned and Deborah. 'All right,' he said. 'I'll talk to the constable. Perhaps I can get you released by Monday.'

'Not sooner?' cried Ned, sounding almost tearful.

'I know you're disappointed,' Rees said. 'I'll do my best, but realistically I think it will be Monday.' Unless Rouge needed the jail for drunken men tearing up the town on a Saturday night. Rees walked back to the wagon and climbed in. It was still early but he hoped Mr Golightly was already in his office and had managed to find the information Rees needed.

The traffic on the main road was, if possible, even worse than it had been previously. Rees had barely driven into it when he began thinking he should have left his wagon at the jail and walked. But the vehicles began turning off at the road to the fairground, and after that Rees moved forward more quickly. He drove into the small mews behind the lawyer's office. Mr Golightly himself opened the door.

'I knew it would be you,' he said. 'You are not a patient man. But I do have news.'

Rees looked at him. 'Well?'

'The Elders have agreed to meet with me to discuss your bid for the Ellis property.' Mr Golightly sounded pleased with himself and spoke with the air of a man demonstrating a magic trick.

'Bid?' Rees repeated, momentarily diverted from his present purpose. 'I'm not bidding to buy it. I already own the damn farm!'

'Language, Mr Rees, language.' Mr Golightly held up a forefinger. 'These legal matters take time.' Rees began grinding his teeth.

'It shouldn't take any time to prove I already own that property,' he shouted. He had never had any patience for this kind of hairsplitting, especially when the facts were as plain as the nose on one's face.

'I'm certain we shall overcome,' Mr Golightly said, motioning Rees to follow him into his office. Rees felt like continuing to argue, but with a supreme effort of will he kept silent and followed the lawyer.

Golightly held the door open for Rees and then crossed to his desk. Rees wanted to scream with impatience as the lawyer fumbled for his spectacles and then spent a few seconds adjusting them before he bent over the papers on his desk. 'I discovered the deed to that farm,' he said. 'Also, that the taxes have continued to be paid. Otherwise the farm might have drawn more attention than it has.'

'Who owns it?' Rees said, his voice rising.

'The Johnson family.' He looked at Rees as though that should mean something. Rees stared back.

'Who was the final owner?' He could hardly put 'the Johnson family' on a tombstone.

'Aaron Johnson.'

'Aaron Johnson,' Rees repeated. Then he knew. 'Brother Aaron?' His voice rose to a squeak.

Why had he allowed that man to leave Zion? He could be anywhere now.

'I assume you know this individual,' Mr Golightly said, removing his spectacles.

'I do,' Rees said. As his initial astonishment faded, he was beginning to ask himself some questions. He turned to the lawyer. 'Why did that property not transfer to the Shakers? The donation of all worldly goods to the community is part of joining.'

Mr Golightly shrugged. 'I'm afraid I can't answer that,' he said. 'All I can tell you is that Mr Johnson owns that farm. He owns it still. No transfer has taken place.'

Rees bid the lawyer a brusque goodbye, too caught up in his own thoughts to be polite, and left. As he walked to his wagon he recalled the question he'd asked himself earlier that morning. Could Brother Aaron still be in the area around Durham? Maybe he slipped into Zion and smothered Elizabeth? In his blue Shaker vest and broad-brimmed straw hat identical to the vest and hat worn by all the other Brothers, he might not have been noticed. Aaron's presence nearby would explain everything.

He fought his way back into the traffic, but turned off at the first opportunity and took the back streets to the jail. He parked his wagon there and returned to Rouge's tavern. It was still busy, but most of the customers had now been served and Rouge was leaning on his forearms, his face drawn with weariness.

'What do you want now?' he asked Rees as

he shoved his way through the mob bellied up to the bar.

Rees bent forward. He tried to speak loudly enough to be heard over the thunder of male conversation, but not so loudly everyone could listen in. 'I found out who owns that abandoned farm. Aaron Johnson.'

Rouge looked at him with a blank expression. 'Who?'

'Brother Aaron. Remember? I asked you to keep a look out for him.' Rees sounded impatient. He took a deep breath and tried to moderate his tone. 'The Palmer boy had nothing to do with it. He was meeting Deborah all right, but for the usual reason – young love.'

'Are you sure he didn't harm the girl? Maybe a quarrel that went wrong?'

'He's worried and he admits he was meeting her. So no. I think Aaron took her.'

'Aaron? Just because he owns the farm?' Rouge shook his head, whether in disbelief or denial Rees could not tell.

'We know Deborah found out about the farm from someone. And she came to this part of the world to search for her father. I think Aaron is her father. And Aaron could easily have murdered Jabez and Calvin. As a Shaker Brother, he had the opportunity.'

Rouge stared at Rees for several seconds. 'But he hasn't been home for, what, several days?'

'Do we know where he's gone? He could be within an hour's drive and we wouldn't know it,' Rees said. The constable did not speak for several seconds, automatically wiping down the wooden slab as he stared at the ceiling above Rees's head.

'Well, you've persuaded me,' Rouge said at last, his forehead wrinkling in thought. 'I'll collect some men and we'll look for him on Monday. I'm too busy today, and tomorrow is the Sabbath.'

'I thought you were already looking for him?' Rees said, scowling at the other man.

'Well, I told people to keep an eye open and I wrote to the constables around.' Rouge grinned weakly. 'It didn't seem that important then. You just wanted to ask him a few questions. But now that we think he might be the guilty party . . .' His words trailed away.

'You must know,' Rees said angrily, 'that if we had questioned him earlier we might have prevented Elizabeth's death.'

Rouge stared at Rees. 'But we might find the girl with him now. Think of that.'

'And we might not.' Rees did not want to imagine what could have happened to Deborah. The girl's fate hung over him like a dark cloud. 'Maybe you should send out the men today, right now,' he said. 'Just in case he has the girl and she is . . .' He stopped. He did not want to finish his thought. Rouge's black brows drew together, meeting in the center, and he nodded.

'I didn't realize the girl was so important to you. Very well. I'll do what I can. We can both pray your Shaker fellow is still nearby and that the girl is with him.' Rouge looked at Rees's expression. 'Don't worry,' he said with awkward sympathy. 'If we find him or I learn anything new, I'll come to Zion and tell you.'

Rees nodded, not trusting himself to speak. He turned and muscled his way through the crowd of men, mostly farmers and hired men, congregated around the bar. He had just a little more than an hour to reach Zion before the noon meal. The bells would be ringing now to call the Shakers to prayer, and if he wanted to be on time he needed to hurry.

He sprinted through the inn yard and vaulted over the fence. Once on the other side, he trotted around Bernadette's house and down the dusty lane to the jail. Although wagons and buggies still filled the street, Rees thought the congestion was slightly less than before. He stopped at the jail and through the open grate said, 'I talked to the constable. I think he'll be releasing you soon.'

Ned pressed himself up against the door. 'Did he find Debbie?'

'Not yet,' Rees said. 'But we are all searching for her.' Despite his attempt to comfort the boy, Ned still looked worried. He kept his face pressed against the bars as Rees waved goodbye.

The journey toward Zion was easier than the trip into town, since few vehicles were traveling away from Durham. Rees whipped Hannibal into a rapid trot. As they approached the turn south on to the Surry Road, the wagon began to shiver a little. Assuming the motion was from the uneven ground, Rees paid it no attention. But the shake and judder of the front wheels increased and the wagon started to sway, making Rees wonder if one of the wheels was damaged.

Suddenly a sharp snap sounded from the front – so loud and so sudden that Hannibal shied and broke into a gallop. Rees sought to pull the gelding back, but as they made the right turn on to the Surry road, still at a gallop, another shattering crack from the front sent the wagon jolting forward. The front seat dived into the road and stopped, sending Rees into flight headfirst over the reins and traces. He sought to protect his head with his arms and curl into a ball, but hit the dirt with a hard jolt to his left shoulder. Rees screamed. His legs came down with a thud, the left one smacking into a rock by the side of the road. The agonizing pain sent him into merciful unconsciousness.

Twenty-Six

Rees awoke to find Lydia bending over him, her face contorted with worry. She had a moist rag in her hand, and from the dampness on his forehead he guessed she had been laying cool cloths upon his face. Pillows behind his back elevated his head and shoulders. He was pleased to see he was in his bedchamber in Zion.

He tried to smile at his wife. When she saw he was conscious and aware, she burst into tears. He tried to move a comforting hand to her wrist, but couldn't. His left arm and shoulder were stiff and too sore to move.

'What . . .?' He stopped and wet his lips. His

mouth was so dry it felt stuffed with wool. 'What happened?'

Lydia tried to stop crying. 'You had an accident . . .' she said with a quaver in her voice, wiping her eyes on her apron. Rees had a vague memory of flying through the air. He looked down and saw that his left foot was encased in bandages. 'A farmer on the way to market saw you and brought you back to Zion. The Brothers moved you into your room. Esther doesn't think there's anything broken, but your shoulder is badly bruised and might be sprained. You cut your ankle on something. Oh, the blood . . .' Sobs overtook her once again and she turned away, lifting her apron to her face.

'Thirsty . . .' Rees said. He was thirsty, but more than that he hoped to distract his wife from her anxiety. It worked. Although still weeping, she poured a beaker of water from the jug and held it out to him. His arms and hands felt so weak the glass was almost too heavy to lift. Lydia sat down beside him and reached over to support the bottom. He drank it slowly, in sips, and felt better once he'd finished it.

'Where's Sharon?' he asked. Lydia nodded to the side, and when he turned his head he saw the cradle and the tuft of red-gold hair on the white linen. He realized Lydia had moved into his bedchamber to nurse him. 'How long have I been unconscious?' he asked.

'It is Sunday morning,' she replied. Tears filled her eyes and threatened to begin falling once again.

'My wagon?' He knew something had broken.

'The Brothers brought it back and put it in the stable.' She turned a fierce gaze upon her husband. 'You are not to worry about it, mind. Jonathan promised they will repair it as soon as they can.' Her mouth pinched together as her cheeks paled, and Rees suspected she was visualizing what the wagon looked like. Just how much damage was there? He couldn't support his family without that vehicle.

'I'm very hungry,' he said, trying to forestall her tears. He spoke the truth, he was suddenly ravenously hungry.

'Esther said you would be once you began to heal,' Lydia said, laughing and crying at the same time. She jumped to her feet and hurried to the door. Rees heard her speaking to someone on the other side. 'Annie will get some soup for you from the kitchen,' she said, as she closed the door and returned to his side. 'We've all been so anxious.'

'Soup?' Rees said, moving his head fretfully on the pillow. 'I don't want soup. I want meat. And bread.'

'Only light meals until you are on your feet,' Lydia said. In response Rees tried to swing his legs round to the side of the bed. The movement made him both nauseous and dizzy, and he was suddenly aware of the bruises all over him. His shoulder and ankle throbbed – well, after what Lydia said, he'd expected that. But his entire body ached, he felt like one large ache and his back throbbed, too.

'Must have twisted my back,' he muttered, allowing his legs to relax back on to the sheet.

'Once you've eaten, I'll make you some willow-bark tea,' said Lydia. 'I hope that will help. Or there's straw tea—'

'No opium,' Rees said flatly, his memories of his experiences in Salem still fresh in his mind. But he remembered both his mother and her mother before her making willow-bark tea for him when he was a child and felt comforted.

A tentative knock on the door brought Lydia to her feet. She disappeared for a few seconds into the hall. When she returned she carried a simple oak tray, made with the Shakers' usual careful perfection. On it were a bowl of soup and a slice of buttered bread. Lydia added another pillow behind him and put the tray on the bedside table. Although Rees felt he could feed himself, she spooned the soup into his mouth as though he were an infant. When he had eaten all he could, and there were only a few drops remaining in the bottom of the bowl, Lydia broke the bread into two pieces.

'I can manage,' Rees said, trying to raise his left hand. He barely achieved a few inches before the agony in his shoulder would allow no more movement. He then reached across with his right hand. Although his back complained, his right arm and hand still functioned and he was able to feed himself the bread.

He thought he must be in terrible shape if the ability to use one arm (merely for lifting bread to his mouth!) was a cause for rejoicing. However, he did feel better when he was done, although very tired.

'Will you be all right if I go and make the tea?' Lydia asked, her forehead furrowed.

'Fine,' Rees said, closing his eyes. He heard the faint rustle of her skirts as she moved away from the bed, and smelled the subtle scent of lavender and honey that clung to her. The door clicked shut behind her.

Although closing his eyes brought every ache and pain into sharp focus, Rees found his mind was already shaking off the fog of unconsciousness and reflecting upon the accident. First, there had been nothing wrong with his wagon. Because his livelihood depended upon it, he was conscientious about keeping it in good repair. Had he hit a rock in the road? With sickening clarity, Rees remembered the two sharp cracks and the drop of the wagon's undercarriage and seat to the ground. The axle had broken; it had to be that. But the axle was made of solid hickory and unlikely to break unless the wagon went headlong into a ravine or over a large boulder. Rees could not remember either occurring. So what had happened? Rees's eyes popped open. He needed to examine that wagon axle.

He slowly – oh so slowly – turned himself around to face the wall. Elevating his head and shoulders just a tiny bit more left him dizzy and breathing hard. It was incredible how weak just one day in bed had left him. He struggled to move his legs to the edge of the bed and drop them over the side on to the floor. The suddenness of his left leg landing on the floor sent a shaft of fire shooting up all the way to the hip.

Rees bit back a curse and sat there for a moment trying to catch his breath.

He was still perched on the side of the bed when Lydia came back into the room. She gasped when she saw him and jumped, the tea slopping into the saucer. 'What are you doing? Get back in that bed this instant.'

Rees suspected she would not consider examination of the wagon a reasonable excuse to leave his sickbed, and tried to think what would serve. 'Chamber pot . . .' he said. It was a partial truth. Now that he'd eaten soup he was feeling some need.

'You couldn't wait for me?' she demanded. She put the tea down on the table. The steam carried with it the willow bark's sharp astringent scent and Rees's mouth puckered. 'I'll help you.'

She pulled the chamber pot out from under the bed and helped him undo the buttons on his breeches. She held him up on the edge of the bed. He closed his eyes, hating his dependency. This would be the last time he needed her help, of that he was determined.

When he was done, she buttoned him back up and helped him swing his legs back on to the bed. Rees didn't fight her. His legs felt weak and for a moment the room tilted. 'I want you to drink this tea,' she said, picking up the mug, 'and go to sleep.' She held the beverage to his lips. He drank down the pale-green liquid, screwing up his face at the taste. Lydia made him swallow the entire glassful. Then she pressed him back against the pillows. 'Sleep!' she commanded, as she picked up the mug in one hand and the chamber pot in the other. The person on the other side of the door opened it for her at her call, and then Rees was alone.

Rees did not feel like sleeping. In fact, he felt more and more clear-headed. And the urge to examine his wagon had taken possession of him to such a degree he could think of nothing else. He listened hard, trying to hear if Lydia or anyone else was still outside. He did not hear a sound. Again he swung his legs to the side of the bed. This time he held his knee with one hand and lowered it very gently to the floor. Clutching the bedstead, he carefully pulled himself to a standing position. Swaying, he fought down the threat from his stomach – both tea and soup were trying to come back up. But the longer he stood the better he felt, and after several seconds he took a step. Then another. His back protested but he ignored the pain. He limped cautiously across the floor. Although he still felt weak and vertigo hovered at the edge of consciousness, he successfully circled his room. His ankle ached – God, how it hurt! – but he could walk on it. The pain was localized in the cut on the outside, and as long as he did not go too fast his leg held up. What he needed was a stick for support, but a quick glance around the room did not reveal anything that would help. He slid his bare feet into his shoes. He did not think he could bend over to put on his stockings.

Taking a deep breath, Rees approached the door, opened it a crack, and peeked out. The hall was empty. He went out.

He made it through the door to the outside without difficulty. Then he looked at the steps.

Although there were only four of them, there was no handrail. Would his ankle support him as he descended the stairs? Rees hesitated, unsure. How strange to tremble at the top of a short flight of steps, one that he usually ran up and down without even elevating his heart rate. The steps were granite and if he fell . . . Well, he wouldn't know if he could do it if he didn't try. He put his weight on his good leg, the right one, but the few moments of standing on his left were so agonizing he let out an involuntary grunt. But he was committed now. He ventured down another step, jarring his back, and groaned. Just two more steps. Rees paused to catch his breath. He knew now how stupid he'd been, but it was too late. He wasn't sure he could climb back up again even if he wanted to, so his only choice was to go on. He made it down the third step and then, very quickly, down the fourth to the dirt road. Now that he'd begun, there was really no doubt that he would continue. For good or ill, once he was determined to do something he did it.

He paused at the bottom of the steps to catch his breath, but only for a few seconds. He knew most, if not all, of the community would be in the Meetinghouse, but he was still afraid someone would see him and force him back into bed. Then he would have to do this all over again.

He looked at the street in front of him. The main road was only wide enough for two wagons abreast, but it looked enormous right now. Rees sucked in his breath and started across. At least he no longer felt so dizzy, and his right leg had recovered its strength.

Rees shuffled across the street as rapidly as he could and went into the barn. He paused just inside the door to let his eyes adjust, leaning against the side beam to relieve the throbbing in his back. That short walk had exhausted him. Fatigue dragged his eyes down, and if he had not been so determined to look at his wagon he would have lain down in the hay and gone to sleep.

His wagon had been pulled into its usual place and had its front to the back wall. Rees limped forward and grasped the side. Using that as his support, he pulled himself the remaining distance to the front. Although the wheel appeared undamaged, the driver's seat sagged to the ground. Rees dropped to his right knee and attempted to peer under the wagon. At first look, the bolsters and plates all appeared intact. Because the front wheels were smaller than the back wheels, a common wagon feature, the axle was invisible from this perspective. He would have to get down very low to see anything. Groaning, he lay down. With his back flat on the ground, he was able to worm his way underneath.

Dust and straw disturbed by his actions made him sneeze convulsively several times. His eyes began to water. But there was nothing wrong with his fingers. He reached forward and ran his right hand along the solid hickory that made up the axle. Instead of the splintering he would have expected if it had broken, he felt the cuts and grooves made by an axe.

This was no accident. Someone had tried to kill him.

Twenty-Seven

Now even more determined than ever, Rees wiped his eyes on the tail of his shirt and leaned over to look at what he had found. He had to hunch his shoulders lest he bang his head on the underside of the wagon. Because it had been drawn in head first, the front wheels were in shadow. Every time Rees shifted, his shoulder blocked the light from the door, but he saw enough to know his fingers had not lied. The hickory had been chopped almost through, and the last bit of solid wood had not been able to take the stress of Hannibal's trot. Rees felt a full body chill shivered over him. He had been amazingly lucky. Saturday's traffic had kept him from driving into town at his usual break-neck speed. A different day, with less traffic to slow him down, and he probably would have been killed.

'Will? What are you doing? Why are you out of bed?' Lydia's voice rose. 'You were fortunate not to break a bone. Are you trying to fall now?'

Rees made an instant decision not to tell Lydia that someone had tried to kill him. 'I wanted to check my wagon,' he said, trying to squirm out from underneath.

'Why? I told you Jonathan said the Brothers would repair it,' she said, her face appearing at his feet.

'I know,' he replied. But he was not sure he wanted them to work on his wagon. Someone had chopped the axle. It was possible none of the Brothers were guilty – after all, he had left his wagon in both the inn's yard and in front of the jail, and in both of those locations it was likely that there would have been witnesses. But here in the barn, especially late at night, someone could have worked on the axle without anyone seeing. And that fitted with the rest of the evidence – with Brother Jabez's death in the laundry tub and the fact that it was one of the Brothers who had taken Calvin to see the horses. No, Rees was persuaded he would find the murderer here, in Zion, and he did not want to put the wagon's repairs into a murderer's hands.

'Come out,' Lydia said, pulling at his right leg impatiently. Rees used his right hand and shoulder to push himself toward Lydia. She moved away, moving to the side so he could inch his way out. Once his head had cleared the underside of the wagon, he sat up, realizing all at once that he was not sure he could stand. 'Let me help you,' Lydia said, tugging at his right elbow.

'Not yet,' Rees said. 'Let me think.' After a moment's cogitation, he rolled over on to his right knee. Then, leaning on the wagon wheel, Rees used his right arm to pull himself up on to his right leg. Sweat streamed down his face. For a moment his back throbbed and his wrenched left shoulder felt as though it were on fire.

'Back to your room, now,' Lydia said. 'You're in pain, aren't you? Well, you deserve it! What possessed you to behave so foolishly?' Rees knew she was barely holding on to her temper. He meekly leaned on her shoulder, putting more of his weight on her than he wanted. He was suddenly so tired he didn't think he could make the walk. Only the fact that he didn't wish Lydia to know how weary he felt kept him on his feet.

'I'm fine,' he said, but the tremble in his voice gave a lie to his words.

As they approached the Dwelling House, the sound of the baby's piercing wails was clearly audible. Lydia did not speak, but she began to push Rees along faster.

With her assistance, Rees got up the stairs. By now the bandage surrounding his ankle was streaked with red. He could feel the wetness on his skin and it felt like his ankle was being severed. Rees could not repress a groan as they went through the front door. Several Sisters were clustered in front of Rees's door, but none of them dared enter. 'I'm sorry,' Lydia said. 'So sorry.' She turned a look of fury upon her husband. 'He thought he was well enough to walk.'

Esther opened the door and Lydia propelled Rees through it. Inside, Sharon's screams were deafening. Lydia helped Rees on to the bed, lifting his legs to put them up, and removed his shoes. Then she picked up the baby. Sharon's cheeks were scarlet and her eyes screwed into slits with the force of her cries. Lydia kissed the baby's head, shooting an accusatory glare at her husband over the lace cap covering Sharon's golden downy hair and carried her to a chair. As

Lydia removed her bertha and began unbuttoning in preparation for nursing the baby, Rees closed his eyes. He dropped instantly into sleep.

When he awoke, his room was dim with shadows. Lydia was gone. Rees looked over at the cradle. It too was empty. But there was a fresh bandage on his ankle, and when he cautiously sat up he felt only a moment of vertigo before the room righted itself. His ankle hurt and his shoulder ached, but the terrible fatigue had left him. Rees looked for his shoes. Lydia had put them next to the bed. Once he'd slid his feet into them, he pushed himself upright. He spent a moment testing his balance before walking to the door of his room and peering through it. A few Shakers – two Sisters walking toward the women's door and one Brother about to go through the men's door – were leaving the Dwelling House. Rees followed the Brother outside.

Other people were walking to the Dining Hall. Rees would have liked to join them but as he stared at the steps he recalled the effort it had taken him to descend them earlier.

'Do you need help?' Jonathan separated himself from the crowd of identically garbed men and came over to where Rees was standing. He eyed Jonathan suspiciously. The Shaker had been hostile from the beginning. Now that Rees knew someone had almost severed his axle, he no longer trusted anyone here. But would Jonathan hurl Rees down the steps? Common sense asserted itself; there were, after all, plenty of witnesses, and he nodded. Jonathan came up the steps and put his arm under Rees's right side. With his help, Rees managed to hobble down the steps. 'I'll make you a cane,' Jonathan said. 'I know our Sister Lydia feels you need to remain in bed, but to me you look ready to get back on your feet.'

'I am,' Rees said. He was more determined than ever to find the wolf in the sheepcote.

Although Jonathan could have increased his speed and left Rees behind, the Brother chose not to. Instead he walked next to Rees, matching his stride to the other man's hesitant limp. They went into the men's chamber outside the Dining Hall together.

Since Sunday was a day filled with services, tonight's supper was almost entirely cold – cold chicken and garden greens – but the squash had been boiled. Rees stared at it on his plate, the orange mash reminding him of the squash flowers he'd seen behind the abandoned house and the bones he'd found so soon afterwards. He had not believed those bones were connected to the more recent murders here in Zion, but now that he knew the farm was owned by Aaron Johnson he suspected they might be. The why of it still escaped him, but Aaron had plenty of opportunity for killing Brother Jabez and Calvin. The boy trusted Aaron, so he could easily have lured Calvin across the road to the pasture and struck him down. The smothering of Elizabeth was harder to explain.

Perhaps Aaron had slipped into Zion purposely, intending to cut the wagon axle? Rees considered that alternative but found it difficult to believe.

For one thing, if Aaron had taken Deborah, what would he do with her while he was engaged in mischief? Or was she already dead? Probably. Rees shuddered. Maybe if he'd been smarter or worked faster, she would still be alive.

A sudden touch on his shoulder brought him out of his reverie. Rees turned, meeting Jonathan's worried gaze. The last week had been hard on the Brother. Light lines in his face had deepened into furrows and the gray in his hair seemed more plentiful. He looked much older than he had when Rees had first met him. Rees acknowledged Jonathan with a nod and applied himself to his supper. Although Rees was now more concerned with Brother Aaron, Jonathan was almost as likely a candidate. Rees did not like feeling he could trust no one here except his wife, but he couldn't. He was glad that the Shaker's prohibition on unnecessary speech kept him from making polite small talk with men he thought might be murderers.

He did not see his wife until the end of the meal when he heard the mewling cry of a newborn baby and looked over. Lydia, rising from her seat with the baby in her arms, sped rapidly from the room. But she did not disappear through the door before darting a disapproving glance at her husband. Rees knew he would catch the rough side of her tongue the next time he saw her. She thought he had gotten out of bed too early. And maybe he had, but knowing that someone had tried to kill him served as a spur to rapid healing. Wounded, he was vulnerable.

As the community separated, heading to evening

270

chores, Rees had a clear view of his children. And they of him. 'My father, oh, my father,' Nancy cried and bolted across the floor straight to him. Judah tried to follow, but the Sister clutched his arm and held him. He began to scream. While Simon followed his sister, Joseph joined Judah in bawling. The usually peaceful Dining Hall reverberated with their shrill cries.

Since Rees didn't trust his balance, he remained in his chair. He tried to angle his body so that Nancy ran to his right side. She tried to climb into his lap and Rees put his hand on her head. The thin Shaker cap had come off during her mad dash across the room and her fine hair, falling from the braids, flew around her face. 'I'm fine,' he said.

'We heard you were hurt,' Simon said, coming up behind his sister. He looked at the bandage on Rees's ankle.

'I was,' Rees said. 'But it wasn't serious.' Simon looked unconvinced. Rees pulled Nancy into his lap, stifling a groan as his left shoulder twisted.

'Are you sure you're all right?' Jerusha asked.

'I'm fine,' Rees said. 'I wouldn't be here, in the Dining Hall, if I wasn't.' Jerusha stared at Rees with wide worried eyes and took Nancy's hand as the two caretakers came up behind the children. Although the young Sister and Brother said nothing as they hustled away their charges, Rees knew they would scold them when they reached the Children's House.

Rees limped back to his room. Although he walked slowly and his shoulder still ached, he was beginning to feel more like his usual self.

The short distance from the Dining Hall to the Dwelling House was perfect. Any further and he would have had difficulty managing it.

When he entered his room, it looked different. At first, he didn't know why. Then he realized that the spot that had been occupied by the cradle was empty. He guessed Lydia, who was probably still angry with him, had returned to her own room. Although he was inclined to cross the hall and speak with her immediately – he wanted to explain himself – he didn't dare. Not when the Believers were all about. He especially did not want the Shaker Family to hear their voices being raised, which was a distinct possibility even if the conversation between himself and Lydia did not become a quarrel.

Instead, he settled himself by winding his warp. But as the shadows crept across the floor and finally reached his bed, Rees felt himself tensing until he was as taut as a bowstring. He kept expecting someone to come through the door. Finally, he took the chair and wedged it under the knob. He did not want to fall asleep and leave himself defenseless. The murderer might sneak into his room while he slept and try to smother him; or since subduing Rees would be much more difficult than suffocating Elizabeth, the villain might stab him.

Rees tried to calmly and logically consider the murders, the bones, and Deborah's abduction, but he couldn't. He was too nervous to focus. Instead, his eyes remained glued to the door.

Although he hadn't intended to sleep, he couldn't help it. Some time in the middle of the night, Rees couldn't tell exactly when without the light necessary to see his pocket watch, he dropped into sleep. The sound of someone trying the handle of his door woke him. Sitting up in panting, sweaty terror, Rees stared at the door. When nothing happened, he began to think he had dreamed it. After all, this last week of nights had been tortured by one nightmare after another. He began to relax, leaning back against the pillow once again. Then the handle rattled again. The door shifted slightly, but the chair prevented it from opening. Rees's heart began pounding like a drum. 'Lydia?' he whispered, fumbling for the dinner knife on the table. He was determined to defend himself if he had to. And even if he failed to kill the rogue, he would give as good an account of himself as he could.

But the person on the other side withdrew. Rees scrambled as quickly as he could out of his bed, almost falling when his weak leg buckled. He limped to the door and pulled away the chair. He peered through the crack. The hallway was in darkness except for the receding light of a candle disappearing through the front door, which closed behind it with a soft click, plunging the hallway into darkness once again. Although Rees could see nothing of the person who had tried his door, he knew it wasn't Lydia. Something about the shadow hinted at a man's form. Besides, Lydia would have no reason to go outside, not now, in the middle of the night.

There could be little doubt about it. The murderer had made a second attempt on his life.

* * *

273

Fear kept Rees awake for the remainder of the night. He kept his mind occupied by considering how he might best move his family from Zion to the Ellis farm. The first problem was driving into town. Not only did Rees not have a functioning wagon, he also wasn't sure he could handle the reins with an injured shoulder. Could he borrow a buggy? He knew Lydia was experienced enough to drive a buggy that short distance. Maybe instead of borrowing a buggy, he should ask for a wagon and move his family to the farm before driving into Durham. Rees moved restlessly on the bed. He didn't want the murderer threatening his family, and he already had ample proof they were not safe in Zion.

He dreaded talking to Lydia. He knew she would not do as he asked without demanding an explanation. So far he had refrained from telling her about the axle, but now he was reconsidering that hasty decision.

He fell into a light doze as the birds began chirruping to greet the dawn and was only awakened by the loud clang of the breakfast bell. He wriggled out of bed, realizing that both his shoulder and ankle felt much better, and jammed his feet into his shoes. He pulled the chair away from under the knob and opened his door. A few Sisters were walking down the other side of the hall. Ignoring them and the disapproving stares they directed at him as he crossed to the women's side, Rees headed toward Lydia's room. She was just exiting, with the baby in her arms. A crisp white bertha made a pleasing contrast to her navy dress.

'What are you doing?' she asked, throwing a quick glance at the Sisters. They had turned and were regarding husband and wife with disapproving frowns.

'We need to talk,' Rees said. He stared at the Sisters, daring them to object. One of the younger ones took an involuntary step backwards. The older women were made of sterner stuff; the elder of the bunch met Rees's eyes with a severe and unyielding stare.

'You should not be on this side of the hall,' she said in an icy tone.

Rees took Lydia's elbow and drew her toward the back door. 'Go on to breakfast,' he told the Sisters. 'This is not your affair.'

'Will!' Lydia said, pulling her arm from his grasp.

'Go on,' he shouted at the Sisters. Lydia gasped. The women turned and hurried away like a flock of chickens. The only difference? Unlike the chickens, the Sisters were temporarily silent, but Rees was certain they would have plenty to say as soon as they were through the front door.

'You don't understand,' he said to Lydia, turning to face her.

'Then help me understand,' she said. 'I know you believe you're protecting me, but I really do need to know.' Rees inhaled and blew out his breath. He agreed, but how should he begin? She grabbed his wrist and shook it. 'Tell me.'

'Someone's trying to kill me,' he said.

Lydia's face blanched and Rees thought that only the baby in her arms kept her from screaming. 'Here,' he said, grabbing her arm and drawing her through the back door. He could feel the resistance in her reluctant body, but she did follow him after a moment of fight. Once outside, he gently lowered himself to the top step. He was sitting on the women's side, but since almost everyone was at breakfast he thought they would be safe. After a few seconds of hesitation, she lowered herself to the stone beside him.

'How long have you known?' she asked.

'Only since I saw the wagon axle,' he replied. He turned to meet her eyes. 'I suspected something. That's why I had to look at it. It was hacked almost through. With an axe, I think.'

Lydia did not speak but her body tensed and the baby let out a wail. Lydia put her hand on Sharon's head and murmured soothingly, without words.

'Then last night,' Rees continued, 'someone tried to break into my room.' Lydia tried to stifle a gasp. He looked at her and nodded. 'I braced a chair against the door and he didn't get in. But I want to get a ride into town. We need to move to the Ellis farm today. I can't allow the murderer to threaten . . .'

He stopped abruptly when he saw Lydia's terrified expression. 'Don't worry,' he said. But of course he knew she would be frantic with apprehension now that she understood the danger, not only to him but to the entire family.

They were so intent upon their conversation they did not notice two men approaching. 'Rees,' said one of the men. Rees struggled to his feet.

'I found him wandering down the main street looking for you,' Jonathan said. He directed a suspicious frown at his companion and withdrew.

'I expected to find you in bed,' Rouge said.

'I'm not good at lying around,' Rees said. 'Do you have news?'

'Guess who one of my deputies found lurking around Zion first thing this morning?' Grinning, Rouge fixed a stare on Rees.

'Who?' Rees felt a tingle of anticipation.

'Your friend, Brother Aaron.'

Twenty-Eight

For a few seconds Rees did not understand what Rouge was telling him. Then, as he processed the information, he turned to Lydia. She met his gaze and he saw she was aware of the significance of this news. Aaron had been found near Zion. That meant, Rees thought in rising excitement, that Aaron could have crept into the village any time within the last few days. He could have smothered Elizabeth and attacked Robert, hacked Rees's axle apart, and most certainly tried to slip into Rees's bedchamber the previous night.

'We can't be certain,' Lydia said, putting her hand on Rees's freckled forearm.

'I know,' he said. 'We don't know how long he's been loitering nearby.' Although that was true, Rees felt positive that Aaron was the murderer.

277

'Have you spoken to him?' he asked, turning to face the constable. Rouge shook his head.

'I didn't want to waste time. I figured it was more important to come for you. I knew you would want to ask him questions. Why go through that twice?'

Rees nodded, although he thought Rouge's response had more to do with his innate laziness than any consideration for Rees.

'Go on,' Lydia said. 'This may put an end to the murders.' And the fear. Although she didn't say the last, Rees knew what she meant.

'I'll return as soon as I can,' he said. Turning to Rouge he added, 'I hope you brought a buggy. My wagon has been damaged.'

Rouge nodded. 'I heard. Your accident is a nine days' wonder in town. And it is a wonder – a wonder you weren't killed.'

'It wasn't an accident,' Rees said, after a quick look around to make sure he would not be overheard. 'Someone hacked my axle almost all the way through. I was fortunate I made it as far as I did.'

Rouge turned a searching gaze upon Rees. 'You think it was Aaron?'

Rees shrugged and nodded at the same time. 'I think it's probable.'

Once again Rees visited the noisome Durham jail, only this time Ned Palmer was gone and Brother Aaron languished inside. Rees would have had a hard time recognizing the Shaker. One eye was swollen shut, blood from a cut over his eyebrow had crusted into a reddish film, and bruises marked his left cheek. Rees turned to Rouge. 'Why did your deputy beat him? The Shakers are pacifists. Aaron would not have given any trouble.'

Rouge lifted his shoulders and said indifferently, 'He's a murderer. And a kidnapper. Where's the girl?' His sudden barked question made Rees jump. Aaron only looked confused.

'What girl?'

'Deborah went missing at the same time you took your little trip,' Rees said.

'Who? I don't know anyone named Deborah.'

Rees thought Aaron might be lying but couldn't tell. The man's face was too swollen and discolored. 'All right. Let's talk about you lurking around Zion. Slipping in to murder Sister Elizabeth. And taking an axe to my wagon axle.'

'Sister Elizabeth is dead?' Aaron shook his head. 'A woman who surrendered to sin but saw the error of her ways and returned home. At least we can be certain she is now enjoying her Heavenly reward with Mother Ann.'

This was so unexpected a response that Rees just stared at the other man.

'So, you claim you had nothing to do with her untimely death?' Rouge jumped in.

'Of course not.' Aaron sounded more irritated than guilty.

'Then why were you creeping around Zion?' Rees asked. 'That's where the deputy found you, isn't it?'

'I sold all my goods, didn't I? So I came home. But I reached the village so early in the morning

279

I thought I would wait until everyone was awake before driving in.'

Rees had to admit the explanation was plausible.

'And what about the bones?' Rouge demanded, his voice rising in frustration.

'Bones? What bones? What are you talking about?'

'We were on your farm,' Rees said. 'We found blood all over the floor of the kitchen, and we found bones in the stream.'

'My farm? I don't own a farm. Haven't for years. Not since I joined the Believers.' Aaron sounded genuinely surprised. But there was something . . .

'You are the owner of record for the farm near the Fitches,' Rees said. 'I know. I checked.'

'I sold that farm more'n ten years ago,' Aaron said. He brought his hands up to the window grate. Any other man's hands would have been marked with scrapes and cuts, the marks left by a fight. But not his. Aaron had not tried to defend himself.

'Who did you sell it to?' Rouge asked.

Aaron hesitated. For the first time Rees seriously considered the possibility that the man had been telling the truth. Now, faced with a question he did not want to answer, his manner had changed. His long, tanned fingers clenched and unclenched on the bars, and he would not meet Rees's gaze.

'Who did you sell the farm to?' Rees asked. 'Tell me, Aaron.'

'I don't remember.' He took his hands down

and stepped back. Rees turned to look at Rouge.

'He's lying,' Rouge said.

'Yes,' Rees agreed. Aaron could not have made his falsehood more obvious if he'd told them outright that he was not telling the truth. But why? 'He's trying to protect someone,' Rees muttered.

Nodding, Rouge stepped up to the grate. 'Listen, you sanctimonious bastard, if you don't tell us who bought the farm I swear I'll send in the deputy for another session.'

'I don't think that will be necessary,' Rees said, knowing he sounded disapproving. He leaned closer to the door and said, 'I think you should tell us, Aaron, not because the constable here is threatening you, but because whoever you are trying to protect might be guilty of murder. Loyalty is all very well, but do you want to protect a murderer from justice? Does God want you to?'

Rees couldn't be sure but he thought that under the dark bruising overlaying his skin Aaron had paled.

'Abraham,' Aaron muttered, so softly Rees could hardly hear him. 'Abraham Vors.'

Rees and Rouge exchanged glances. 'Who?' Rees asked.

'That's who I sold the farm to,' Aaron said in a louder voice.

'Never heard of him,' Rouge said, sounding as surprised as Rees felt.

'Why isn't his name on the deed then?' Rees asked.

'How should I know?' Aaron sounded annoyed. 'I joined the Believers shortly after, so I was no longer interested in the affairs of the World.'

Rees absently passed his hand over his forehead, trying to fit this new piece into the puzzle. 'Have you ever seen Mr Vors again?' he asked.

'No. But then I wouldn't, would I? He is not a Believer?'

'Have you been paying the taxes on the farm?' Rees knew he was missing something, but couldn't figure out what. He hoped his random questions would help.

'No. Why would I? It didn't belong to me. And I don't have any cash money, anyway.'

'You do now,' Rouge said, leaning forward. 'You just returned from a trip where you sold goods.'

'But that money isn't mine,' Aaron said, almost triumphantly in Rees's view. 'It belongs to Zion. And I surrender all of it to the Elders, every last farthing, every sou, and every piece of eight. So no, I did not pay the taxes on a farm I no longer own.'

'Have you stopped by the property recently?' Rees asked, feeling his hope that Aaron would have all the answers curl up and start to die.

Aaron stared at Rees through his one good eye. 'Now why would I do that? I sold it and gave the money to the Elders. I have no interest in that farm anymore.' He turned and stomped back to his stone bench. Unable to think of any more questions to ask, Rees let the man go.

'You know,' Rouge said as he and Rees returned to the buggy, 'the members of this new faith are supposed to be gentle pacifists. Why, that Brother Solomon – butter wouldn't melt in his mouth. How did this sour old fellow,' and he tipped his head at the jail, 'find his way to the Shakers?'

'It is strange,' Rees agreed. 'That doesn't make him a murderer, of course. But I know Aaron lied to us at least once. I think that bears further examination.' Rouge nodded in agreement.

Since Rees's journey into town had cost him the rich breakfast he would have had in Zion, he elected to eat in the tavern. He had to stop there anyway since he was dependent upon Rouge for his ride back to Zion. Rees found a table and seat easily; Monday morning was not a busy time in the inn. Save for a few farmers following up negotiations made at the market on Saturday and five travelers waiting for the stage, the taproom was empty.

Rouge had hired two new maids. A lanky blonde child of fourteen and an older girl: French if her muttered imprecations were to be taken at face value. She scowled at all the customers, and Rees was glad to be served by the child. Although clumsy, she was polite. She slapped a mug of hot coffee down with such force the steaming liquid sprayed across the table and spattered Rees with hot drops. 'I'm sorry, I'm sorry,' she cried, her face crumpling as though she might burst into tears.

'It's all right,' Rees said, pushing himself to his feet as he scrubbed ineffectually at the front of his shirt. 'Just fetch me a rag.'

The girl pulled a length of tattered cloth from

283

the ties of her apron and handed it to Rees. 'Go on now and fetch the sugar and cream,' he said in a soft voice.

As she scurried away, he quickly mopped up the spill with the grimy towel and returned to his seat.

Although the room was not crowded, loud conversations at nearby tables distracted Rees from his own thoughts. The farmers to his left kept increasing the volume of their conversation to drown out the complaints of the stage passengers sitting to Rees's right. One gentleman in particular, dressed inappropriately for this warm day in a tall beaver hat and fitted jacket, drawled on and on without seeming to take a breath.

'One of the worst I've seen, don't ye know,' he was saying. 'A mean little village and this inn, well, I can only be glad I did not sleep here last night. And the food! Well, I suppose it is edible if one likes homey peasant fare.' A woman companion in white muslin, rather crumpled from the journey, tittered in response. A second man grunted. Instead of eating, he was drinking his breakfast. A jug of whiskey sat before him and he was on his fourth – or was it his fifth? – glass. He seemed determined to empty the jug before they were called back to the stagecoach.

'A good year for buckwheat,' shouted one of the farmers, directing a judgmental stare at the speaker in the other group. 'And my wife's bees did well. We'll have honey to sell.'

'Are you sure? I expect those nine kids of yours could devour that honey in a few days.'

'And another on the way? You're keeping busy. Trying to produce your own hired men?'

'Ah, five of them are girls,' said the first man to a round of chuckles. They subsided into silence when the young barmaid returned with Rees's cone of sugar and the cream jug.

As Rees began fixing his coffee, the coach driver came through the front door shouting, 'Time to go. Time to go. Stage to Boston.'

The passengers rose to their feet, the beaver hat man still complaining in a high whiny voice. There was a flurry of activity as they collected their parcels and other possessions and moved to the door.

With their departure, the taproom seemed suddenly very silent.

Rouge came out from the back with a plate for Rees: three eggs with fried bread and a heap of bacon. A fork had been dropped across the bread. Rees took out his knife.

Wiping his forehead with his apron, Rouge sat down across the table. 'Getting low on bacon,' he commented.

'The farmers will be butchering soon,' Rees replied through his full mouth. He swallowed. It was good bacon but he knew the Shakers had better. 'When can you take me back to Zion?'

'Whenever you're ready,' he said. 'But I couldn't leave that Mr Spencer to the girls.'

'Mr Spencer? That the fellow in the beaver hat?'

'That's him. Mr High-and-Mighty. Thinks he's a prince at least. Travels back and forth to Boston every summer. It's always the same story, nothing's good enough for His Royal Highness.'

285

'He likes the food whether he complains or not,' Rees said in sympathy. He'd done weaving for a number of women whose complaints were unending. 'Oh, is this a loose thread? I expected the weave to be tighter. I don't like the color.' Some people just couldn't be happy.

Rouge nodded and jumped up to attend to the farmers, who were now leaving as well. Finally, Rees was alone with his thoughts.

Twenty-Nine

It was almost ten before Rouge finally detached himself from his responsibilities at the inn. Rees, feeling the effects of his broken sleep the night before, was groggy and disoriented. When he climbed into the buggy and they started out, the rocking motion was well on its way to putting him to sleep when Rouge spoke.

'I'll keep Aaron in jail for now. He's clearly guilty.'

Rees dragged his eyes open and tried to concentrate. 'We don't know that for certain,' he said. 'I am not yet convinced.'

'But you were the one who wanted him found,' Rouge said, darting an irritated glance at his passenger.

'Yes,' Rees agreed.

'He could have slipped into Zion with no one the wiser.'

'That's true,' Rees agreed.

286

'And he lied to us.'

'Also true. But . . .' Rees's voice trailed away. Why couldn't he think? 'I know there's something we haven't thought of yet. Or something I've heard.' Rees stopped in frustration.

'Now I remember how you are,' Rouge said, his voice tight. 'Nothing is enough. Ever. You have to keep picking at it.'

'I want to be sure,' Rees said, annoyed in his turn. 'If Aaron isn't guilty, I don't want to see him hang. That isn't justice. He'd only be another victim.'

'Well, if not him, who?'

'I don't know,' Rees muttered, wishing he could think. He yawned, a jaw-cracking stretch that widened his mouth to its limit. 'I just feel something is wrong. And until I work that out, I won't be convinced Aaron is the guilty party.'

Rouge grunted, his wordless exclamation telling Rees quite clearly the constable did not agree, and lapsed into silence.

He stopped in front of the Dwelling House and helped Rees climb the steps. Rees went into his room and, although the Sisters had not finished cleaning, closed the door and put his chair under the knob. Kicking off his shoes, he dropped down on to the bare sheet and fell almost instantly asleep.

The clang of the dinner bell woke him. His face was pressed into the pillow and he'd been drooling. He rolled over, his injured shoulder protesting with a twinge of pain, and sat up. He still felt tired but his head had cleared. He was conscious of several thoughts banging together.

He'd been thinking of bees as well as Brother Aaron. Wondering why his sleeping mind had dredged up such an unlikely pairing, Rees slid out of bed and shoved his feet into his shoes. He looked at the door, but the chair was still wedged firmly against it. A handmade cane was leaning against the wall, so Jonathan had visited previously, probably while Rees had been in town. Rees picked up the cane, admiring the smooth finish. Even on such a plain and homely object, the workmanship was perfect. He tried walking a few steps. Jonathan had gotten the height right, too. He hoped Brother Jonathan was not the murderer; it would be a loss to hang such an expert carpenter.

Using the cane, Rees went out, navigating the stairs with only a little bit of difficulty. He walked to the Dining Hall and into the waiting room. Jonathan was already there. Rees held up the cane. Jonathan did not smile, but Rees thought those stern lips relaxed a little.

'I'm working on your wagon,' he said.

'Can it be patched?' Rees asked. Jonathan shook his head.

'I thought about sistering another piece of hickory to the axle, but it wouldn't last. One hard stop and it would break again. I'll need to put in a whole new axle.' The target of several disapproving glances, Jonathan lapsed into silence. Rees sighed. Another delay in his plans to leave Zion.

Dessert was a cake liberally topped with honey and butternuts. In Rees's opinion, the honey did

288

not taste as nice as his wife's. She always planted lavender, which gave the honey a slightly different flavor. When he looked for her on the Sisters' side, he found her sitting staring at the pastry on her plate. Her mouth was turned down and her eyes looked unusually liquid, as though she might burst into tears at the slightest provocation. She was missing her bees, Rees was sure of it, and he swore they would set up some more hives as soon as they were settled.

Solomon dismissed the Shakers with unusual speed and left quickly. As the Family began to scatter to their afternoon chores, Rees limped outside, where he could wait for Lydia. With Sharon in her arms, Lydia came out at the end of the flood of Sisters. She smiled at Rees but he could see tears still trembling on her lashes. 'Don't worry,' he said, 'we will start more hives when we move to the Ellis farm. Surely the Elders here will sell you a few queens.'

Lydia nodded but she sighed. 'It takes a while to establish the colonies,' she said. 'To plant the flowers they like and set up the skeps . . .' She sighed again and Rees knew she was remembering the hives she had left behind in Dugard – the few remaining after a malicious fire had destroyed the rest.

'Do you remember when we met here?' Rees asked, smiling down at her and running his hand over his daughter's head. 'You lived in the cottage up there . . .' He stopped abruptly and turned to look over his shoulder. The slope up to the cottage was invisible behind the stable. Although he had walked through the cottage when he'd been searching for Calvin, Rees had not done so when Deborah went missing. 'I wonder,' he murmured. From this angle the beginning of the path could not be seen, but Rees knew exactly where it began next to the blacksmith's. Had Robert the blacksmith managed to find his way home after his wife's death? Pushing away that question, he said, 'I have to look at the cottage right now.'

'What? Will, what are you talking about?' Lydia tugged at his shirtsleeve.

'I never looked in the cottage for Deborah,' Rees said. 'I'll return, I promise you. But I have to search that cottage now.'

'You're scaring me,' Lydia said.

'I just want to satisfy my curiosity,' Rees said. But he knew he hadn't reassured her. Pulling his sleeve free, he turned and hurried across the street. He didn't think he had much time left to find Deborah, if indeed she was still alive. Turning by the huge boulder and starting up the steep track felt familiar, almost like coming home. He increased his speed and felt his left ankle sting in response. Rees leaned hard upon the cane to give himself additional lift. His heart began to thud in his chest.

As Rees climbed the hill, soon reaching a height above the stable roof, he looked down upon Lydia. She was still standing in front of the Dwelling House but she was not watching him. Instead, she was talking rapidly to Esther. The Eldress was nodding. The women dropped out of sight as Rees followed the overgrown path around the curve.

Rees struggled up the last incline, blessing the cane. He could not have climbed this steep path successfully without it. Before he reached the bluff upon which the cottage sat, he paused and tried to catch his breath. He had fond memories of this little house, which had been Lydia's home when he first met her. Rees picked his way carefully up the overgrown path, trying not to upset the bees as he negotiated his way through the overgrown flowers.

He stopped outside the door and listened. But, over the hum of bees and the flutter of leaves in the breeze, he heard nothing.

He went inside, to the main room. It was empty except for the bee swarm. It looked to Rees as though the comb they had constructed over the shelves was even larger than it had been a few days previously. The buzzing filled the room, almost deafening in its volume. The entire space vibrated with it. Rees again thought that while the hum of a solitary bee was pleasant and comforting, the sound of this many bees was ominous and frightening.

He turned to leave but then thought he would peek into the smaller room to the side. He skirted the hive very carefully, and pressed his ear to the door. Over the loud drone, Rees thought he heard speech. He couldn't be sure. He flung open the door and froze.

Jonathan was kneeling in front of Deborah, trying to press bread into her mouth. Her face was dirty and streaked with tears, and her hands had been tied in front of her with a strip torn from her bertha. She'd been blindfolded and gagged, although the dirty piece of cloth had been pushed down from her mouth and now circled her neck. A leather strip was fastened around one ankle and fixed to the far wall under the window so she could barely reach the door. Despite the open window, the small room smelled terrible; the odor from a small bucket was almost solid in this tiny area.

Jonathan jumped up. 'Help me . . .' he began. Rees hurled himself at the Shaker Brother. But his weak ankle turned beneath him. He toppled to the floor, grabbing at Jonathan and clutching him in a hug. As Jonathan fought to keep his balance, the plate left his hand and sailed through the door. It smashed into the wall near the bees. A cloud of startled insects rose up, completely obscuring the surface behind them.

Jonathan went down on one knee, and pushed Rees hard to make him loosen his grip. He rolled away but, as Jonathan jumped up, Rees swung his cane and smacked it with a satisfying thwack against the Shaker's legs. Jonathan screamed and lunged toward the door. As the Shaker hobbled into the other room, the alarmed bees surged toward him. Rees was dimly conscious of another person hurrying past him, but was too focused on Jonathan to recognize the owner of the blue skirts rushing past. The drone of the bees increased to an angry roar as the honey-gatherers became soldiers, ready to defend their hive. Rees felt a sharp hot sting on his hand and another on his neck. Screaming, Jonathan ran from the cottage, with the bees in pursuit.

'Will. Hurry, Will. In here.' When Rees turned

toward Lydia's voice, he saw her crouching with her bertha held over her head. She had covered Deborah's head with the girl's white cape. Rees could hear Deborah crying. 'Hurry.' Lydia gestured at him. Rees crawled to Lydia. She swept the bees away from him and covered his head and neck under her white cape. Then she stretched out her foot and kicked the door shut, trapping most of the remaining bees outside.

'Are you all right?' she asked. In the dim light that penetrated the bertha, Rees could just see her wide eyes and wrinkled forehead.

He nodded, breathing too hard at first to talk. He had received more than a few stings and they burned. Besides that, the wound on his ankle had opened up again and begun to bleed. And Lydia?

The back of Lydia's dark-blue dress was outside the drape. He frowned at his wife. 'What are you doing here? You had a baby only a few days ago. You shouldn't have come after me.'

'I'm fine,' Lydia said. 'Many women would already be returning to housework and their gardens. I'm not ill.' She stopped and took a breath.

'You could have been killed.'

'Me? By what? This swarm might have stung you to death if I hadn't arrived. But these are the descendants of *my* bees. They will never hurt me.' Her chin jutted out in defiance.

Rees stared at her through the gloom. His generally sensible and practical Lydia had, to his mind, an almost mystical attitude toward her bees. On the other hand, her years of keeping bees had saved both him and Deborah.

'How did you know Jonathan was . . .?' Lydia couldn't get the words out accusing him of murder. 'That Jonathan had abducted Deborah?'

'I didn't,' Rees said. 'I just suddenly realized that I hadn't looked in the cottage. No one comes here anymore, and it's close enough for a member of the community to slip away to it. To feed a prisoner, for example.' He turned to look at Deborah, but could see only the white cape that draped over him and Lydia.

'We should leave now,' said Lydia, 'but it won't be safe to go through the main room. Deborah, can you hear me?'

'Y-yes.' The girl's voice quavered.

'Stop crying and listen.' Lydia sounded stern. 'We're going to climb through the window.'

'But I'm tied up.'

'I'll cut the leather strap with my knife,' Rees said. He fumbled under the hem of Lydia's bertha until he found the edge of Deborah's. He slid his hands underneath. 'Put your hands as close to me as you can.' He felt her movement and her warm skin touched him. Trying to keep Lydia's white bertha over his vulnerable neck, he thrust his head after his hands. He could see her, her hands outstretched. She was so small and slight her cape covered her crouching form almost to the ground. Only a narrow band of light illuminated the hem of her dress. He sawed at the leather until it parted and she was able to brush away the strips that had bound her wrists together.

'Move to the window,' said Lydia, 'keeping the bertha over your head and shoulders.'

As Deborah began to move crabwise toward the window, Rees hastily retracted his head back under the linen cape sheltering him and Lydia. 'There aren't many bees left,' Lydia said, putting her hand on Rees's arm and beginning to draw him upright. 'Most of the hive followed Jonathan.' She glanced at Rees's lower legs. 'And they won't see your white stockings.' Tense and expecting burning stings with every step, Rees followed Lydia to the window. But, as Lydia had promised, he received no additional stings, although he could hear buzzing all around him.

When they reached the window, Rees and Lydia found that Deborah had already scrambled over the sill and was standing outside with the bertha still draped over her head like a hood. Although the bees' abandoned skeps were not more than twenty feet away, only a few bees foraged here. The lavender remained and the roses, but the garden was going over to goldenrod and Queen Anne's lace.

'Go on,' Rees said to Lydia. With a nod, she hitched up her skirts and swung a leg over the sill. Rees held her left hand tightly, for support, although she didn't seem to need it. Once she was safe outside, Rees scrambled awkwardly through the window after her. Although his back throbbed with the movement and he struggled a little with his cane, he soon found himself standing by her. Without the bertha covering his head, the air felt cool and clean.

Rees looked around. He could neither see nor hear anything of Jonathan.

Thirty

Deborah began running down the rocky hill toward the main street. 'Wait,' Lydia called to her. But the girl did not hesitate. Rees took Lydia's arm, more for his own support than hers, and they started after the girl. 'We've got to find out what happened,' Rees said.

Lydia nodded. 'I can hardly believe Brother Jonathan . . .' Her voice faded.

'I know,' said Rees. Since the combination of loose rocks and low-growing blueberry bushes made the footing treacherous, neither of them spoke while they negotiated the slope. Rees's ankle ached, and he was grateful he had the cane. It seemed a cruel irony that the tool had been made by Jonathan. When he finally reached level ground, he bent over and just breathed.

'How did you know the murderer was Jonathan?' Lydia asked again as they circled the stable and started for the street.

'I didn't. I thought I might find . . .' Rees shrugged. 'Well, I don't know what I thought I would find . . . It was simply that when I realized we hadn't searched the cottage, I hoped we might find Deborah.'

Lydia looked across the street at the girl. She was leaning against Esther, who was trying to comfort her while holding baby Sharon. 'Well, you did find her. And she is still alive.' Squeezing her husband's arm, she smiled up at him.

'I hope Deborah is able to identify her kidnapper,' Rees said in a low voice as they crossed the last piece of road.

'She may not be able to,' Lydia said. 'She was blindfolded. And terrified, as well she should have been. But why, I wonder, didn't he kill her?'

'I don't know,' Rees said. What did he know of the child? She had come to Zion searching for her father, who had left the family to join the Shakers. 'Do you think Jonathan could be her father?'

Lydia began to shake her head but then paused, chewing her lower lip. 'He would barely be old enough,' she said, sounding uncertain. 'And they don't look anything alike.'

'Well, he is dark and she's fair,' Rees agreed as they crossed the road. 'But Aaron is dark-haired, too—'

Lydia flashed a warning glance at him, and they covered the last few steps in silence.

While Lydia reached out for her daughter, Rees said to Esther, 'I must find Brother Solomon immediately.'

'He's in the workshop, I think,' the Sister said, tipping her chin toward the north part of the main street. 'Who took Deborah? Was it Jonathan? He came flying down that hill like Satan himself was after him.'

Without replying, Rees squeezed Lydia's arm in farewell and began limping toward the workshop as fast as his wounded ankle would allow.

Lydia's voice rose and fell behind him, as she struggled to deflect Esther's questions without revealing what they suspected.

Rees heard Jonathan's voice as soon as he neared the steps into the workshop. 'I found the girl,' Jonathan was saying in a loud, agitated voice. He took a deep breath. 'She was in the cottage.' Rees hauled himself up the three steps and entered the workshop. Jonathan stopped short. Bright-red swollen bee stings blotched his face and hands.

'He had Deborah,' Rees said. 'He's the murderer.'

'I'm not,' Jonathan shouted, his face turning an ugly mottled reddish color. 'And I didn't have her. I found her.' His hasty trip into the village from the cottage had left him sweaty and panting and he kept touching the stings, as though they were bothering him. Rees suddenly remembered seeing bee stings on someone else, but could not remember who.

'I saw you,' he shouted at Jonathan. 'You were right in front of her.'

'You saw me because I found her,' Jonathan said, his own voice rising in volume.

'Lower your voices, please,' Solomon said, taking a few steps forward so that he stood between them. 'Such anger is not seemly.'

'If you aren't the murderer, how did you know she was there?' Rees asked, turning a suspicious stare upon Jonathan.

'I thought I heard something last night,' he said. 'You know how sound travels late at night.

It sounded like sobbing, but muffled. I listened for it this morning but I couldn't hear anything so I thought I'd imagined it. But I couldn't stop thinking about it. We still hadn't found Deborah and I wondered whether I'd heard her. So when I had a chance, I searched the stables and then the smithy. Then I thought of the old cottage. So I went up the hill to the cottage, and there she was.' He looked up at Rees. 'I tried to tell you when you came bursting in, but you wouldn't listen.'

'Enough,' said Solomon. He glanced at Jonathan and then turned to Rees. 'Do you have any proof Jonathan took the girl? His explanation for finding her sounds plausible and could very well be what happened.'

Jonathan nodded emphatically. 'It happened just as I told you,' he said.

Rees stared at the two Brothers, standing shoulder to shoulder and regarding him with identical serious expressions. He couldn't think of anything to say, and was aware that even if he could find the right words they wouldn't do any good. He was the outsider here, the one who didn't belong. Of course Solomon would believe Jonathan before he believed Rees.

Trying to determine what he could do, he retreated. He needed the constable, but no matter how hard he tried he couldn't think of a way to drive to Durham.

Esther and Deborah had apparently gone inside the Dwelling House – at least they were nowhere around – but Lydia was still waiting for him. She turned, her forehead puckering.

'What happened?' she asked as she brushed her lips over the baby's head.

'I need to talk to Deborah,' he said.

'Esther just took her inside to get her cleaned up.' Lydia paused. 'Anyway, I'm not sure how much she'll be able to tell you. She's so frightened.'

'I'm very much aware of that,' Rees said. 'But she's the only proof we have. Jonathan is sticking to his story and Solomon is supporting it.'

Lydia switched the baby from her left shoulder to the right. 'But Will, Deborah has reason to be frightened. How will we be able to protect her from Jonathan?'

Rees nodded. 'I know. But she is already a threat to him. At least, if she tells us what she knows she won't be the only one who knows it.' Lydia stared at him and then, almost imperceptibly, she nodded.

'I'll fetch her then.' She handed the baby to Rees and hurried up the steps into the Dwelling House. Rees settled Sharon against his right shoulder and felt her weight increase as she relaxed once again into deep sleep.

A few minutes later Esther and Deborah followed Lydia outside. Deborah had changed into clean clothing and her face and hands had been washed. But the fair hair visible under her cap was still full of leaves and dirt. Her eyes were red and swollen from recent crying.

'I know you're frightened,' Rees said to her, 'but we're trying to determine who abducted you.'

'I don't know,' she whispered, tears forming in her eyes.

'It wasn't Ned Palmer, was it?' Rees asked, just to be certain. She shook her head decidedly.

'He had no reason.'

Esther looked at Rees and then turned her gaze upon the girl. 'You were meeting him?' Deborah lowered her eyes and nodded.

'So, who abducted you? Did you see anything?' Rees asked.

'He – he grabbed me from behind.' She began to shake.

'What happened?' Rees asked. She shook her head, her lips trembling. 'You were on your way to meet Ned Palmer?' Rees knew that, but asked the question in the hope of calming her down. She nodded, and for a brief second the ghost of a smile touched her lips. 'Where were you meeting him?'

'The laundry.'

That was just as the Palmer boy had said. 'Did you see anyone?' he asked. She shook her head. 'What about the night Brother Jabez was killed?'

'We didn't see anyone,' Deborah said, biting her lip. Rees stared at her.

'But . . .?'

'We heard someone arguing.' She lowered her eyes to the ground. 'But we didn't know who it was. And we hid under the trees until the Brothers went inside – so we couldn't see who they were, either.'

'Why didn't you say something, you silly girl?' Esther said angrily.

'I didn't want to get in trouble.'

Rees wanted to shake the girl. If only she

301

had said something previously he might have been able to save both Calvin's and Elizabeth's lives!

'Then what happened?' He didn't care that he sounded furious.

'He came up behind me and put his hand over my mouth and said, "Don't scream!", then he tied a rag over my mouth.' She put her hand up to her mouth and stared at Rees over it, her eyes wide and staring.

'What did you see?' Rees asked. 'What was he wearing?'

'A light shirt. Homespun.'

Esther gasped. All the Brethren wore homespun linen shirts, bleached white. Rees looked at her sympathetically, realizing she had continued to hope the kidnapper did not belong to the community. 'Then what happened?' Rees asked, returning his attention to the girl.

'He tied on the blindfold. He told me to behave and I would not be harmed.'

'He already had the gag and blindfold with him?' Rees wanted to be sure. Deborah nodded. So the abduction was premeditated. But why, if Jabez's murderer had seen Deborah and Ned Palmer that night, had he let the girl live?

'And then?'

'He pushed me. And when I struggled, he picked me up and carried me. When we started going uphill, he made me walk in front of him. I didn't know where we were going – not then, anyway – but I realized when we went inside. He tied me up. He told me I wouldn't be hurt but . . . he had to . . .'

She stopped, her voice catching. Rees waited a few seconds.

'Had to what?' he asked. Lydia shook her head at him as she put an arm around the girl.

'Had to what?' Rees repeated, his voice rising in spite of himself.

'. . . decide what to do with me.' Deborah's voice trembled so much Rees could hardly understand her. He met Lydia's horrified stare. He did not want to consider what those words might have meant. What if this had been Annie? Or Jerusha? He swallowed convulsively.

'Are you sure he didn't hurt you?' Lydia asked, her voice barely above a whisper.

'N-no. He didn't hurt me.'

'What are you people doing, standing talking here in the street?' Jonathan and Solomon had come up behind them. Awkward, with the baby tucked into his shoulder and holding the cane in his other hand, Rees turned to face Jonathan, startled by his question.

'This is not proper,' Solomon said in a high and breathy voice. 'We must go inside.'

'Is this the man who abducted you?' Rees asked, gesturing at Jonathan. Deborah looked at him. But his face was so red and so swollen with bee stings he was almost unrecognizable, even to Rees. He was not surprised when the girl shook her head.

'I don't know,' she said. But then, frowning, she stared at Jonathan's tanned hands and the dark hair visible at the edge of his cuffs. 'I think the man who kidnapped me might have been older.'

'I'll prepare the room upstairs,' Solomon said.

'Yes,' Jonathan agreed, as his fellow Elder went up the steps into the Dwelling House. 'Let's finish this in the office.'

Everyone walked up the steps and went inside, with Rees following slowly behind. Climbing stairs was by far the most difficult activity and, although the cane helped, Rees did not move fast.

By the time Rees reached the front hall, everyone else was already in the Elders' room on the second floor. Sighing, Rees paused at the bottom of the staircase. Although there was a handrail, there were many steps and he wasn't sure he would be able to climb them all. But he had to. Filled with determination, Rees put one hand on the rail and hauled himself up, using the rail and cane for balance. He had to ascend, using only his right leg, one step at a time like a child. The left buckled when he put all his weight on it.

He had almost got to the top when Lydia came out on the landing to see what was delaying him. 'Oh dear!' she said.

'I can make it,' Rees said, sweat bathing his face and pouring down his back.

He was tiring, and he still had four more stairs to climb.

'Your ankle is bleeding again,' Lydia said, staring at his leg.

'Can't be helped.' Rees hauled himself up the next step. 'Four. Three. Two. Last one.' He paused to catch his breath. Then, leaning on Lydia's shoulder, he limped into the office and collapsed into the nearest chair.

Esther turned to stare at him in amused disapproval. At which point he realized that he was sitting on the women's side – directly across from Jonathan, who was the only Brother on the opposite side.

Rees looked around the room. 'Where's Solomon?' he asked.

Thirty-One

Where was Solomon? Had he gone for more chairs? Or maybe to answer a call of nature? Rees stared into space over Jonathan's head, thinking. Facts crowded into his mind. Bee stings on Solomon's hands, Aaron saying he'd sold the farm to Abraham Vors, the midwife mentioning a little girl, Robert talking about two brothers named Abraham and Solomon . . .

'It's Solomon!' he said aloud, cutting across Jonathan's rambling explanation. 'He's the murderer.'

His statement was met by several seconds of silence. Then the objections began.

'That's impossible!' Esther said. 'Elder Solomon is a gentle and saintly man.'

'He has no reason,' Jonathan said at the same time. 'You were wrong about me, and you are mistaken again.'

'Well,' said Rees, electing not to argue, 'that may well be. But I need to get into town and find the constable.'

'You aren't planning to arrest the Elder?' Jonathan protested, his voice rising. 'And put him in jail?'

Rees took in a breath. 'Jonathan, Solomon is on the run.'

'That can't be,' Jonathan repeated. 'I'm certain you've misread the situation.'

'Lydia, help me,' Rees said, struggling to stand. She bent down, ostensibly to support him.

'Are you certain?' she whispered. 'Solomon is a respected Elder of the community.'

'We have to find him,' Rees said. 'Perhaps I'm wrong, but I don't think so. We need to speak with him to reveal the truth of the matter.'

'Why did he kidnap me?' Deborah asked in a plaintive voice. 'He never spoke to me.'

'He's your father,' Rees said, wishing as soon as the words left his mouth that he had softened that bald statement. 'He knew you were looking for him. And he probably saw you one of those nights when you were meeting the Palmer boy.'

'That's why he didn't kill her?' Lydia asked, her mouth rounding. 'Because she's his daughter?'

'I think so.' Rees suspected that eventually Solomon might have pushed himself to the murder of Deborah, but refrained from saying so aloud.

'But that doesn't make sense,' Esther objected. 'He could have just ignored her.'

'She knew about the farm,' Rees said. 'She lived there as a child, remember? She knows her last name. And if I'm right, well, Jabez wasn't Solomon's first murder.'

'You must be unhinged!' Jonathan said in a loud voice.

'There was a tree with a branch,' Deborah said in a faraway voice, 'that looked like a hand. I used to believe the tree was waving at me.' She looked at Rees. 'I knew I was in the right place the first time I met Ned at the farm. I saw the tree.'

'He couldn't risk you recognizing him,' Rees said. 'Uncomfortable questions would have been asked of him.' He limped to the door. 'Come on. We've got to find him. And he's already had a head start.'

Jonathan jumped to his feet. He quickly overtook Rees and started down the stairs. Cursing his injury, and the effect it had on his speed, Rees hobbled after the Brother.

Jonathan was already in the street, looking up and down, when Rees finally made it through the Brethren's door. He started across the street toward the stables, calling to the young boy standing by the paddock, 'Did you see Elder Solomon?'

'Yes. I helped him harness a horse to the buggy.' The young boy sounded proud. Rees turned around and looked at Jonathan.

'I'm sure there is a reasonable explanation,' Jonathan said in a weak voice. 'But I suppose I better go after him.'

'We,' said Rees. 'We will go after him.' He went to the paddock and whistled for Hannibal.

'You are the most stubborn man I have ever met,' Jonathan said.

'The constable needs to know,' Rees said. 'Especially if we can't find Solomon.'

While Jonathan harnessed Hannibal to a buggy, Rees fidgeted, tossing the cane from hand to hand. The process seemed to take forever; it felt as if hours had passed before they were finally on their way. He kept a sharp look out for Solomon's buggy as they drove out of the village, but he saw nothing. Of course Solomon could have gone south, either through the center of Zion or along the Surry Road. In which case he would have been visible to witnesses, so Rees was betting on north.

He wondered if anyone in town would even recognize the Shaker Elder, especially if he'd changed his appearance. Once he shaved his beard off and made a few adjustments to his clothing, he could disappear with no one the wiser.

'We need to go faster,' Rees told Jonathan. 'Much faster.' Jonathan directed a glance at Rees but said nothing. He didn't flick the whip at the horse, or in any other way encourage Hannibal to gallop. 'Solomon will escape,' Rees shouted.

Jonathan might have been deaf for all the attention he paid.

He slowed to a stop at the fork in the road. Rees looked north, up the Surry Road; and then left, up the main road that went into Durham. He saw only a horse and rider who, as they approached, resolved into the constable.

Rouge trotted up to the buggy. 'What are you doing here? I was just on my way to tell you I released Aaron.'

'You did?' Jonathan said, sounding pleased. He looked past Rouge. 'Where is he?'

'Walking—' Rouge began.

'Did you see anyone?' Rees interrupted. 'A buggy perhaps?'

'There's a buggy pulled up alongside the road,' Rouge said, pointing back toward Durham. Rees nodded at Jonathan and he slapped the reins down on Hannibal's back. 'Wait. Where are you going?' Rouge called after them as they started down the road.

'It's Solomon!' Rees shouted at the constable. 'He's the murderer.'

Rouge quickly caught up and together they rode west toward town.

They were almost at the city limits when they came upon the buggy, tucked into a hollow and almost invisible from either side. There was no horse standing between the traces.

'He's heading for the abandoned farm,' Rees said. 'Go after him, Jonathan. Go.'

Jonathan looked at Rees doubtfully but began to pull on the reins. Rees stared down at the dust moving underneath him. Did he dare jump and risk injuring his ankle once again? He wanted to, but caution kept him in his seat.

The buggy skidded to a stop. Jonathan jumped down with an ease Rees envied and came around to the side. He stretched out a hand but Rees brushed it off. 'Go after him. I'll follow as soon as I can.'

Jonathan nodded and ran into the trees, disappearing within seconds into the thick greenery. Rouge dismounted from the bay. He looped the reins over a branch and followed Jonathan. Cursing softly, Rees lowered himself on to his good right leg and carefully brought the left one down behind it. He limped to the edge of the road and stared longingly into the screen of trees. He, not Jonathan, should be in there, pursuing the murderer.

A few minutes later Solomon came out of the trees, running toward the road, heading straight for the buggy, where Rees was standing. The Elder had lost his hat, and his white hair stood up in tufts, thickly sprinkled with leaves and grass stems. He ran in a wild, frenzied surge, too alarmed to notice Rees, who was standing in the buggy's shadow. The sound of his panting breath was so loud it was almost painful to hear.

Rees understood what Solomon wanted to do – to take the buggy and horse and drive away. Rees hobbled round to the back of the buggy, where he was screened from view by the high hood. As Solomon ran in front of the horse and turned toward the driver's seat, Rees limped up the side of the buggy as fast as he could. When Solomon saw him, he tried to turn aside. But Rees was on him. Before the Shaker could even fling up an arm to defend himself, Rees smacked the cane across Solomon's leg. With a scream, he fell to the other knee. 'You!' he said when he recognized Rees. 'You!' In one smooth motion, the Elder flung a handful of dirt at Rees. The fine silt blew into his eyes and mouth. He began coughing. Through his watering eyes, he tried to watch Solomon, who'd begun crawling to the buggy. Muttering an epithet – this time Rees vowed to floor the other man completely – he smacked the cane down upon Solomon's head. The perfectly made hardwood snapped in half and the Brother dropped unconscious to the road.

'Jonathan,' Rees shouted. 'Jonathan, Rouge. I've got him.' Using his teeth, he tore the hem off the bottom of his shirt and sawed it into strips with his dinner knife so that he could tie Solomon's hands behind his back. By the time Rees had wrestled his prisoner on to his belly, Solomon was beginning to regain consciousness. 'No, you don't,' Rees said, looping the linen around and around the Elder's wrists. He had to work quickly since he could neither overpower Solomon nor run him down. Even the exertion required to rip the linen left Rees panting. The effort of bending over and securing the strips left him so dizzy he almost fell over, and his ankle and shoulder were throbbing.

With Solomon finally immobilized, Rees staggered back to lean against the buggy. For the moment, he did not possess the breath to shout for help.

'Rees? Rees?'

That sounded like the constable. 'Here,' Rees tried to shout in reply. He paused, inhaled, and tried again. 'Here. I've got him.' And then he just rested while he waited.

Rouge was all for dragging Solomon straight to the Durham jail but Jonathan, who seemed more concerned with the health of the man he revered as an Elder, refused to permit it. 'Brother Solomon must go home to Zion,' he said. He darted a quick glance at Rees and added in a lower tone, 'Despite the weaver's gift for

311

unraveling tangled webs, I think he may be wrong in this case. Besides, I have the buggy. What would you do, constable? Throw him over your saddle?'

'I'm not wrong,' Rees said. Even now, Jonathan grated on him. 'Solomon ran, and if we hadn't captured him he would have kept on running. Isn't that proof enough?'

'No,' said Jonathan, with just the faintest thread of uncertainty in his voice. 'I daresay he was frightened of you, Mr Rees. I don't think you realize how intimidating you can be, all red hair and bluster.'

'I would prefer to have him safe in jail,' Rouge said, exchanging a glance with Rees. But short of leaving Jonathan standing in the middle of the road while Rees drove the buggy into town, neither saw a choice other than doing as Jonathan wished. And Rees did not think he could manage the drive, though he seriously considered it for several seconds.

As they drove into Zion and Rees saw the number of people waiting, he wished he had attempted the drive after all. He began to fear that this community, for all that they were pacifists, would attempt to wrest Solomon from the constable's custody. By now the Shaker Elder had come awake. When Rouge took him out of the buggy and they started up the stairs to the office, Rees, who was a short distance behind, distinctly heard whispered comments such as 'Persecution!' and 'Tyranny!' running through the crowd.

So many members of the community followed

Solomon up the stairs that Rees was almost knocked down. He was unsteady without the cane and would not have succeeded in ascending the stairs without the handrail. When he reached the top, he had to fight his way through those who had not been able to fit into the room. Fortunately, Lydia and Rouge were looking for him and helped him push through the crowd.

One chair next to Solomon was vacant, saved for Rees. He did not go immediately to it, even though his leg was aching. Instead, he paused at the door. The room was crammed. All the Elders and Eldresses, all four of the Deacons and Deaconesses, and a good number of community members were present – and all of them were staring at Rees as if he was the guilty party. Even Brother Aaron. And when Rees made his case, what if the Shakers refused to believe him? What would happen then? From Jonathan's posture and the skeptical arms-crossed stance of several other members, Rees knew that the community would believe no wrong of their Elder without overwhelming proof, and he had nothing but conjecture and circumstantial evidence to offer.

'Sit down,' Jonathan said, gesturing to the chair. Slowly Rees made his way into the chamber and around to the men's side.

Despite the open windows, the air inside the office was stuffy and smelled of human sweat, horses and manure.

'What proof do you have?' demanded Jonathan before Rees had even sat down on the chair. 'Not even the girl can identify her captor.'

Rees looked around the room. Deborah was still there, half-hidden behind some of the other Sisters. And there was Lydia, holding their baby daughter. Lydia smiled at him with love and trust and nodded slightly in encouragement.

As Jonathan seated himself next to the Elder, Solomon said, 'You know I am innocent. I've done nothing wrong. While I wish you had found the villain who murdered our Brothers and our Sister, fixing your attention on me is not justice.' He sounded so reasonable Rees couldn't blame the people around them who began murmuring in agreement.

'You were running,' he said. 'Trying to escape.'

'I was attempting to reach Durham,' Solomon said softly. 'I planned to fetch the constable to take you, Rees, into custody. Everyone knows your temper. We've seen several examples of it this past week. I was afraid for my life.'

Despite, or because of Solomon's taunt, Rees could feel his temper beginning to rise. He knew Solomon was lying, but didn't know how to refute it. 'Someone abducted Deborah and tied her up in the cottage,' he said. 'Someone in this community. And that individual was feeding her.'

Solomon turned to look at Jonathan. Without speaking, he managed to imply that his fellow Elder was the guilty man. 'She was kept well-fed and unharmed,' Solomon added after a brief pause. It sounded as if he was trying to defend Jonathan, but Rees knew better.

'Now how did you know that?' Rees asked, feeling his entire body tense.

'Why, I saw her,' Solomon said, 'when you brought her down.'

'No you didn't,' Rees said. 'She was already down from the cottage when you arrived. And no one had examined her yet. She could have been injured. And how did you know there was food there?'

'Jonathan told me.'

'No, I didn't,' Jonathan said, sounding like he couldn't catch his breath. 'I told you I found her. Nothing more.'

'Let's go through the timeline,' Rees said, raising his voice slightly. 'I haven't yet worked out why you murdered Brother Jabez, but you did. And Calvin knew it, didn't he? He accused you in front of everyone.'

'No, he didn't,' said Esther. 'He couldn't . . .'

'Yes, he did,' Rees interrupted. 'Calvin had some difficulty with pronouns but he knew what he saw. He stood up and told Solomon he saw his wet shoes. Rees looked at Solomon. 'Wet, no doubt, from your efforts to push Jabez into the tub.'

'That's hardly proof,' Solomon said, with a smile. 'Testimony from an idiot.'

'So, you murdered Jabez,' Rees said as if Solomon had not spoken. 'When Calvin accused you, you panicked. You were afraid someone would translate Calvin's speech, so you used his trust in you to bring him across the road to see the horses. And then you struck him with a rock and killed him.' Rees had to pause. His voice had thickened with emotion and he had to take a few seconds to master himself. He heard a

315

muffled sob. 'You sent Aaron away. He was close to Calvin and if anyone could interpret Calvin's speech, it was Aaron.' Hearing the movement of someone behind him, Rees paused. But no one else spoke. 'Besides, Aaron had a piece of information that could hurt you.'

'And what was that?' Solomon asked, as if he was amused.

'Brother Aaron,' Rees said, turning to look at the Brother. 'You told us that you sold your farm, a farm that is now abandoned, before you signed the Covenant.' Aaron nodded, his Adam's apple bobbing up and down. 'To whom did you sell it?'

'I . . .' Aaron paused. 'I . . .'

'Tell him,' Rouge said, reaching out and shaking the Shaker's shoulder.

'Abraham Vors. I sold it to Abraham Vors.'

'Who?' Jonathan looked around at the other Believers.

'I don't think we need witness anymore of this harassment of our Family,' Solomon said. 'It is not necessary for you to answer any more of Mr Rees's questions.'

'No need,' Rees said to Solomon. 'Just listen. Both Brother Robert and Sister Elizabeth knew you in the days when you were all new converts. In fact, they knew you and your brother. The Vors brothers, Robert called you.'

'I am not responsible for my brother,' Solomon said. 'I've lived among the Believers since the early days with Mother Ann. Everyone knows that.' Droplets of perspiration beaded his forehead and sparkled like silver in the light from the window.

'So,' said Rees, who was following his own train of thought. 'If your brother owned the abandoned farm, who do the bones we found in the stream belong to?' Solomon shrugged. Although the smile never left his face, his shoulders tensed. 'I believe,' Rees said, his voice harshening, 'they belong to your brother Abraham.'

'I don't understand why that is important—' Jonathan began. Rees raised his voice and talked over him.

'Because Solomon murdered his brother.' Rees swept his eyes around the room and then fixed them upon the man sitting next to him. 'And that's why you smothered Elizabeth and tried to murder Robert.' Solomon shook his head. As he began to speak, Rees raised his voice to a shout. 'They knew that Abraham was your brother and that your surname was Vors. After I found the skeleton, Elizabeth wondered about Abraham. Did she ask you about the bones? I suspect she did.'

'How do you manufacture such lurid tales?' Solomon asked, trying to smile.

'She also knew you were married. Is that the secret you murdered to protect? I think she assumed you had put aside your wife when you joined the Shakers. But that's not what happened, is it?'

'Of course it is,' Esther said, throwing desperate glances at everyone around her.

'No, it isn't. Although Abraham bought the farm, he abandoned it shortly after and another family moved in. Your family, Solomon.'

'He was a failure at everything he turned his

317

hand to,' Solomon said. He'd begun clasping and unclasping his hands – fidgeting with remembered anger, Rees thought. Not fear or guilt.

'So you, Solomon, brought your family to the farm, visiting them whenever you could. Deborah remembers the farm, don't you Deborah?' She nodded, white-faced, but Rees did not give her an opportunity to speak. 'What happened Solomon? Did Abraham return? Did he find you enjoying all the pleasures of wife and family, but at the same time serving as a pious celibate among the Shakers? Did he threaten to expose your secret? Am I correct, are those your brother's bones buried under the cairn of rocks?'

By now everyone was staring at the Elder. He did not seem to realize it, his attention was entirely fixed upon Rees. Solomon affected a laugh that was meant to be mocking. 'This is a silly tale, Mr Rees. The farm, the bones – they have nothing to do with me. As God is my witness, I have done nothing but follow the precepts of Mother Ann Lee and do my best to labor for this Family.' Although some of the community nodded, Rees was heartened to see most did not. 'I've served as Elder since my arrival here.' Solomon continued. 'Before that, I was a Deacon in York Village. My life has been a simple one, wholly devoted to God. I have no secrets.'

'Why did you strike down Brother Jabez?' Rees asked. 'I understand about Elizabeth and Robert. Even Calvin, although his murder displayed a depth of wickedness . . .' Rees

318

stopped and struggled to control his voice. 'And, oh yes, you tried to kill me, because I was getting too close.' Solomon remained silent. 'But why Jabez?' Still the Elder did not speak.

Rees abandoned that line of questioning. 'You couldn't quite force yourself to do away with your daughter, could you? But you were afraid she would find you and then all the secrets would be revealed. That's why you hid her in the cottage. But the bees betrayed you. I saw the stings on your hands and neck, though I didn't understand their importance at the time.'

'Bee stings are common here—' Solomon began. But he did not get the chance to finish.

'You killed that boy?' Aaron's voice resounded around the room. 'I saw you talking to him. Did you lure him to the field? You did, I know it.' He went for Solomon, hands outstretched. Everyone was taken by surprise – everyone but Solomon, who leaped to his feet and backed away. He tripped over Daniel's feet but managed to right himself and make for the door and the stairs. The Shaker community parted before him. Rees tried to stand up, but he wasn't quick enough and his injured ankle wavered beneath him as he took his first step.

Impeded by no such infirmity, Aaron took several long strides behind the chairs and flung himself at Solomon. They both went down in a flurry of arms and legs, with Aaron on top, pummeling Solomon for all he was worth. 'You killed that poor boy,' he shouted. 'How could you? That poor innocent boy.' It took both Jonathan and Rouge to pull Aaron away. By then, his knuckles were bloody and a rivulet of blood was snaking down his chin from a split lip.

'Both of you should be expelled!' Jonathan said loudly. 'Fisticuffs! Such behavior, here in a community dedicated to the Lord.' But Rees clapped Aaron on the shoulder, thinking that he'd never liked the man as much as now.

Jonathan and Deacon Daniel pushed Solomon back into his chair. All the fight had gone out of him and he sagged against the back. 'Is this true?' Jonathan asked in a trembling voice. 'Is Rees telling the truth?'

Solomon looked up at his fellow Elder and nodded very slowly. Jonathan sat down with a thump.

'But why?' Esther asked.

'The pleasures of the flesh,' Aaron said, his lip curling into a sneer.

'No. No,' said Solomon. 'It was never about that.' He turned his gaze to Rees. 'He understands.'

'I do?' said Rees in surprise.

'I wanted my own hearth and home and my family around me,' Solomon said, looking straight into Rees's eyes. 'Just like you do.' Rees nodded, feeling an unexpected pang of sympathy.

'I do understand,' he said.

'I love my God and this faith,' Solomon said. 'It is all-important. But I wanted my family. I couldn't sacrifice my wife and children. My brother had left by then, for good I thought. I'd given him money, you see.'

'You took community money?' Jonathan asked, turning a look of utter disgust upon Solomon, who shifted slightly in his seat, unable to meet Jonathan's gaze.

'I didn't know where Abraham was,' Solomon continued. 'But there was the farm. So I moved my family there. And for a few years it worked well. But one day he returned. My brother, Abraham.'

'You killed him?' said Rees.

'I had to. He was threatening to tell.' Solomon shook his head in recollection. 'We were arguing in the kitchen. He called me a milk-and-water man. He never expected me to hit him with the axe.' Solomon sighed. 'My wife left me then. She was willing to pretend I was a traveling preacher and see me only when I could get away. But after Abraham's death, she was frightened of me. So I became a celibate Shaker in truth . . .'

'And Jabez? Why murder him?'

'He met my wife. I don't know what she told him but he threatened me.' He looked up to meet Rees's eyes. 'He wouldn't listen. I couldn't allow anyone to take away everything I'd worked for. I'd already lost so much. And I was a good Brother and a good Elder. You understand, don't you?'

'I understand about wanting your family,' Rees said. He glanced over at Lydia. She was jiggling Sharon, who'd awakened and begun to fuss. 'But when you signed the Covenant, you made your choice. You murdered all these people because you didn't want to abide by the rules of this Millennial Church.'

'Mother would never talk about you . . .' Deborah murmured, staring at her father.

'You'll hang for this,' Rouge said, pushing his

321

way down the aisle between the men and the women. He grabbed Solomon by the arm and hauled him to his feet. Jonathan jumped up and moved away so hurriedly his chair fell over. 'I'll need someone to drive the buggy.' Daniel, with tears in his eyes, stood up. No one spoke as the three men left the room.

'I suppose we owe you our thanks,' Jonathan said to Rees. He sounded as though the words were choking him.

'I would rather have the use of my farm, the Ellis property, for a little while, than thanks,' Rees said.

'That will have to be discussed by the Elders,' he began.

'Oh stop it,' Esther broke in. 'That property belongs to him. Let Rees and his family reside there until they no longer have need of it. We owe him much more than that.'

'Very well. I don't have the strength to argue.' He raised his eyes to Rees. 'We will give you whatever assistance you require.'

'Thank you,' Rees said. He looked over at Deborah. 'Ned Palmer is still in town, waiting for you.' With no other heirs, she too would have a farm, the so-called Johnson farm, if she wanted it – though, thought Rees, it would be no surprise if she sold it and purchased a property that had no memories attached to it.

The Shakers began to drift from the room, back to their chores and the other routines of their lives. Lydia crossed the floor to join her husband. 'Can we go home now?' she asked. Rees looked down into her face.

'To the Ellis property,' he said. 'For now. I hope we will all be safe there.' She nodded and both were silent for several seconds. The security of the Shaker village had turned out to be an illusion and it would take some time for both of them to recover. 'Later this week I'll return to Dugard to check on David. Won't he be surprised to see me after less than two weeks away!'

He grinned down at her, inviting her to see the humor of it. She smiled. 'He will be surprised to hear about the Ellis farm,' she said. 'To hear we've found a new home at last.'

Author's Note

MONEY

Although the early United States had its own money (Alexander Hamilton set up the first US bank in 1793), money from other nations remained in common currency. English coinage (shillings, pence, farthings and so on), French sous and Spanish pieces of eight would have been in Rees's pockets. 'Pieces of eight', by the way, was an exact description of a Spanish coin that was scored so it could be broken into eight pieces.

PROPERTY TAXES

Property taxes have a long history. Our modern tax structure is based on feudal obligations to kings and landlords dating from the fourteenth and fifteenth centuries. Tax assessors at that time used their own estimates of a taxpayer's ability to pay. (I would imagine there was a lot of abuse!)

By the Revolutionary War, the colonies already had a well-developed tax system, although it varied from colony to colony. In the South, for example, slaves could be taxed as a form of property. During the war tax rates increased and became a matter of heated debate, and in 1794 the imposition of a tax on whiskey provoked the Whiskey Rebellion.

By 1796, seven of the fifteen states levied capitation taxes (taxes levied at a fixed rate on adult males). Twelve taxed livestock. Only four taxed the mass of property by valuation. But as new states joined the union, that changed and by 1900 thirty-three states required all property to be taxed according to value.

An interesting note: the Federal Congress had the ability at this time to exact property taxes. In 1798, faced with the possibility of war with France, Congress set up a formula to tax slaves, houses and property. When the war did not occur, the tax lapsed. Congress levied another direct tax to fund the war of 1812 with Great Britain.

THE SHAKERS

The official name of the community is The United Society of Believers in Christ's Second Coming, but 'the Shakers' is how they are popularly known.

Like any culture, they were not static and various fashions came and went.

Shaker communities ate meat, became vegetarian, and returned to eating meat. The use of tobacco was approved and forbidden several times. In the early days both Brothers and Sisters smoked, and for some of the communities pipe-making was a source of income. Their attitude toward the consumption of alcohol was something else that changed over time. The Shakers were famous for their cider, a hard cider, and both wine and beer were permitted. But with the rise of the Temperance movement, the Shakers became teetotal.

In 1821 the Shaker authorities created the Millennial Laws, which forbade tobacco, alcohol and eating pork, among other behaviors. Additional rules were added in the revised Millennial Laws of 1845.

Burial customs also evolved. Eschewing the elaborate coffins and practices of the World, the Shakers buried their dead as simply as possible. Later on, simple pine coffins and plain stones were used. To the outside world, the lack of elaboration seemed 'disrespectful'. During the course of the nineteenth century Shaker practices became more elaborate, and more in line with those of the outside world.

The wearing of beards was another custom subject to change. During some periods of their history, the Brothers were permitted to wear beards. At other times they were expected to be clean-shaven, and permission from the Ministry was needed in order to wear a beard. Obedience being a cornerstone of Shaker culture, some men left the Shaker community when permission was denied (I saw letters detailing one such event on display in New York State Museum's exhibition on the Shakers).

One of the buildings in my fictitious community of Zion is an infirmary. In the early days, prayer was the accepted method of curing illness. But the Shakers developed a thriving business in medicinal herbs and the patent medicines made from those herbs, too. When an archeological dig in Canterbury, New Hampshire, revealed the existence of an infirmary in the Shaker village there, the archeologists theorized that very ill Family members were nursed in the infirmary instead of their rooms in the Dwelling House. For someone like Elizabeth suffering from the white plague (tuberculosis), separating her from the other Sisters would make sense.

Granny cradles were also used (I saw one on display at a Shaker exhibition). Exactly how they were used is not known, but one of the theories is that they were used as a form of comfort, to promote healing, and I have adopted that explanation here.